'A head-spinning thrill ride, a cautionary tale about the most salient emotion of the 21st Century . . . *Hater* will haunt you long after you read the last page'

Guillermo del Toro on *Hater*

'As with *Hater*, Moody deals with larger themes – notably here, how far will a parent defend the indefensible actions of their child – within the tropes of a post-apocalyptic novel, elevating it above the multitude of such books currently on the shelves. The final part of the trilogy can't come soon enough. Another bleak and powerfully uncomfortable journey for the reader'

Total Sci Fi

'What it does redefine is just how utterly ruthless and down-right vile one human being can be to another on the written page. Moody knows only too well that when a line is drawn between life and death people will do whatever they can to stay on the right side of that line. The results are displayed in a language that is all the more brutal for its simplicity. Moody tells it like it is, the scale and nature of his apocalypse deserves no less. A worthy successor to *Hater*'

Graeme's Fantasy Book Review

'A brilliant, post-apocalyptic romp of a book that manages to ask big questions about the nature of humanity. Moody delivers plenty of blood and guts, but it's the ideas that really pack a punch. A book that thrills on every level' *Big Issue*

DAVID MOODY

The right of David Moody to be identified as the author of this work has
been asserted by him in accordance with the
Copyright, Designs and Patents Act 1988.

First published in Great Britain in 2010 by
Gollancz
An imprint of the Orion Publishing Group
Orion House, 5 Upper St Martin's Lane, London WC2H 9EA
An Hachette UK Company

This edition published in Great Britain in 2011 by Gollancz

1 3 5 7 9 10 8 6 4 2

A CIP catalogue record for this book is available
from the British Library

ISBN 978 0 575 08475 9

Typeset at The Spartan Press Ltd,
Lymington, Hants

Printed and bound in the UK by CPI Mackays,
Chatham, Kent

The Orion Publishing Group's policy is to use papers that
are natural, renewable and recyclable products and made
from wood grown in sustainable forests. The logging and
manufacturing processes are expected to conform to the
environmental regulations of the country of origin.

www.davidmoody.net
www.orionbooks.co.uk

Dedicated to the memory of Dr Brian Barnes (1942–2006)

PART I

The cause of the Hate (as it had come to be known on both sides of the uneven divide) was irrelevant. At the very beginning, when the doubters had been forced to accept that something was really happening and that the troubles weren't just the result of media-fuelled, copycat mob violence, the usual raft of baseless explanations were proposed; scientists had screwed up in a lab somewhere, it was an evolutionary quirk, it was a virus, a terrorist attack, aliens or worse . . . Thing was, people were quickly forced to realise, *it didn't matter*. You could bullshit and postulate and hypothesise all you wanted – it wouldn't do you any harm but it wouldn't do you any good either. Within days of the belligerent population finally beginning to accept that the shit had indeed hit the fan with almighty force no one talked about the cause of the Hate any more. Hardly anyone wasted time even thinking about it. The only thing of any importance to the non-Hater section of the populace now was survival. And the so-called Haters? The one-third of society who *had* changed? Those previously 'normal' people who, without warning, had each become savage, brutal and remorseless killers? The only thing that mattered to any of them was destroying every last one of the Unchanged (as they labelled their enemy) until none remained alive.

Before it had actually happened, the popular assumption in most apocalyptic films and books was that the population as a whole would immediately bind together against their common enemy and either stand united and fight back or take cover and hunker down when it became clear that something of Armageddon-like proportions was looming on the horizon.

They didn't. Whether it was because many of them simply chose to bury their heads in the sand through fear or denial until it was too late, or whether it was instead just their stubborn refusal to abandon their homes, material possessions and daily routines, no one knew. No one cared. A cynic might suppose that the effects of the Hate had been camouflaged by an inherently bad-tempered, mistrusting, selfish and greed-driven society, but the exact reasons for society's lack of reaction were neither clear nor important. The bottom line was that the extent and implications of what was happening weren't fully appreciated until it was far too late, and the repercussions were devastating. This, it was painfully apparent, was no ordinary war.

In many ways the situation the Unchanged found themselves facing was indefensible. This conflict wasn't faction versus faction or army against army: it was individual versus individual, more than six billion armies of one. And the Hate didn't care who you were, where you were or what you were. You were simply on one side or the other, your position in this new, twisted, fucked-up world decided by unknown variables and fate, quite without your involvement. Within weeks command structures at every level were compromised. Organisations fell apart. Families crumbled. The Haters were everywhere and everyone; the whole world beaten-up from the inside out.

The ratio of Unchanged to Haters was generally thought to have settled somewhere between 2:1 and 3:1. In spite of their enemy's ferocity and apparently insatiable bloodlust, their greater numbers and pre-existence gave the Unchanged an early advantage which was quickly squandered. With no time or inclination to look for a cure (could the condition even be reversed?), separation and eradication soon became the only viable option for survival. Conveniently ignoring lessons learnt through history and any moral arguments, a half-hearted attempt to cull the Haters failed dramatically. Almost overnight the Unchanged plan of attack was forced to become a plan of *defence*, and their first priority was to make their

4

people defendable. Civilians were herded together, major city centres quickly becoming swollen, overcrowded, under-supplied, understaffed refugee camps. Once they'd successfully separated 'us' from 'them', the Unchanged theory went, they'd head back out into the wastelands and hunt the fuckers out.

Less than four months ago, when the last frosts of winter had finally thawed and the first green buds of the year's new growth had tentatively started to appear, this public park had been a frequently empty and underused oasis of lush greenery buried deep within the drab grey concrete heart of the city. It was a place office workers used to escape to during lunch breaks or take a shortcut through on their way to or from work. A place where kids bunking off school would hide and drink stolen alcohol and smoke fags and carve their names on wooden benches and tree trunks. A place where elderly shoppers with too much time and too many memories would sit and talk to anyone who'd listen about how the country had gone to ruin and how things used to be so much better back in their day . . . and it had to be said, they were right.

Tucked away in the long shadows of office blocks, shopping malls, convention centres and multiplex cinemas, what used to be a vast and open expanse of grass was now covered in cramped rows of ragged, refugee-filled tents. Two football pitches had become helicopter landing pads, constantly in use. The patch of soft tarmac where children's swings, roundabouts and slides used to be had been commandeered to house heavily guarded and rapidly dwindling stockpiles of military equip-ment and supplies. The changing rooms on the far side of the park were now a hopelessly inadequate field hospital. Next to the small, square redbrick building, a tall wooden fence had been erected all the way around the park's four concrete tennis courts. They had, until three weeks ago, been used as a make-shift morgue but, by then, the number of stacked-up corpses awaiting removal had reached such a level that the cordoned-off area had become a permanently lit funeral pyre. There was no longer any other way of hygienically disposing of the dead.

Before his mother had tried to kill him and he'd been dragged screaming into the war he'd desperately tried to isolate himself from, Mark Tillotsen had sold insurance in a call centre. He'd worked hard and had enjoyed (as much as anyone enjoyed selling insurance in a call centre) the job. He'd liked the anonymity of the role and he'd taken comfort from the safety of the daily routine, the procedures and regulations he hid behind and the targets he worked towards. In his last development review, just a month or so before the Hate, his manager had told him he had a bright future ahead of him. Today, as he trudged slowly through the afternoon heat towards a convoy of three battered trucks bookended by heavily armed military vehicles, he wondered whether he, or anyone else for that matter, had *any* kind of future left to look forward to.

Mark hauled himself up into the cab of the middle truck and acknowledged the driver. His name was Marshall and they'd travelled outside the city together several times in recent weeks. Marshall was a stereotypical trucker, more at home behind the wheel of his rig than anywhere else. His arms were like tree trunks, fading tattoos hidden beneath a thick covering of grey hair. He gripped the steering wheel tight in his leather-gloved hands even though they weren't moving. His head remained facing forward, his expression sullen and serious. To show no emotion at all was better than letting Mark see how nervous he really was. This wasn't getting any easier.

'All right?'

'Fine,' Mark replied quickly. 'You?'

Marshall nodded.

'People today, not supplies.'

'How come?'

'Helicopter spotted them on infra-red, about three miles outside the zone.'

'Many?'

'Don't know till we get there.'

And that was the end of their brief, staccato exchange.

Nothing more needed to be said. Although it was widely believed that the Change was over and by now you'd know whether the person standing next to you was going to rip your fucking head off or not, conversations between strangers remained brief and uncomfortable, and happened only when necessary. You constantly trod a fine line; to ignore someone was dangerous, to overreact was worse. You didn't want to give anyone reason to believe you might be one of them. All that Mark knew about Marshall was his name, and that was how he wanted to keep it.

Time to move. Marshall started the engine of the truck, the sudden rattle, noise and vibration making Mark feel even more nauseous and nervous than he already was. Remember why you're doing this, he repeatedly told himself. Apart from the fact that going outside the so-called 'secure zone' allowed him to escape the confines of the shitty, cramped hotel room where he, his girlfriend and several other family members had been billeted, willing militia volunteers like him were paid with extra rations – a slender additional cut of whatever they brought back. But, more importantly, going out into the open and watching those evil bastards being hunted down and executed was as close to revenge as he was ever going to get. And Christ, he needed some kind of revenge or retribution. Through no fault of his own his life had been turned upside down and torn apart. Like just about everyone else, he'd lost almost everything, and he badly wanted someone to pay for it.

The truck lurched forward, stopping just centimetres short of the back of the vehicle in front, then lurched forward again as the convoy began to move. Mark glanced back across the park as a helicopter gunship took off from its football pitch landing pad before taking up position overhead, their escort and their eyes while they were outside the city.

A single strip of grey tarmac weaved through the park from a central point, running through a large, rectangular car park (now filled with military vehicles) then continuing on as a half-mile-long access road with copses of trees on either side. As the track curved around Mark shielded his eyes from the relentless afternoon sun and looked out across this bizarre militarised zone. How could it have come to this? He'd played here in school holidays as a kid, now look at it. The village of tents and Portakabins made it look more like a third-world slum than anything else. Or perhaps a badly organised humanitarian response to some devastating natural disaster – the aftermath of a hurricane, tsunami, earthquake or drought? But nothing like that ever happened here. He forced himself to look up from the never-ending crowd of refugees which covered every visible square metre of land, forced himself to shut out their constant cries and moans which were audible even over the rumble of the truck, and forced himself to ignore the foul, rancid smell which filled the air. He concentrated instead on the tops of the trees swaying lightly in the lilting, early summer breeze. That was the only part of the world which looked like it used to in the days before the Hate.

It was a relief when they reached the access road and Marshall followed the other vehicles round to the right. But even here there were people everywhere, crowded in and around the trees, desperate to find shelter and shade. There were more of them here than when he'd last been out with Marshall. He focused on one particular woman who sat cross-legged on the grass, desperately trying to hold onto a hysterical, squirming, screaming child. Surrounded by her few remaining possessions gathered up in carrier bags, she gently rocked her terrified, inconsolable little girl. He found himself wondering what had happened to this woman to bring her here. Had she had a partner? Had they turned against her? Had there been more kids? She looked up and caught his eye and he quickly looked away. He forgot her almost immediately, suddenly preoccupied with his own insurmountable problems instead. Mark's girlfriend Kate was pregnant. Much as he tried to deny it, he wished she wasn't.

*

The convoy moved away from the densely occupied heart of the city and out through the exclusion zone. This was a bizarre and unsettling place. In the wake of the panic and terror caused by the onset of the Hate, under military orders the authorities in cities like this had pulled the remaining population inwards, housing them temporarily in shops, office blocks, high-rise buildings and anywhere else that space could be found. The exclusion zone (which was generally between half a mile and two miles wide) was an area of dead space: a desolate strip of no-man's land wedged between the overcrowded refugees and the city border which was patrolled from the sky. It was a place which had been abandoned rather than destroyed and which now stood like a vast and dilapidated museum exhibit. They drove past the front of a modern-looking school, its buildings empty when they should have been filled with students, the knee-high grass making its athletics track look more like a field of crops overdue for harvest. At the front of the convoy a military vehicle which had been fitted with a make-shift snowplough-like attachment cleared the road of a number of abandoned cars which had been stuck in a frozen, unmoving traffic jam for weeks.

The closer they got to the border, the worse Mark began to feel. Desperate not to let his anxiety show (for fear of Marshall misreading his reaction) he leant against the window and forced himself to breathe in deeply, trying to remember the relaxation and stress-control techniques he'd been taught on the 'Dealing with Customer Complaints' workshop he'd been sent on last December. Christ, it didn't matter how many times he did this, he still felt woefully underprepared. No amount of relaxation methods and calming techniques were going to prepare him for what he was about to face.

'Couple of miles,' Marshall said, startling Mark. He sat up straight and readied himself, his heart thumping ten times faster in his chest than it should have been. They were well outside the exclusion zone now, and even though there were no signposts, physical boundaries or other warnings marking the change, he suddenly felt a hundred times more vulnerable and exposed.

'Did you say we're out here for people today?' Mark asked, remembering their brief conversation when he first got into the truck.

'Yep.'

'Great.'

A double-pisser. Excursions outside the city were always more risky and unpredictable when civilians were involved. More importantly, if they weren't out here collecting supplies, there'd be nothing for them to take a cut from when they got back.

'Look on the bright side,' Marshall said under his breath, sharing Mark's disappointment, but almost managing to smile, 'loads more of those cunts die when the public are involved.'

He was right. As soon as the first civilian took a step out of their hiding place, Haters would inevitably descend on them, piling in from every direction. Maybe that was the plan? Easy pickings for the helicopter and the forty or so armed soldiers travelling with them in this convoy. He wondered what kind of state the survivors they rescued would be in? Would they even be worth rescuing? He couldn't imagine how they'd managed to last for so long out here. Christ, it had been hard enough trying to survive back in the city. If these people thought their situation was going to get better after they were rescued, they were very wrong.

The road they followed used to be a busy commuter route into town, permanently packed with traffic. In today's baking afternoon heat it was little more than a silent, rubbish-strewn scar snaking its way between overgrown fields and rundown housing estates. Sandwiched between the first military vehicle and the squat armoured troop transporter bringing up the rear, the three empty high-sided wagons clattered along, following the cleared path snowploughed through the chaos like the carriages of a train following an engine down the track. Still bearing the liveries and adverts of the businesses which had owned them before the war, their bright colours left them conspicuously obvious and exposed as they travelled through the dust-covered grey of everything else.

Mark stared at the back of a row of houses which they thundered past, convinced he'd seen the flash of a fast-moving figure. There it was again, visible just for a fraction of a second between two buildings, a sudden blur of colour and speed. And then, as he was trying to find the first again, a second appeared: a woman of average height and slender build. She scrambled athletically to the top of a pile of rubble then leapt over onto a parched grass verge, losing her footing momentarily before steadying herself, digging in and increasing her pace. She sprinted alongside the convoy, wild hair flowing in the breeze behind her like a mane, almost managing to match the speed of the five vehicles. Mark jumped in his seat as a lump of concrete hit the truck door, hurled from the other side of the road and missing the window he was looking through by just a few centimetres. Startled, he glanced into the wing mirror and saw that they were being chased. His view was limited but he could see at least ten figures in the road behind the convoy, running after them. They were never going to catch up, but maybe they sensed the vehicles would be stopping soon? They kept running with dogged persistence; though the gap between them was increasing, their speed and intent remained undiminished. He looked anxiously from side to side and saw even more of them moving through the shadows towards the road. Their frantic, unpredictable movements made it hard to estimate how many of them there were. It looked like there were hundreds.

Marshall remembered the place they were heading to from before the war: a modern office building in the middle of an out-of-town retail park. As part of his job in his former life he'd made deliveries to a nearby depot on numerous occasions. He was glad he was following and not leading the way today. It was getting harder to navigate out here, and he'd convinced himself they had further to go than they actually did.

Everything looked so different beyond the exclusion zone,

the landscape overgrown and pounded into submission after months of continuous fighting. A reduction in the number of undamaged buildings was matched by a marked increase in the level of rubble and ruin. There were more corpses here too. Some were heavily decayed, sun-dried and skeletal, others appeared fresh and recently slaughtered.

Christ, he thought to himself, not wanting to voice his fears, what would this place be like a few months from now? There were already weeds everywhere, pushing up through cracks in the pavements and roads and clawing their way up partially demolished buildings, no council workers with weed-killer sprays left to halt their steady advance. Recent heavy rain storms and the relative heat of early summer had combined to dramatically increase both the rate of growth of vegetation and the rate of decay of dead flesh. Everything seemed now to have a tinge of green about it, like mould spreading over spoiled food. The outside world looked like it was rotting, and the stench which hung heavy in the air was unbearable.

High above the line of trucks, the helicopter suddenly banked hard to the right and dropped down. Mark leant forward and watched its rapid descent, knowing that the sudden change in flight path meant they'd reached their destination. Despite an irrational fear of heights, at moments like this he wished he was up there picking off the enemy from a distance rather than trying to deal with them down at ground level. Not that he was expected to fight unless he had to, of course. His role was simply to get as much food, supplies, civilians or whatever they were out here to acquire into the trucks in as short a time as possible.

But he wasn't stupid. He knew that these missions were often little more than thinly veiled excuses to stir up as many of the enemy as possible, draw them into a specified location and blow the shit out of them. Their uncoordinated, nomadic behaviour and apparently insatiable desire to kill made them surprisingly easy to manipulate and control. Any activity outside the exclusion zone would inevitably cause most of them within an unexpectedly wide radius to surge towards the disturbance, where they could be taken out with ease. And if civilians, soldiers or volunteers like him got hurt in the process? That was an acceptable risk he had to get used to. Anyone was expendable as long as at least one Hater died with them.

The convoy swung the wrong way around a traffic roundabout, then joined the road which led into the business park. Once well maintained and expensively landscaped, it was now as run-down and overgrown as everywhere else. The snow-plough truck smashed through a lowered security barrier then accelerated again, bouncing up into the air and clattering heavily back down as it powered over speed humps. Mark could see the office block up ahead, the sun's fierce reflection on its grubby bronzed-glass fascia. He tried to look for an obvious entrance, but it was impossible at the speed they were approaching. He clung to the sides of his seat and lurched forward as Marshall, following the lead of the driver in front, turned the truck around in a tight arc and reversed up towards the building. He slammed on the brakes just a couple of metres short of the office, parallel with the other vehicles.

Mark didn't want to move.

Marshall glared at him. 'Shift!'

He didn't argue. The tension and fear was suddenly evident in Marshall's voice. Mark jumped down from the cab and sprinted around to open up the back of the truck. He was aware of noise and movement all around him as soldiers poured out of their transports and formed a protective arc around the front of the building and the rest of the convoy, sealing them in. More soldiers, maybe a fifth of their total number, ran towards the office block's barricaded entrance doors and began to try and force their way inside. A burnt-out car surrounded by dustbins full of rubble blocked the main doorway.

'Incoming!' a loud voice bellowed from somewhere far over to his left, audible even over the sound of the swooping helicopter and the noise of everything else. Distracted, he looked up along the side of the truck towards the protective line of soldiers. Through the gaps between them he could see Haters advancing, hurtling forward from all angles as they converged on the exposed building with deadly speed. Like starving animals desperately hunting food, they tore through holes in overgrown hedgerows, clambered over abandoned cars and scrambled through the empty ruins of other buildings to get to the Unchanged.

Mark watched, transfixed, as many of them were hacked down by a hail of gunfire coming from both the defensive line and the helicopter circling overhead, their bodies jerking and snatching as they were hit. For each one that was killed, countless more arrived to take their place, appearing to wrestle with each other to get to the front of the attack. Some of them were oblivious to the danger, more concerned with killing than with being killed themselves. Their ferocity was terrifying.

Mark heard the sound of pounding feet racing towards him. He spun around, ready to defend himself, but then stepped aside when he saw it was the first of a flood of refugees who were pouring out of a smashed ground-floor window. He tried to help them up into the back of the truck, but his assistance was unwanted and unneeded: sheer terror was driving these people forward. Every man, woman and child was fighting to get into one of the transports, desperate not to be left behind. After weeks of living in unimaginable squalor and uncertainty, and with their hideout now open and exposed, this was their last – their only – chance of escape.

The relentless gunfire and the thunder and fury of the helicopter overhead continued undiminished. Mark tried to block out the noise and concentrated on getting as many people as possible into the truck. Ahead of them, the soldiers were being forced back. Marshall revved the engine, letting Mark know he was about to leave. Terrified of being left behind, Mark ran forward and hauled himself up into his seat, leaving the remaining refugees to cram themselves into the truck as best they could.

'This is getting shitty,' Marshall said, looking at a section of the defensive line of soldiers which appeared dangerously close to being breached. 'We're going to—'

Before he could finish his sentence, a gap appeared in the line. A Hater woman had taken out a soldier as he reloaded, knocking him to the ground, leaping onto his chest and caving his head in with a football-sized lump of concrete. As the soldiers on either side tried to react and defend, one gap became two, and then three and then four. In awed disbelief Mark watched as a huge beast of a Hater manhandled another soldier out of the way and smashed him up a wall. The soldier continued to fire at his attacker but the Hater, oblivious to the bullets which ripped into his flesh, continued to fight until he finally dropped and died.

The speed and strength of the enemy was bewildering and terrifying. Marshall had seen enough. Following the lead of the truck to his right, without waiting for order or instruction, he accelerated. Unsuspecting refugees fell from the back of the truck and immediately began sprinting after the disappearing vehicle, but they didn't stand a chance. Haters rushed them from either side, taking them out like animal predators praying on the plentiful, slow-moving game of the savannah. In the distance the last few civilians spilled out of the building like lambs to the slaughter.

The third truck – the one which had been parked on Marshall's left – hadn't moved. Mark watched in the wing mirror as Haters yanked the doors of the truck's cab open and dragged the driver out, swarming over him like maggots over rotting food. Within seconds they'd enveloped the entire vehicle and were massacring the refugees who'd fought so hard to get in the back, expecting to be driven to safety. As the distance between the truck he was in and the building behind him increased, all Mark could see was what was left of the refugees and the last of the stranded soldiers being wiped out in brutal, lightning-fast attacks.

Above them all, the helicopter continued to circle and attack, the gunners' orders now simply to destroy anything on the ground that still moved.

Those Haters who had escaped the carnage outside stormed into the building, looking for more of the Unchanged to kill. Some twenty of them moved from room to room, sweeping over every last square metre of space, desperate to kill and keep killing. One of them sensed something, in a narrow corridor, and he stopped beside an innocuous doorway which the rest of them had ignored. There were dirty handprints around the edges of the door, and he was sure he'd heard something moving inside. It was the faintest of noises, barely audible among the chaos of everything else, but it was enough. He grabbed the handle and pulled and pushed and shook it, but the door was locked. He took a hand-axe from an im-provised holster on his belt and began to smash at the latch. One of them was still in there, he was certain of it. He could almost smell them . . .

The short corridor was empty and the noise of his axe splintering the wood temporarily drowned out the sounds of fighting coming from elsewhere. Ten strong strikes and the wood began to split. He barged the door with his shoulder and felt it almost give. Another few hits with the axe and another shoulder-barge, and it gave way.

He flew into the dark, foul-smelling room and tripped over a child's corpse which had been wrapped in something – it looked like an old rolled-up projector screen. An Unchanged woman – the dead child's mother, he presumed – ran at him from the shadows. Instead of attacking, she dropped to her knees in front of him and begged for mercy. He showed her none, grabbing a fistful of hair then chopping his axe down into the side of her neck, killing her instantly. He pushed her body over. She collapsed on top of her child and he looked down into her face, her dead, unblinking eyes staring back at him. He felt a sudden surge of power and relief; the unmistakable, blissful, drug-like rush of the kill.

The room was filled with noise again as the circling helicopter returned. He took cover behind a concrete pillar and peered out through a small rectangular window, watching as more of those fighters still out in the open were taken down by machine-gun fire from above. Then, suddenly, the helicopter turned and climbed and disappeared from view. He listened as its engines and the thumping of its rotor blades faded into the distance.

Danny McCoyne knew he had to get out of the building before they came back. He'd seen these tactics before. He knew what was coming next.

1

Have to get away from here. It's too dangerous to stay. If there's one thing I've learnt about our piss-weak, cowardly enemy, it's that they always deal their deadliest blows from a distance.

The leaden feet of the woman's corpse are blocking the door and stopping me from getting out. I drag her out of the way then shift the kid's body, kicking it back across the cluttered floor. The kid's bloodstained projector-screen shroud unrolls, revealing his lifeless face. Jesus, he was one of us. I uncover him fully. His wrists and ankles are bound. Can't see how he died but he hasn't been dead long, a few days at the most. Probably starved. Another pitiful example of an Unchanged parent refusing to accept their kid's destiny and let go. Did she think she'd be able to tame him, or find a 'cure' or something? Dumb bitch.

Back out into the corridor. Most people have gone now but I can still hear a few of them moving about, hunting down the last kills before they move on. I automatically head towards the back of the building, hoping I'll find more cover going out that way. A small kid darts past me, moving so fast that I can't even tell if it's a boy or a girl, then it doubles back when it can't get out.

I keep moving forward until I reach a T-junction. There's a fire door to my left but it's been blocked and I can't get through. I follow three men and a woman the other way into a dank toilet which smells so bad it makes my eyes water. The sudden darkness is disorientating and the man in front of me takes the full force of a clumsy but unexpected attack from an Unchanged straggler who's hiding in the shadows under a sink.

There's hardly room to swing a punch in here, but between the five of us we get rid of him quickly. I smash his face into a cracked mirror with a satisfying thump. He leaves a bloody mark on the glass, just another among many.

In a wide disabled cubicle there's a narrow window high on the wall above the dried-up mustard-brown-stained toilet pan. One of the men, a small, suntanned, wiry guy, climbs onto the pan then uses the pipe-work to haul himself up. He opens the window and squeezes out through the gap. We take turns to follow him, impatiently standing in line like we're waiting for a piss. The fighter in front of me has a wide belly and backside and I can't see him getting through. I'll be damned if I'm going to get stuck in here behind him. I push him to one side, ignoring his loud complaints – for all his girth I'm stronger than he is – and climb past, knowing I'll be long gone before he's done whining. I throw my rucksack out first, then force myself through the narrow window frame. I drop down into a flowerbed overrun with brambles and weeds. A pile of waste and emaciated corpses cushions my fall. I quickly get up, swing my pack back onto my shoulders and start to run. Won't be long now before they—

'Oi, Danny!'

Who the hell was that? My heart sinks when I look back and see Adam hopping after me with his ski-pole walking stick, his useless, badly broken left foot swinging. I found this poor bastard trapped in his parents' house a few days back and I haven't been able to shake him yet. He can hardly walk, so I could leave him if I wanted to, but I stupidly keep letting my conscience get the better of me. I tell myself that if I get him away from here he'll be able to kill again, and anyone who's going to get rid of even one more of the Unchanged has got to be worth saving. I run back, put my arm around his waist and start dragging him away from the building.

'Thanks mate,' he starts to say. 'I thought I—'

'Shut the fuck up and move.'

'Oh, that's nice. What did I ever—?'

'Listen,' I tell him, interrupting him mid-flow, 'they're coming back.'

I pull him deep into the undergrowth behind the office block. Although the canopy of leaves above us muffles and distorts the sound, I can definitely hear another aircraft approaching. Whatever's coming this time is larger, louder, and no doubt deadlier than the helicopter that was here before.

Adam yelps as his broken ankle thumps against a low tree stump. I ignore him and keep moving. His leg's already fucked; a little more damage won't matter.

'Sounds big,' he says through clenched teeth, trying to distract himself from the pain. I don't respond, concentrating instead on putting the maximum distance possible between me and the office. Other people run through the trees on either side of me, illuminated by shafts of sunlight which pour through the gaps between the leaves. They're all overtaking us. The noise is increasing, so loud now that I can feel it through the ground. It must be a jet. Christ, what did I do wrong to end up saddled with a cripple at a time like this? Maybe I should just leave him here and let him take his chances?

I look up and through the trees I catch the briefest glimpse of the plane, streaking across the sky at incredible speed, so fast that the noise it makes seems to lag way behind it.

'Keep moving,' I tell him. 'Not far enough yet . . .'

I stop and hit the deck as soon as I hear it: the signature whoosh and roar of missiles being launched. Adam screams in agony as I pull him down, but we'll be safer on the ground. There's a moment of silence – less than a second but it feels like for ever – and then the building behind us is destroyed in an immense blast of heat, light and noise. A gust of hot wind blows through the trees, and dust and small chunks of masonry begin to fall from the sky, bouncing off the leaves and branches above us, then hitting the ground like hard rain. The thick canopy of green takes the sting out of the granite hailstones. The shower of debris is over as quickly as it began and now all I can hear is the plane disappearing into the distance and our laboured breathing. Adam sits up, struggling with his injuries. Crazy bastard is grinning like an idiot.

'Fuck me,' he says, 'that was impressive!'

'Impressive? I could think of other ways to describe it. If you'd been any slower we'd have had it.'

'Whatever.' He leans back against a tree, still panting heavily.

We should keep moving, but the idea of resting is appealing. The Unchanged won't come back here for a while. Even here in the shade the afternoon heat is stifling and, now that I've stopped, I don't want to start walking again. I give in to temptation and lie back on the ground next to Adam. I close my eyes, replaying the memory of today's kills over and over again.

2

We keep walking as the daylight slowly fades, the darkness finally bringing some respite from the heat.

'What time is it?' Adam asks.

'No idea.'

'What day is it?'

'Don't know that either.'

'Don't suppose it matters,' he grumbles as we limp slowly down a long dirt track which curves around the edge of a deserted farm. He's right – the time, day, date, temperature, position of the moon . . . none of it really matters any more. Life is no longer about order and routine, it's about the hunt and the kill and just getting through each day unscathed. When the war began killing was all that mattered, but things feel like they're changing now.

I would never tell him, but I've enjoyed travelling with Adam. Having someone like him to talk to has proved unexpectedly beneficial. Maybe that's why I went back for him earlier, and why I've put up with him for the last few days. Without even realising it, he's helping me make sense of what's happened to me since the onset of the Hate. Before I killed them, Adam's parents had him locked in their garage, chained to the wall like a dog. He'd spent months there, in total isolation. I've had to explain everything that's happened to the rest of the world while he'd been locked away, and going over it with him has helped me to understand a little myself.

Adam's first direct experience of the Hate was similar to mine, but in some ways the poor bastard had it even tougher than me. He was caught off-guard when he realised what he was, and what he had to do. He tried to kill his family but he was filled with the same fear and disorientation that I remembered feeling after I'd killed my father-in-law, and while he was all shaken up, his father was fighting back, and managed to smash Adam's right hand and his left ankle with a lump hammer.

But rather than finish him off or turn him over to the authorities, Adam's parents locked him up and locked themselves down. They hadn't got the strength to kill him, even though they knew he'd kill both of them in a heartbeat. I understand why they did it. It's like that tied-up kid I found earlier today. The Unchanged just can't let go. They hold onto the people that used to matter to them in the vain and pointless hope they'll somehow be cured, or change back by themselves.

But how can we be cured? We're not the ones who are sick. Adam's parents had the whole thing planned out. They starved the poor sod for days, then fed him drugged food to keep him subdued and under control. Finding him was like something out of a fucked-up Stephen King book. Wonder if Stephen King's like us or like them . . . ?

'Can we stop soon?'

'Suppose.'

'You got any idea where we are?' Adam asks. His voice is weak.

I glance across at him. His face is white and his skin looks clammy. 'Roughly,' I answer.

Truth is I'm not exactly sure but, for the first time in ages, I actually do have a fair idea of where I am. For weeks I've travelled everywhere on foot. Like most people, I've shunned cars and other similar means of transport – they make me feel conspicuous, when all I want to do is disappear. Anyway, most roads are blocked now, pretty well impassable. I knew we were getting close, but it was yesterday afternoon, after we'd spent almost an hour waiting on the outskirts of a vicious battle for a kill which never came, when I caught sight of the Beeches on the horizon. This is a natural landmark: a distinctively shaped clump of ancient trees perched on top of an otherwise exposed hill. I used to pass the Beeches on the motorway travelling back home from rare daytrips out with Lizzie and the kids, and my best guess is that we're three or four miles away from them, and they're another five miles or so from the edge of town.

'So where are we?'

'Close to where I used to live.'

'So why do you want to go back there?'

'What?' I mumble, distracted.

'Back home? Why do you want to go home?'

'I lost my daughter and I want to find her again,' I tell him. 'She's like us.'

He nods his head thoughtfully. Then, from out of nowhere, a huge grin spreads across his tired, sweat-streaked face. 'So how many did you kill today, Dan?'

'Two, I think. You?'

'Beat you! I got three. You should have seen the last one. Speared the fucker on my stick. Took more effort to pull it out again than it did to skewer him!'

'Nice.'

'I tell you, mate,' he continues, the tiredness gone and his voice suddenly full of energy and enthusiasm, 'it's the *best* feeling. When I first see them they scare the hell out of me, but as soon as I'm ready and I've got my head together, all I want to do is kill. Does that feeling ever go? Tell me it doesn't . . .'

Adam's still living off the buzz of sudden power and freedom that comes with understanding the Change and experiencing your first few kills. I felt the same when it happened to me. It'll be a while before he comes down again. It's like a drug, and we're junkies. I don't get the same highs I used to any more, just the cravings. The euphoria has faded and life's more of a struggle now. It's getting harder to find food and I'm tired. The gaps between kills are increasing, and all that's left to do in those gaps is think.

'The feeling doesn't go,' I answer, 'it just changes.'

'Wish I'd been there at the start . . .' For a few seconds he's quiet again, daydreaming about all the opportunities he's convinced he's missed. The silence is only temporary; he's already thinking of the next question to ask. 'So what are we?'

'What do you mean?'

'All I want to do is kill, mate. I'm addicted. Am I some kind of vampire?'

'Don't be stupid.'

'I'm not, think about it . . .'

'Believe me, I have thought about it. We're not vampires. We don't drink blood, we just spill it. I like garlic in my food, I'm okay with sunlight and I can see my reflection in mirrors.'

'You sure? You seen the state of yourself recently?'

I ignore his cheap jibe. He's right, but he looks no better. It's months since I cut my hair and weeks since I last shaved. I did manage to wash in a stream yesterday, or was it the day before?

'What are we then? Werewolves?'

I shake my head in disbelief. This guy's relentless. But what's even more disturbing is the fact I've already had this conversation with myself and I've got my answers prepared. Truth is, at the beginning there were times I felt more like an animal than a man. In some ways I still do, but now I scavenge more than I hunt: less like a wolf, more like a rat.

'We're not werewolves. We don't change when the moon comes out.'

'I know that, you prick,' he says, catching his breath as the toes on his broken foot drag on the ground. I stay quiet for a moment, wondering if I should tell him what I really think, or whether it's just going to pointlessly prolong this stupid conversation.

'Here's what I reckon,' I say, deciding just to go for it. 'You want to compare us to a type of monster? Look at the evidence . . .'

'What evidence?'

'Look at how we live and what we do.'

'I don't get you . . .'

'We drag ourselves around constantly, looking for Unchanged to kill. It's almost like we're feeding off them. When you're killing you feel alive, like you can do anything, but the rest of the time it's like you're in limbo. Just existing. Not really living, but not dead either . . .'

'So what are you saying?'

'I'm saying we're like zombies,' I finally admit. 'Being out here is like being one of the undead.'

He doesn't react. For a minute everything is quiet and deceptively peaceful, the only sound our slow, uneven footsteps on the dirt track.

'Do you know what I always used to wonder?' he eventually says.

Do I really want to know? 'What?' I say.

'I used to wonder what happened to the zombies after the end of the film. You know what I'm saying? When all the living have been infected and there's no one left to kill, what happens next? Does the hunger ever go away, or is rotting all that's left for them?'

3

Adam is struggling, his battered body a wreck, but he keeps moving. The light's almost completely gone and we need to stop. Apart from a single helicopter in the distance and a fast-moving truck a few miles back we haven't seen or heard anyone for hours.

Things have changed – when the fighting first started there were people everywhere. Maybe it's because I'm moving at a fraction of my normal pace that the world seems empty? Part of me still thinks I should just dump Adam and go on alone. We'll find somewhere to stop and rest for the night. When I'm ready to get moving again I'll decide whether I'm going to take him with me.

'Over there.'

'What?'

'There,' he says, pointing across the road. He uses his broken hand and because his fingers jut out at unnatural angles I can't work out what he's gesturing at. 'Look . . . through the trees . . .'

The road we're following runs alongside a dense forest. I squint into the semi-darkness to try and see whatever it is he thinks he's spotted. He hops away from me, moving towards a gap in the trees. I look down and see that there are muddy tyre tracks curving onto the road from the mouth of a barely visible track.

'What do you reckon?' he asks.

'Got to be worth a look. There wouldn't be a track if it didn't lead somewhere.'

'Might be more of them down there . . .'

He tries to speed up again, keen to kill, but I pull him back.

I'm not sure. This doesn't feel right. I can see the outline of a large building up ahead on the edge of a clearing and I cautiously edge closer. The building is huge, box-shaped, like a warehouse. But why here, out in the middle of nowhere? I take another few steps forward and realisation slowly begins to dawn. Shit, I know what this place is.

'What's the matter, Dan?'

I don't answer – *can't* answer. My mouth's suddenly dry and my legs feel like lead. I should turn around and walk away, but I don't. Instead I keep moving forward, on autopilot, my mind racing. We enter a dusty, gravel-covered yard. Lines of maze-like wooden queuing barriers make it look like an out-of-season tourist attraction. Up ahead the building's doors hang open like a gaping mouth.

'What is this?'

'You don't know?'

He shrugs his shoulders. 'Should I?'

'Slaughterhouse.'

Adam uses the nearest barrier, working his way along it to get to the open door. 'You told me about these places, but I . . .' His voice tails off.

'What? You didn't believe me?'

'It's not that . . .' He stops talking and I stop listening.

Like a character in a bad horror movie I walk into the building. It's almost pitch-black inside, but I can see enough to know that we're in a narrow corridor with a set of heavy double doors directly ahead. It's musty and damp in here, faint scents of the forest and wood-smoke mixing with the heavy, acrid stench of chemicals and decay. I wish I'd got a torch. The gloom makes it too easy to remember the night I almost died in a place like this. Standing here in the dark I can still see the helpless, terrified faces of the people crammed around me as we were herded like cattle towards the killing chamber. I remember our expressions: lost, desperate, confused, the frustration and pain so evident. I remember my own terror, the conviction that I was about to die . . .

'You okay?' Adam asks, finally catching up and nudging into me from behind. I hadn't even realised I'd stopped walking. I feel like I've stepped out of my body and now I'm watching from a distance. It's a nauseous, unsettling feeling, like the nervous relief you feel when you walk away without a scratch from a crash that's just written off your car. You're thinking, how did I get away with it? How close was I to biting the bullet? And then your mind starts with the 'what ifs?' and 'if onlys' . . . I know that if I'd been another hundred or so people further along the queue that night, I'd be a dead man now.

I lean up against one of the doors in front of me. It moves freely and I shove it open and walk into what must have been the gas chamber. The dark hides the details, but I know what is all around me. There are bodies here. I have no idea how many, but I can see them, stacked up in featureless piles. The cavernous room is filled with the buzzing of thousands of flies gorging on dead flesh. I keep looking up to avoid looking down. There's a hole in the roof three-quarters of the way down the length of the room, and I can just about make out metal gantries and walkways high up on either side. Wide-gauge pipe-work weaves in and out of the walls of the building and an enormous exhaust fan has been mounted at the far end of the room. Its blades are still turning slowly in the gentle evening breeze.

'Let's get out,' Adam whispers from somewhere close behind me. 'Fucking stinks in here.'

I move forward again, dragging my feet along the ground so I don't trip over anything I can't see. I am convinced that the entire floor is covered with gore and bits of bodies. I kick chunks of wood and twisted chunks of metal out of the way – remnants of the fallen section of roof – and finally reach the far wall, my pace almost as slow as Adam's. As I work my way along, I am trying to find a way out. In the furthest corner, hidden from view by another unidentifiable pile of rubbish, is a wide door, half-open and hanging off its hinges. I duck underneath it, then turn back and prop it open fully so Adam can get through. His uneven footsteps and his grunts of effort make him sound like a monster in the shadows.

'We can't stay here,' he says.

'Might be some other buildings around.'

As soon as he's completely outside I put my arm around him and support his weight.

We've taken only a few steps when he stops.

'Fuck me,' he mumbles. 'Would you look at that . . . ?'

To the side of the long building is another clearing, out of sight until now, and the ground is almost completely covered with bodies, for as far as I can see. There are hundreds of them, thousands probably, stacked up in massive piles. I leave Adam again and move towards the nearest one. From a distance the gloom makes it look like a single, unidentifiable mass. It's identifiable as human remains only because of the countless hands, arms and legs which are sticking out at awkward angles.

As I get closer, a level of sickening detail is revealed. These bodies have been dumped – not even laid out – and those at the bottom have been crushed by the weight of the rest, leaving them unnaturally thin, almost like they've been vacuum-packed. Higher up, the countless squashed, waxy faces stare back at me unblinking. Their discoloured flesh, hollow cheeks and sunken eyes give them grotesque, nightmarish expressions. Seeing them makes me think about my own mortality. I don't feel anything for any of the people here – they're just empty shells now, each of them a spent force – but I swear I won't end up like this.

'Look on the bright side,' Adam shouts across the clearing.

'There's a bright side?'

''Course there is. You got away. That could have been you, that could. Could have been me . . .'

I ignore him and keep walking further into the clearing, following a narrow pathway between another two fifty-metre-long piles of death. Distracted, I lose my footing when I reach the end of the rows and the ground suddenly starts to crumble beneath my boots. I fall back and find myself sitting on my backside on the edge of a vast hole, at least twenty metres square, and deep enough for me not to be able to see the bottom in some parts. I know immediately what it is: a mass grave, filled with an incalculable number of people like Adam and me.

I get up and carefully walk around the edge. There's a bulldozer up ahead, fitted with a massive metal scoop. At first I think they must have used it to dig the pit, but then I see there's a scrap of cloth caught on the teeth of the scoop and I realise they were using it to fill the pit. Directly below me there are corpses piled almost as high as the ground. They look like they're climbing over each other to get out.

I jog back over to Adam, forcing myself to look away from the dead. How many sites like this are there, and are any still in operation? Even now, as I'm wasting time here, are more of our people being killed elsewhere? And then another thought crosses my mind, one which makes me go cold: my daughter, Ellis. Did she end up in a place like this? Is she there now, waiting to die? Is she *here*? For a few desperate seconds I turn back towards the corpses and start looking through them, terrified that the next face I see will be my little girl's. But then, as quickly as sudden panic just took hold, common sense takes over again. If she's here, there's nothing I can do. I have to believe she's still alive. She's all I've got left.

'So where are they all?' Adam asks.

'Who?'

'The fuckers who did this. Where'd they go?'

'I don't know,' I answer as I lead him out behind the main building towards a group of three square-shaped, light-coloured, prefabricated huts which look new in comparison to everything else. 'Just abandoned the place, I guess. Maybe they were attacked?'

'Hope the bastards got what they deserved.'

Two of the almost identical shed-like buildings are locked. The corrugated metal roller-door on the front of the third is not. I open it fully and go inside. It's small, cramped, and half-full of bags of chemicals. Doesn't matter. It'll do for tonight. No one with any sense will come here, and even if they do, we'll just play dead. I'd have fought side by side with any of the thousands of people who died here, but they're just rotting meat now and we'll use them as cover.

Adam sits down on a pile of sacks, struggling to get comfortable and still talking nonstop about nothing of any importance. I close the door, then find myself a scrap of space in the far corner of the hard concrete floor and try to sleep, resting my head on another plastic sack full of Christ knows what. It could be poisonous or corrosive, but it doesn't matter. I cover it with my coat and close my eyes, too tired to care.

4

I'm woken by a crash and a muffled cry of pain. I sit up quickly and look around the dark room, struggling for a second to work out where I am. The combination of the acrid chemical smell and the stench of decay helps me remember. Where's Adam?

I catch a momentary glimpse of him outside through the open door, hobbling back towards the main building. I grab a knife from my rucksack and run after him, but I've taken barely two steps out of the chemical store when I hear other voices up ahead. There are people around the front of the cull site. I drag Adam out of the way, stopping only when we're both pressed up tight against the outside wall at the back of the main killing chamber.

'It's Unchanged,' he whispers, voice full of nervous excitement. 'I saw them.'

'How many?'

'Don't know. Heard engines.'

What the hell do I do now? Despite what Adam probably thinks, we can't risk taking them on until we know how many we're facing. There could be hundreds of them here, and if they've dared come out into the open like this then they're probably armed to the teeth and ready to fight. What do they want? Maybe they've come to try and get this place restarted? Shit, maybe they're here looking for us?

'Wait here,' I tell him, pushing him towards an alcove. 'Keep yourself under control and don't do anything until I come back, okay? I'll try and get a better look.'

Adam nods and does as I say. There's a metal ladder running up the side of the building, from ground level to an access hatch up high. Before I can talk myself out of it I start climb-ing, trying to keep down the sound of my heavy boots on the metal rungs. I pause when I'm two-thirds up and lean over to one side to peer in through a grubby window. The early morning sun is blazing through the windows along one side of the slaughterhouse and the hole in the roof, filling it with light, uncovering every gruesome detail that was hidden in the darkness last night. The Unchanged are inside the building now. I can see a couple of them slowly picking their way through the bodies and debris.

At the top of the ladder I open the hatch and carefully ease myself inside. I'm on one of the narrow gantries running around the edge of the vast room, and I know I'm all too visible up here through the metal grilles. I move towards the side of the room which is still in shadow. I'm right above one of the intruders now. Looks like he's wrestling with a corpse. He's trying to prise a rifle from the death grip of a decaying soldier. Fortunately he's preoccupied, and I keep moving to-wards the front of the site undetected.

Further ahead I notice that this walkway's loose. Several brackets and supports have come away from the wall and it's already feeling unsecure. I'm less worried about my safety and more concerned that the creaking and groaning of the metal will cause one of the scavengers below to look up. They don't look like typical Unchanged military or militia. They're wear-ing mismatched clothing and they're both weighed down with weapons, far more than they need. They look more like mech-anics than soldiers.

A sudden noise makes me catch my breath. I look back over my shoulder and stare down, worried they've found Adam, but it's nothing, just another Unchanged helping themselves to a dead man's gun.

I turn around to try and get off this unstable walkway, but stop when I glimpse something happening through the large dust- and cobweb-covered window at my side. The reason for the enemy being here has suddenly become painfully apparent.

Outside, under the protective gaze of five armed militia fighters, two young women and a white-haired elderly man are working their way along the nearest pile of corpses, stripping them of anything of value. Inhuman bastards. There must be a hell of a black market somewhere for them to be risking this, but the fuckers look well organised and they know what they're doing. They're wearing yellow washing-up gloves, and the three of them move along the bodies at speed, each of them working at different heights, snatching rings and watches from the dead hands which are sticking out of the massive mound of rotting flesh, filling buckets with their stolen booty.

A teenage boy grabs each bucket when it's full, replacing it with an empty one and carrying the stash away out of sight. What I'm watching makes me seethe with hate and anger, but what can I do? There are too many of them to risk taking on alone (and even though Adam's with me, in terms of fighting I still think of myself as being alone). All I can do is wait for them to disappear.

Hang on, something's caught the attention of the grave-robbing bastards below me. One of them stops scavenging and calls to his mates. Carrying several weapons each, they head towards the door in the corner we exited through last night. I run back along the gantry but before I get to the hatch I know it's Adam. I hear the stupid kid before I see him through the window. Should have known he'd struggle to keep himself under control.

The Unchanged are outside now, heading straight for him as he limps aggressively towards them, the sharp tip of his ski-pole walking stick held out like a bayonet. Fortunately the rest of this gang are either unaware or too interested in their haul to get involved. I climb back out through the door and down the ladder. Adam and the Unchanged are out of sight now, but I can still hear them fighting. With half a dozen rungs left I jump down and run around the corner to help, knife in hand. Adam's on the ground, taking a heavy beating from two of them. To his credit he's already taken the other one out. The scrawny little fucker is slumped up against the side of the building, impaled with his metal stick.

I grab the shoulders of one of his attackers and slam him down onto the dusty ground. His body rattles with the impact and the look on his face is one of surprise more than anything else. Before he realises what's happening I stab my knife into his chest, aiming for his heart. The blade's wedged stuck in his breastbone.

No time to pull it out. I run straight at the other one, punching the side of his head with enough force to knock him over. He scrambles back up, shakes his head clear and rushes at me, holding a rifle by the barrel and swinging it around like a club. I duck his first clumsy strike then, while he's still off-balance, I thump my axe into the base of his spine. I shove his face down into the dirt to muffle his screams until I'm sure he's dead.

Need to get under cover. We're out of sight and there's no sign of them yet, but the others will come looking for their people before long. Adam's out cold and my already slim chances of winning this one-sided fight have just been slashed even further. All I can do now is get out of the way and wait for the rest of these fuckers to move on. Trouble is, I realise as I shove my arms under Adam's shoulders and start dragging him back towards the chemical store, when they find the bodies of three of their own they're not going to go anywhere. And then, as I reverse through the door and look back, I realise the tracks Adam's feet have left in the gravel and dust will lead them straight to us.

I dump his useless, groaning bulk in the space on the floor where I slept last night. There's a dribble of blood running from the corner of his mouth but I can't tell if it's just his mouth that's cut or whether his injuries are more serious. The way they were laying into him, I wouldn't be surprised if his insides were well and truly fucked.

I stand up to lower the roller-door back down but it's too late. There's already another one of them standing over the bodies, and this one looks like he actually knows how to use the powerful rifle he's carrying. He's calling for reinforcements but he hasn't seen me.

I duck down behind more of the acidic-smelling chemical sacks and watch him through a narrow gap between two waist-high piles. All I can see are his boots. As I'm watching, another two pairs of feet approach. I don't think they've seen the tracks in the dirt yet, but it's only a matter of time. It's not like there's anywhere else around here I'd be hiding. I try to stay calm and prepare myself mentally for the fight, working out which one I should attack first and which way I should run. Maybe running is the only option? Sorry, Adam, I think this is where we say our goodbyes. Can't see any way of getting him out of here now. Poor bastard's three-quarters dead anyway.

Another two of them join the first three. Five to one – those are bad odds in anyone's book. I'd have been better off taking my chances and laying flat on a pile of corpses. Wish I'd thought of that sooner. Perhaps I can still get over to that open grave . . . ?

Here they come. One of them starts to walk towards this building. Christ, I don't even have my knife with me. It's still buried to the hilt in the gut of one of them. Maybe I can reach my rucksack from here . . .

Wait. They've stopped.

Something's distracted them. Figuring I've got nothing to lose, I slide across the floor to try and get a better view of what's happening. They're starting to move back towards the front of the building now. Can't see why, but their weapons are raised. This is my chance to make a break for it. I get up, grab my rucksack and run back outside, then stop when one of the enemy scavengers goes flying past the front of the chemical store. He skids along the ground, thrown like a rag doll, eventually landing in a heap in the dust a few metres from my feet. Another one of them reappears, this one running backwards, trying to fire his rifle while he's defending himself from whatever it is that's attacking him. I'm right out in the open again now, my curiosity and bewilderment forcing common sense to take a back seat, and I can finally see what's happening.

The cavalry have arrived. *Halle-fucking-lujah.* At precisely the right moment a van full of our people has turned up at the site, and they've got two powerful and incredibly aggressive fuckers in tow who are making short work of any of the Unchanged stupid enough to stand in their way. The way these two are fighting is savage and brutal in the extreme and it's awe-inspiring to watch. Ignorant to their own personal safety, they move with an agility and speed which belies their otherwise ordinary appearance. They're totally focused on the kill, oblivious to everyone and everything else around them.

The old man I saw stripping corpses is hobbling towards me, a look of absolute fear plastered across his weathered face. He runs straight at me, yelling for help, too terrified to realise I'm going to kill him.

'Get out of here,' he tries to warn me, barely able to breathe. 'They'll—'

I end his sentence before he has the chance to. I grab his shock of white hair, yank his head back and punch him hard in the throat. He collapses at my feet, choking. I snatch a knife from my rucksack and finish him off. Suddenly feeling fired up and alive, I sprint down towards the battle that's raging at the front of the building, desperate to kill again.

By the time I get there it's over, the suddenly one-sided fight ended with incredible speed, force and brutality by seven other people like Adam and me. None of them question me. There's an immediate, unspoken trust between us and within minutes I'm helping them dump the bodies of the Unchanged with the thousands of others already here.

These people are surprisingly well coordinated. There are seventeen of us here now, including me and Adam, another group having just arrived on foot through the trees to the east of the cull site. I've stumbled into the middle of a pre-planned rendezvous and I'm going to take advantage of it while it lasts. They won't be here long. Sticking together in large numbers is dangerous. It leaves us exposed.

They work quickly, hiding their vehicles in the shadows of the building and stripping the site of weapons and anything else of value. Guards patrol the perimeter constantly; others watch from the roof. The two most aggressive fighters are positioned one at either end of the building. As I walk towards the chemical store with a short, stocky man, I notice that the fighter out back is shackled. She has a heavy-duty chain padlocked around her waist which is anchored to a metal stake that's been driven deep into the ground.

'What's all that about?' I ask quietly, not wanting her to hear. He takes off his glasses and cleans the one remaining lens on the bottom corner of his shirt.

'You not come across Brutes before?'

'Brutes?'

'That's what we call them.'

'Them? You make it sound like they're different to us.'

'Not really,' he sighs, like it's an effort having to explain. 'They're the same as us, but extreme.'

'Extreme?'

'Are you the guy who was hiding here?'

'I wasn't hiding, I just . . .'

'Why didn't you attack?'

'What?'

'When those thieving bastards first turned up this morning, why didn't you attack them?'

'Because I didn't know how many of them there were. I didn't know what weapons they had, and . . .'

'Exactly,' he interrupts, replacing his glasses. 'You knew there was a good chance you'd've been killed if you'd tried anything.'

'It wasn't worth the risk.'

'Don't blame you,' he says, leaning up against the side of the chemical store and shielding his eyes from the climbing sun. 'I'd probably have done the same.'

'So what's your point?'

'The point is a Brute wouldn't have held back. They can't. They catch a scent of Unchanged and they'll hunt them down and attack, no matter what the odds are.'

'Bloody hell . . .'

'Useful, though – they make good guard dogs! Always on the lookout – just look at her . . .' He gestures at the woman tied up at the back of the killing chamber.

She's constantly straining against her shackles, trying to break free and go after the enemy she knows is still out there somewhere. I'm transfixed by her face, flushed red and full of rage, and yet, in a different light, she doesn't look like a killer at all. When she relaxes, her features are surprisingly soft and feminine.

'She could just be someone's mother . . .'

'She was. Her name's Pat. She had someone with her when we first found her, someone who knew her before the Change. She was a teacher in a primary school. Hard to believe, isn't it? A well-respected pillar of society, cornerstone of the community, great with kids, wouldn't hurt anyone . . . you get the picture.'

'Incredible.'

'My brother was a Brute,' he continues. 'From sheet metal worker to a killer like that, overnight.'

'What happened to him?'

'We lost him.'

'Sorry, I—'

'Oh, he's not dead, I don't think. When I say we lost him, I mean we *lost* him. Clever bastard slipped his chains and got away. Christ knows where he is now. Don't suppose it matters as long as he's still killing. Your mate in here, is he?'

He slaps the wall of the chemical store.

'What?' I mumble, still thinking about this guy's missing brother and forgetting what we came out here for. 'Yeah, sorry. He's in the back.'

By the time we clear the doorway and we're ready to move him out, Adam's just about regained consciousness. He's still in a bad way: pale, clammy, and barely able to move. We fashion a stretcher from wood stripped from the walls of the main building and between us we carry him back to the others.

6

'**M**y name's Preston,' a disarmingly confident, oily man says, grabbing my hand and shaking it vigorously. I already know I don't like him. He's too loud and in-your-face. He reminds me of the senior managers I used to despise at work; the higher up the corporate ladder they managed to climb, the more arrogant, obnoxious and smarmy they became. He's wearing a bizarre combination of military garbs and civvies. His clothes make him look like someone's dad going to a fancy dress party as a World War II general.

'Danny McCoyne.'

'Good to meet you, Danny. You had some food?'

'Yes, I—'

'Excellent. Have you been introduced to anyone?'

'I've met a few people. I don't know if—'

'Great,' he says, interrupting me again. Irritating little shit. Apparently he's the self-appointed leader of this cell and I've been granted a personal audience (as, I've learnt, are all new 'recruits'). We're sitting in the back of a beaten-up Transit van, just him and me. The heat is suffocating. He's propped the doors open.

'Look, I—' I start to say.

'So, what have you been up to, Danny?' he asks, his hat-trick of interruptions complete.

'What?'

'Since the war started? What have you been doing with yourself?'

Is this a trick question? What does he think I've been doing? I've fought whenever I've been able, done all I can to get rid of the maximum number of Unchanged. Does this guy think

43

I'm just some lazy shyster, hiding out here in the middle of nowhere, waiting for the war to end?

'Fighting.'

'Good. On your own?'

'Generally, travelling on my own, fighting with others whenever I've had chance. Look, what's all this about?'

'You killed many?'

Now he's beginning to annoy me. Idiot. I've a good mind just to leave. His questions make me feel uneasy, inadequate, almost. I don't think I could have fought any harder, but how does that stack up against everyone else? For the first time it occurs to me that I don't know how 'good' a fighter I actually am. Is my tally of victims higher or lower than average? Does it matter? As long as we're all killing, does anyone care how quickly, enthusiastically or effectively we do it? I suddenly feel like I'm being assessed, like one of those pointless performance reviews I used to have to go through at work. Have I hit my agreed Unchanged corpse target for this month?

'Plenty,' I answer, 'but I haven't been keeping count.'

'Too many to keep track of, eh?' he grins. Patronising bastard.

'Something like that.'

'Have you noticed their numbers are dropping off? That there's fewer of them around to kill?'

'Yes.'

'And do you know why that is?'

I shrug my shoulders. 'Could be any one of a number of reasons,' I reply, suddenly feeling like a little kid put on the spot in class. I'm being deliberately vague, not wanting to give this joker the chance to make me look stupid, playing cat and mouse games with the truth like I used to with my managers back at the council. 'I know it's not because we've killed them all.'

'If only that was the case! No, the real reason is that they're continuing to concentrate themselves together, completely pulling out of areas like this. Tell me, have you heard of Chris Ankin?'

I stop and think. The name sounds familiar. Then I remember: Chris Ankin was the politician who recorded the message I heard when the war first began. After getting away from the slaughterhouse that night, his was the voice that finally explained what was happening to me, and why. I kept that message on a phone I'd found and I replayed it again and again until the battery died and I finally threw it away.

'I know him. I thought he was dead.'

'He wasn't last time I saw him.'

'And when was that?'

'About ten days ago. Have you been following his messages?'

'Haven't heard anything for weeks.'

Preston gets up and moves to the front of the van. He rummages around and pulls out a laptop from under one of the front seats. He turns it on and I watch as it boots up, staring at the start-up screen graphics and messages as raptly as if I was watching a Hollywood blockbuster. It makes me feel unexpectedly nostalgic and empty, remembering things I haven't seen or thought about since my old life ended. After a couple of minutes the machine is ready. With the speed of a computer-phobic two-finger typist, he logs on and opens a video file. At the bottom of the screen a number of small icons and speech bubbles appear and disappear as programs try pointlessly to search for updates via networks which no longer exist. A haggard, tired-looking pixellated face (Chris Ankin, I presume) appears in a small window which, after much cursing, Preston manages to enlarge to fill the screen. By the time he passes the laptop over to me, the politician's already in full flow. The small speakers and the confined space distort his voice but it's still recognisable, and strangely reassuring.

'When your enemy's tactics change, you have to reassess your own tactics too,' he is explaining. 'From the earliest days

45

of this war, fate and circumstance have combined to make us underdogs. We are, however, underdogs in numbers only.'

I glance across at Preston but he doesn't look back. His eyes are glued to the screen. Even though he's probably heard this a hundred times already, he's still hanging on Ankin's every word.

'Since day one, our enemy have been retreating. The way we've fought this war put them on the back foot from the beginning, and it's a position from which they've struggled to recover. The fact that our opposing sides were so closely inter-twined before we realised we *were* two opposing sides has made it all but impossible for them to isolate themselves and defend against us. We're practically invisible to them, and that has strengthened our hand dramatically. But now, now that we're months into this campaign, the position is beginning to change.

'With every day that passes, our people have become more and more diffuse. We each move from fight to fight, from battle to battle, going wherever we're needed. As a result our people are increasingly spread out, and the enemy have taken advantage of this.'

'What's he talking about?'

Preston glares at me. 'Just shut up and listen.'

'They've pulled back into the hearts of their remaining cities, pulling their people closer together and drawing them in from the outside. There's strength in numbers, and we need to do something similar. We need to stop fighting as individuals and form a coordinated attack force, an army, if you will.'

'But they will hunt us out. If we start grouping together in large numbers, they'll find us and . . .'

Preston sighs and pauses the video. He rubs his eyes. 'This is so much bigger than you and me, Danny,' he says. 'We're just cogs in a machine and we're expendable. Ankin's not talking about setting up a military force with sergeant majors and captains and the like. He's just trying to get us to work together and coordinate our efforts.'

'I understand that, but . . .'

'We have to start making better use of the people and resources we've got, and start hitting the enemy where it hurts. If we can do enough damage to start them off, they'll destroy themselves. You heard about London, didn't you?'

'No. I haven't heard anything for weeks—'

'It happened incredibly quickly. We lost thousands that night, but they lost many, many more . . .'

'How? What happened?'

He's surprised that I don't know. 'It was the mother of all battles,' he explains. 'We came at them from all angles, caused so much panic and confusion that they lost control. In the end the only option left for them was to destroy it completely.'

'Jesus . . .'

'And we can make the same thing happen again and again if we learn to fight smarter. We don't have any choice. Our only alternative is to wait out here in the wastelands until they decide to come out into the open again and hunt us down, but by then it'll be too late. We have to act now.'

'So what do you want from me?'

He looks straight at me and puts down the laptop. This feels ominous. He's going to ask me to sign up and join his happy brigade of killers, I know he is. Thing is, apart from Adam, I've spent weeks fighting alone. Do I really want to go back to being one face among hundreds again? I've never been any good at taking orders.

'We want you to fight with us,' he says, unsurprisingly. I bite my tongue. 'The more of us there are, the better our chances will be. Tell me about yourself, Danny. What your skills are, where you're heading?'

'Don't know where to start.' For a moment I truly am flummoxed. No aspect of my former life has any bearing on me today, and as far as skills are concerned, what does he expect me to tell him? That I've got a Certificate in Dismemberment? A Ph.D. in Asphyxiation Techniques? The sudden protracted silence is uncomfortable.

'Well, what did you do before all of this?'

'I worked in an office.'

'Okay. What line of business?'

'Processing parking fines.'

Preston pauses to try and get his head around the banality of my pre-war existence. 'Not much call for that these days,' he says, without a hint of sarcasm in his voice. 'Any special skills? Military or police experience?'

I feel suddenly inadequate. What we do is instinctive, not taught. My answer is automatic and stupid.

'I was in the Scouts for a while . . .'

'Don't take the piss,' he warns. 'I'm serious.'

'No, nothing.'

'So now you're just drifting without a purpose? Spending your time hiding behind the corpses of our people?'

'I wasn't hiding,' I snap quickly, annoyed by his tone. 'We were just passing through.'

'That's what they all say.'

Truth is, I have been as directionless as he's implying. But now I've got a reason to keep moving.

'Actually,' I announce, 'I'm heading home.'

'Home? Why the hell would you want to do that? What possible reason could you have for wanting any connection with your past life?'

'I want to find my daughter.'

He looks up, his interest suddenly piqued. 'Why?'

What do I tell him now? Have I made a mistake admitting I want to look for Ellis – does he think I'm less of a man because of it? A weaker fighter? Or maybe that I'm in league with the enemy? Do I even know why I want to find Ellis? What am I hoping to achieve? Life with her could never be like it used to be again, so why am I bothering? As much as the thought of who and what I used to be now disgusts me, I wonder if that's the real reason I want to be with her again: perhaps I'm just trying to bridge the gap between today and all that happened in the years before now. This uncomfortable silence seems to last for ever. I open and close my mouth to speak, but no words come out.

Then Preston speaks for me. 'She's like us, isn't she?'

7

Preston stares at me intently. What the hell is he thinking? So he knows that Ellis is one of us, so what? Why should that make any difference to him? Whatever the reason, his tone has definitely changed. He's suddenly more serious and direct. He left the van momentarily to speak to someone, then came back and pulled the door shut. It's suffocatingly hot in here now.

'Tell me about her, Danny.'

I don't like this. I'll drip-feed him information and find out why he wants to know. Years of living in the old world have taken their toll and my guard is up. Part of me can't help wondering whether I've managed to stumble on the last remaining paedophile ring in existence. When I don't answer he asks another question.

'How old?'

'Just turned five.'

'And you think you know where she might be?'

'Possibly,' I answer quickly. I can afford to give him some vague details. Even if I knew exactly where Ellis was, I could tell him anything. He doesn't know anything about her. He doesn't know what she looks like. Christ, I haven't even told him her name.

'She somewhere near here?'

'Might be.'

Preston leans over to the front seat and picks up a map which he unfolds. 'Show me.'

'I'm not telling you anything until you tell me why you're so interested in my daughter. What are you, some kind of pervert? A kiddie-fiddler?'

His face remains impassive and serious. There's not a flicker of emotion. 'It's not just your daughter we're interested in,' he says finally. 'Our belief is that children are key to our future. They're important now, and they'll be even more crucial when this war's won.'

'Go on.'

'Have you ever seen a child fight? They're fast, strong, agile . . . completely uninhibited. They're not burdened with years of memories of the old way of things; all they know is now. They accept what they see and experience today, and they accept it without question. *This* is their normality.'

What he says makes some kind of sense, but I don't trust this guy. His slimy, slick way of speaking immediately gets my back up. He comes across like a politician; a sub-par spin doctor. I know we're both fighting on the same side, but how different are our aims and objectives?

'You talk a lot, but you're not actually *saying* anything. Why should I tell you anything about my little girl?'

'Kids are true fighters, Danny, perfect fighters even. Brutes are strong and aggressive, but children are something else entirely. I think—'

He stops speaking suddenly, almost as if he's not sure I can be trusted. I press him, keen to hear what he has to say. He runs his fingers through his greasy, slicked-back black hair.

'I think the line between us and the Unchanged starts to blur when you're looking at very young children. Like I said, they don't carry the baggage and the memories we do. Given the right stimulation and provocation, I think even an Unchanged kid could be taught to fight like us.'

There's another silence as we both think about what he's just said. My initial reaction is that it's probably bullshit, but he might just have a point. A young kid growing up surrounded by all this madness wouldn't know any different. They'd have to learn to fight to survive, whatever their initial allegiance.

'I got separated from my family when the Change happened to me,' I tell him, deciding I've got nothing to lose from opening up a little more, as long as I'm sparing with the details. I take the map from him and tap my finger on the area where I used to live. 'I last saw them here, but my partner managed to get away with the kids.'

'Kids? More than one?'

'Two sons and a daughter. It's only Ellis I'm interested in.'

'That's your little girl?'

'Yes.'

'Don't be so quick to write off the other two . . .'

I slide my finger across the map then stop. 'I think Lizzie would have gone to her sister's house. What are these marks?'

Two circles have been drawn on the map, both centred on the main part of town. My flat and Lizzie's sister's house are just outside the outermost circle.

Preston explains. 'Like Ankin said, the Unchanged have withdrawn into the city centres. Our information's a couple of weeks old, but we think the first circle is the extent of their occupation.'

'What about the second line?'

'The outermost edge of their exclusion zone. It's a strip of empty land smack between them and everything else, pretty well defended. Makes it that much harder for us to get through unnoticed. It's not impossible, just a little more difficult.'

'So how does Ankin plan to march an army through no-man's land without being noticed?'

'He'll find a way,' Preston answers. He's not filling me with confidence. I try and steer the conversation back towards Ellis.

'So that's my plan,' I tell him. 'Check the flat first, then look for Ellis at Lizzie's sister's house.'

'And if she's not there?'

'I haven't thought that far ahead. I don't want to.'

Preston folds up the map and thinks for a moment. 'What if I said we could help you?'

'Help me? How?'

'We've got a group of people heading out that way later today, looking for more recruits. You could go with them. You'll have more chance if you go with our support . . .'

'And what's in it for you?'

'There are just two conditions,' he announces. It sounds ominous. 'First, if you don't find your girl, you forget about her and come back here and fight with us. Second, if you do find her, you *both* come back to us and fight.'

8

'I could've had all three of them,' Adam says, his voice weak and frail, but somehow still filled with adrenalin-fuelled enthusiasm and excitement. 'I didn't need your help. I'd have been perfectly fine if you hadn't come back . . .'

'Sure you would,' I interrupt. 'You're full of shit, you know that?'

'You're the one who's full of shit,' he laughs. 'You were the one hiding up a ladder!'

'I wasn't hiding!'

He coughs and laughs again, showering his bare chest with speckles of blood. There's no two ways about it, Adam's on his way out. His breathing is increasingly shallow and uneven. He was already severely weakened by the injuries inflicted by his dad and the subsequent untreated infections. The brutal beating he took this morning did more than enough damage to push his broken body into total submission. He's covered in bruises, cuts and contusions. He's hardly moved in hours and his condition is continuing to steadily worsen.

It's another swelteringly hot day. The air is dry and the relentless heat makes the smell of thousands of badly decayed corpses even harder to stomach. The insect population is flourishing. It's hard to take a breath without sucking in a lungful of buzzing little fuckers. We're not heading into town until after dark, so there's nothing to do for the next few hours except try to relax and ready myself for the next fight.

'Need a drink,' Adam gasps. I grab a half-empty plastic bottle of water and hold it up to his chapped lips. He tries to swallow, but most of it runs down his chin. He coughs again and winces with sudden pain, but he doesn't complain.

Unbelievably, he's still fired up by the rush of battle. Poor bugger's completely oblivious to the fact he'll probably be dead before the morning.

'Next time,' he says, every word an effort, 'I'm gonna aim straight for the head, know what I'm saying?'

I nod. I don't have the heart to tell him there's not going to be a next time.

'I know,' I lie.

'See,' he continues, trying to prop himself up on his elbows but immediately dropping back down again, 'they'll look at me and think that because my arm and leg are fucked, I'll be a pushover. But they'll be wrong . . .'

His eyelids flutter closed and, just for a second, I think he's gone. I reach out to check his pulse but he bats me away when I touch his skin and mumbles something unintelligible. He's like an animal, blissfully unaware of his own mortality, convinced he's going to go on and on and on. In a way I can't help but envy his ignorance. He fades into unconsciousness.

'He dead?' a woman asks, her voice uncomfortably loud. I stand up and try to usher her away from Adam, but she stands her ground. Her name's Julia. She's coordinating the group of us heading out and from what I've heard from some of the others, she's a hard bitch who doesn't stand for any shit. She has a strong Irish lilt to her voice and I can't help thinking of the IRA and the Troubles when she speaks. It's wrong of me, but who cares? Equality, diversity and political correctness are all things of the past now, condemned to history by the Hate: the great leveller. All the name-calling, insults and dis-criminatory language we used to avoid using – it's all lost its impact now.

'Not yet. He's still hanging on.'

She nods, her stern face devoid of any emotion. 'There's more food in the van. Make sure you eat before you leave. Don't know when you'll get the chance again.'

What with the heat, the flies and the smell, the last thing I want is more food. 'Poor sod,' I say quietly. 'Just look at the state of him.'

Now that I've taken a step back from Adam I can see how bad his condition really is. He has open weeping wounds all over his body and his shattered bones haven't been properly looked at since his father first broke them. It makes me feel uneasy. This is a harsh and unforgiving world we're suddenly all living in. This man is going to die before the day is done, but none of his wounds are truly life-threatening. The medicine, the expertise and the means to save him exist, but it's all out of reach.

Julia seems to second-guess what I'm thinking with uncomfortable accuracy. 'Don't bother beating yourself up about it,' she says, 'there's no point. Face facts, he's useless to anyone like this.'

'I know, but . . .'

'But nothing. We don't have time to waste patching up people like this who aren't going to be able to fight again. It'd take him months to recover, and even then he'll still be next to no good. And who's going to look after him? We don't have the people to spare. Right now there's no such thing as doctors and nurses and surgeons and the like. At the end of the day we're all fighters, and that's all there is to it.'

I feel like I should protest, that I should try and say something in defence of my fallen friend, fight his corner, but I know there's no point. She's right. Christ, it was only this morning that I was thinking about walking out on him anyway.

'A fighter who can't fight,' she continues, preaching at me, 'is just a corpse. If you want to do something to help him, then find yourself a gun and put a bullet in his head.'

9

I'm away from the slaughterhouse and the corpses and the flies and the stench now and the land stretches out in front of me for ever. The sun-bleached knee-high grass shifts lazily from side to side in the warm wind like waves on a gently rolling sea. The world is suddenly absolutely beautiful, calm, and almost completely silent. I feel strong and relaxed, revitalised, ready for the next fight. It'll be time to leave soon.

I take a few steps forward, the blazing sun blinding me and burning my skin, my boots trampling down the long grass and leaving a flattened trail behind me. Considering how close to the cull site this place is, it's remarkably tranquil. Ahead of me there's nothing. The land from here to the horizon is flat, with only a handful of distant trees daring to stretch up from the yellow-green ground into the intense blue sky above.

Wait. What was that?

I hear something. The rustle of grass. Footsteps? I'm starting to think it was just the wind when, a few metres ahead of me, a child-like figure appears, emerging from the long grass where it had been hiding. It's virtually naked and desperately thin, and I can't tell from here what sex it is. It stands upright slowly, swaying slowly, watching me intently. I don't care who or what it is. I know that I have to kill it.

I start sprinting, totally focused on catching the figure up ahead and nothing else. He runs (now I can tell from the way he moves it's a male) and makes a sudden, darting turn to the left. He's moving far faster than me and the gap between us increases as I follow his trail through the flattened grass, round and around in a lazy arc until I end up back where I started. The child disappears momentarily. As I scan the horizon I can see the ruins of my home town that's up ahead of me now. It's been weeks since I've been here, but it's just as I remember, just a little dirtier than before. The dark, ugly buildings are in stark contrast to the beauty of everything else. There's a steady smoke haze hanging over the place: wisps of white spiralling up between the tallest buildings and clouds of dirty grey lying at street level like a heavy fog.

I've completely lost sight of the child now, but the trail of trampled grass will lead me straight to him. I start running again. The chase is getting harder now. The air is scorched and dry and I can feel the fierce sun burning the skin on my bare back. I force myself to keep moving forward, driven on by the thought of killing again. My mouth salivates at the prospect of tearing Unchanged flesh from bone . . .

A thin strip of hedgerow marks the furthest edge of the grassland. I crash through, ignoring the spiteful thorns which slash at my skin, onto an empty street I don't recognise. There are buildings rising up on either side of me now, dilapidated, but still tall enough to block out the sun. It's hard to see anything in the sudden change from light to dark and it's ice-cold in the shadows. Disorientated, I start to slow down. The child I'm chasing is long gone.

I hear footsteps again – more than one person this time, and they're behind me. I turn around and see a huge crowd of people charging up the long straight street after me. There're enough of them to fill the entire width of the road, but their true numbers are masked by the worsening gloom. I start to run again, willing myself to keep moving faster. My energy levels are dropping now I'm the one being chased, and every step takes ten times the effort it did before. My hunger has been replaced with fear as the crowd gets closer. Every time I look back over my shoulder my hunters are nearer still.

There's a gap in the row of buildings to my left – leading to another straighter, even narrower road – and I take it, my aching feet in heavy boots pounding the concrete, sending shockwaves shooting the length of my tired frame. All my strength and energy has gone. Can't keep going much further . . .

I stop halfway down the second street, unable to go any further. I look back and see the crowd still surging after me, like a herd of stampeding animals. They're close enough that I can see their faces now, and they stop suddenly, maintaining an unexpected, cautious distance. I sense they could attack at any moment and I'm scared.

For the first time in months I feel genuinely afraid. I look at the people at the front of the hunting pack and I see that they're like me, but I sense they're going to attack. Why? Do they think I'm one of the Unchanged? I open my mouth to try and explain, to try and make them understand, but I can't force out even a single word. I feel crushed, devastated and humiliated, wishing I was like them again. They look at me with total hatred . . .

I turn around to run and find myself facing Ellis. In disbelief I move closer towards her. She backs away from me, matching every step forward with a single step back, stopping when I stop . . .

'Ellis,' I start to say, my parched voice barely audible, 'I thought you'd—'

She throws herself at me, leaping up with lightning speed and grabbing hold of my throat. I'm down before I know it, my face slammed hard into the ground . . .

10

'Bad dream, Sleeping Beauty?' the man sitting next to me asks. I nod, but don't answer. I rub my head where it just thumped against the window of the van and immediately remember where I am. It's late in the day, I'm on my way back home with three other fighters, and I'm feeling travel-sick. Can't remember the last time I went anywhere by road like this. Is it safe? The confidence of the rest of the people in the van makes me feel out of step with everyone else.

The cocky, sour-faced guy next to me is Paul Hewlitt and he seems to have a far higher opinion of himself and his own abilities than anyone else does. In the front of the van are Carol and Keith, who's driving. As far as I'm aware there's nothing between them, but they bicker and argue like an old married couple. I feel like I don't belong here. I think I'd rather be doing this alone. Maybe I'm just not used to being with groups of people any more?

'Will you put that damn thing out?' Keith moans as Carol lights up a cigarette. She blows smoke in his direction, deliberately antagonising him.

'No,' she snaps abrasively, her voice dry and harsh.

'Don't know where you keep getting them from.'

'You don't want to know,' Paul pipes up.

'What's that supposed to mean?'

'I saw you,' he says, 'checking the pockets of corpses.'

'Well, they don't need them any more,' she argues. And she's got a point. But does that make her any different from the Unchanged I saw fleecing bodies earlier?

'You're disgusting,' Keith sighs.

'I'm addicted,' she answers back quickly, 'and I don't want

to give up. Fags are one of my few remaining pleasures. Where else am I supposed to get them?'

'At least open the window then. Last thing I want to do is be breathing in your second-hand smoke all night.'

'Hold your breath then,' she grumbles, begrudgingly winding down her window. The cool, relatively fresh air which floods into the van is a relief and I breathe it in deeply.

I look around at the three people I'm travelling with tonight and I can't help but feel concerned. I haven't seen any of them in action yet, but I don't hold out much hope. Keith looks like he'd be more at home in his garden than on the battlefield. Carol appears permanently angry. She has bulging eyes and short dark hair which obviously used to be coloured (the dye's grown out, leaving a brassy red tidemark). She has long nails which probably used to be filed and painted but which now look more like talons. She reminds me of a woman I used to work with – a bitter, drink-addled ex-publican. She has the ruddy complexion of a heavy drinker and I suspect she'd be happiest either behind a bar or propping one up. Paul, on the other hand, at least looks like he's ready to fight. He's an arrogant fucker. Since we've been driving he's already told me several times what a great fighter he is and how he's lost count of the hundreds of kills he's made. I can see straight through him. His bragging, aggressive talk is there to hide his insecurities. He's struggling just as much as the rest of us.

So, all in all, not a great team. Still, if they help me get closer to finding Ellis, I'll put up with them.

'Give us a clue then, mate,' Keith says, glancing back at me over his shoulder. I lean forward to try and get a better view of where we are. The van judders and lurches from side to side as we move quickly down a wide, rubbish-strewn road. It's difficult to see very much from where I'm sitting. The fact that Keith's driving without lights on doesn't help, but when the ominous black shape of a huge enemy helicopter crawls across the early evening sky just ahead of us, tail-lights flashing in the gloom, I'm thankful that we're dark.

There's a road sign up ahead. Keith stops the van and all four of us stare up at it, trying to make out the place names and directions. Much of the sign is covered in a layer of green-brown dirt.

'This is Chapman Hill, isn't it?' Paul says. I look in front and behind, trying to get my bearings. He's right. I bought my last car from a garage close to here, but I didn't recognise the place. Now that I know roughly where I am, everything slowly comes into focus and the streets and buildings begin to regain some semblance of familiarity. This is bizarre – everything looks basically the same, but it's all changed too. The landmarks and structures I used to know are mostly still there, but absolutely everything seems to have been indelibly scarred by the war. A long row of once-thriving shops is now a blackened ruin, almost completely destroyed by fire. The forecourt of the garage I remember has collapsed, flattening the few dust-covered cars which remained unsold or unstolen. Next to the garage an office block is surrounded by the mounds of rubble which used to be its top five floors. In the fading light it looks like every road and pavement for as far as I can see is covered with debris. The bodies are the only shapes that are easy to distinguish in among the chaos. Just ahead of us a skeletal hand is sticking up from a pile of fallen masonry, almost as if its dead owner wants to ask us a question, or hitch a ride.

'Well,' Keith says impatiently, 'you just here to sightsee, or are you gonna tell me which way to go?'

'Sorry,' I answer quickly, forcing myself to snap out of my trance. 'Keep going straight for another mile or so, then it's a right. I'll tell you when we get closer.'

Keith's about to pull away again when Carol stops him, leaning across and grabbing his arm. 'Wait. Something's coming . . .'

There's a junction up ahead. She watches it intently.

'There's nothing,' Keith whispers, instinctively lowering his voice. 'You're just overreacting again. It's like the time . . .'

He immediately shuts up when a short but fast-moving convoy races across the crossroads in front of us. It's just three vehicles long: a huge military juggernaut at the front is followed by a battered single-decker civilian bus, with a heavily armed Jeep bringing up the rear. They are moving with reckless speed – going far too fast to notice us.

Keith waits. He glances over at Carol, who remains perfectly still. Eventually she nods.

On her signal he moves off again. 'Can we get through that way?' he asks, slowing down at the point in the road where the convoy crossed our path.

'You want to follow them?' I reply, surprised.

'They've done us a favour and cleared the road. Yes, I want to follow them.'

He's right. There's a clear line through the debris where the vehicles have just been.

'It's a little further but yes, this'll get us to roughly the right place.'

He nods and pulls away and I can immediately see the sense in his actions. We're able to move with more speed now, the cleared channel making it easier to follow the direction of the road.

I sink back into my seat and turn to face Paul. 'Are we safe out here?'

'Truth is, we're not safe anywhere,' he answers quietly. 'But I've not seen much trouble here recently.'

'So what was all that about?'

'Looking for survivors, I guess,' he says, shrugging.

'That's what they'd say,' Carol interrupts, turning around to face us both. She blows smoke out of the corner of her mouth. 'But there can't be many of them left out here now. They just come here to take pot shots at us.'

'Which way now?' Keith shouts, fighting to make himself heard over the noise of the engine. There's another junction looming, but yet again I'm struggling to work out where we are. In the distance I can see occasional flashes of red: the brake lights of the three Unchanged vehicles. They're heading straight into the centre of town, the last place we want to go.

I look around from left to right and back until I spot a large familiar-looking pub and I know where I am again. The building appears intact at first, then I see the back of the structure has been almost completely destroyed, leaving the relatively undamaged frontage standing like something from the set of a movie. I went to a leaving do for someone from work there once. Or was it a birthday party?

'Straight on takes us closer to them, so do we go right or left? Come on, for Christ's sake, Danny. We don't have time to piss around like this . . .'

'Left,' I answer, biting my tongue, determined not to let my anger show. These people don't understand how hard this is for me.

As we follow my directions I recognise this as the route I drove to the flat with my father-in-law, the morning of the day before I killed him. Retracing the last steps I took as one of the Unchanged is unexpectedly unnerving. The road runs past a row of terraced houses before swinging up and left over a bridge spanning the motorway below. Keith stops the van when we're halfway across. I press my face against the window and look down at the once-busy road below. One side of the motorway is relatively clear – all the broken-down and crashed vehicles have no doubt been pushed aside by the heavy, if infrequent, Unchanged traffic. The other side is still a clogged mass of cars, trucks, vans, motorbikes . . . some look abandoned, others as if they've been hurled over the central reservation – it looks more like a rusting scrapyard than a road.

'Busy tonight,' Carol says.

I look up. She's staring down the motorway in the other direction. I follow her gaze and, for the first time, I can clearly see the enemy-occupied heart of the city. Silhouetted against the last golden-yellow light of the rapidly fading sun, the tall buildings in the centre of town are standing proud and defiant. Even from here, still several miles away, I can see that the enemy refugee camp is filled with movement. Planes and helicopters fly through the darkening sky like flies around a dead carcase. The fact that there are lights on in some of the buildings takes me by surprise – they still have power!

Keith starts driving again. I keep my eyes fixed on the buildings in the distance, watching them until they disappear from view.

'All right?' Paul asks, watching me as I crane my neck to keep looking.

'Fine,' I answer quickly, hoping he doesn't pick up on my unease. There must be tens of thousands of Unchanged here, and I know that every last one of them has to die before the war will be over. Seeing their city centre stronghold makes me appreciate the enormity of the task ahead of us. It makes me realise that Chris Ankin might be right. We're going to have to work together to defeat this enemy.

11

'Take a left, then straight to the top of this road,' I tell Keith, my voice so quiet I have to repeat myself twice before he hears me. We're very close now. I used to walk this way when I came home from work at night. When we turn the corner I'll be able to see the apartment block at the top of the hill. I brace myself. I'm not looking forward to going back.

Keith stops the van suddenly and waits. He's finally been forced to use the headlights, and the bright beams of light illuminate several flashes of sudden, darting movement across the road in front of us. We watch in silence as a pack of stray dogs streak through the ruins in search of food. Once probably lazy, well-fed, pampered pets, they're now nervous, thin and savage creatures. One of them, a mangy fawn-brown mongrel with protruding ribs and ragged fur, stops in the middle of the road and stares defiantly at the van, ears twitching, the lights reflecting in its eyes. The stand-off lasts for just a few seconds before something more interesting causes the hound to turn and chase frantically after the rest of the pack.

The interruption over, Keith drives on again and in seconds I can see the outline of the house I used to share with Lizzie and the kids. In the winter I was able to see the lights on in the windows from here, and sometimes I could see the shadows of the kids as they ran from room to room, winding their mum and each other up. I've got to forget about all of that now, but it's hard.

As I get closer, each new wave of familiarity hits me like an undefended punch in the face. And at the same time I feel a nauseous disgust – shame almost – that I was ever a part of this place. I can't believe I allowed myself to stay trapped in such a pathetic, pointless life for so long.

'Lovely spot,' Paul grumbles sarcastically as he surveys the battered remains of the run-down estate I used to call home. The sky's clear tonight and the moon's severe but limited light illuminates all the details I was hoping not to see.

'It's hardly changed,' I tell him, semi-seriously. 'It looked this bad before the fighting.'

Another helicopter flies overhead, the constant chopping of its rotor blades audible even over the rattling engine of this ancient Transit van. The others watch anxiously as it banks high above us then turns around and flies back on itself, but I pay it hardly any attention. I'm focused on the dark apartment block we're fast approaching, wondering what the hell I'm going to find inside. I know Ellis won't be there. I just want to find a trace of her; an indication, no matter how small or how slight, of where she might have been taken.

Keith stops the van in the shadows, nestling it up against a tall wooden fence, and switches off the engine. Two more helicopters drift overhead. Are they tracking us? None of the others seem overly concerned.

'You've got five minutes,' Keith says with a slight trace of urgency in his voice. 'Spend too long pissing around in there and when you come back out you'll find us gone. There's a fair amount of activity around here tonight, and I don't want to get caught in any crossfire. Understand?'

'I get it.'

I reach up to open the door, then stop when Keith speaks again.

'Just remember,' he warns, 'we're here to find other people like us, not just your kid. If she's not here or at the other house, you forget about her. Is that clear?'

Who the fuck does he think he is, talking to me like a bloody sergeant major? I ignore him and get out of the van before anyone can say anything else. I slam the door without thinking and it echoes around the desolate estate like a gunshot.

I stand at the end of the path which leads up to the communal front door of the apartment block, carrying only my rucksack, a torch and a knife. Except for the broken window and the ragged curtains whipping in and out in the wind, the flat looks just like it always did. Seeing this place seems almost to cancel out the last three months. It feels like only yesterday that I was last here . . .

Keith blasts angrily on the horn, the uncomfortably loud sound forcing me into action. I walk down the uneven path and push the door. It sticks at first, but opens when I shove it hard, making the same loud, ear-piercing creak it always did, except it sounds a thousand times louder tonight because everything else is so deathly quiet. I step inside and shine the torch around. The shared lobby has been trashed and the ground beneath my feet is covered in bits of broken furniture and other rubbish. I recognise some of these things. They used to belong to me and my family. The kids used to hate being out here.

The front door of the flat is open. It swings to and fro slightly in a gentle breeze. The wood is splintered, cracked across its width, and there are several dirty boot marks, most probably left by the soldiers who were forcing their way in as I was trying to get out when I was last here.

With trepidation I push it open and go inside, and immediately I'm sucker-punched by the familiarity of everything again. I kick my youngest son's upturned pushchair out of the way and move further down the hall. The first room I reach is the kitchen. I go inside and I can smell my father-in-law's corpse before I see it. He lies exactly where I left him, still covered in his blood-soaked duvet shroud, decay having deflated his lifeless bulk down to half its former size. Hard to believe that this rancid, shrunken, germ-filled mass is all that's left of Harry. When I think of him I still remember the man who used to look after the kids and who always gave me such a hard time: a crotchety, white-haired old bastard who did all he could to make my life difficult. In spite of everything that's happened, it's hard to look at him in this state.

I look up and shine the torch back across the room towards the doorway, suddenly remembering the screams and the terrified faces of my family when they saw what I'd done. I remember Ellis' frightened face clearest of all, desperate for answers which I didn't yet know I could give her.

I retrace their steps, moving back along the hallway until I reach the living room, the small circle of light from the torch providing more than enough illumination. I step over what's left of the furniture Lizzie stacked up to keep me out. It's cold and damp in here, the broken window having left the room open and exposed to the elements. There's black mould on the walls and the paper's peeling. The flat has been ransacked, but I don't think Lizzie did this. Our things have been trashed by scavengers looking for food, weapons and valuables. They were wasting their time here. We never had anything worth taking.

A missile or jet roars through the air above the flat with a piercing scream. Silence returns in seconds, but Keith blasts the horn again and I pick up my pace. I don't bother with Edward and Josh's room. Instead I go into the bedroom Lizzie and I shared and I look down at our bed. The thought of being so physically close to her makes my skin crawl. Surprisingly, the thought of being so far from her now makes me feel equally bad.

I grab a change of clothing from the wardrobe (all of Lizzie's clothes are still here – proof that she never came back) then run through to Ellis' room. I shove some of her belongings into my rucksack – a doll and a rainbow-coloured jumper she used to live in – figuring that the familiarity will help when we're together again. Didn't matter what she was doing or where she was going, when we asked her to get dressed, this jumper was what she always chose. I hold it to my nose and sniff it, hoping to remember her scent. It just smells of the flat, damp and musty.

I take one last look around then make my way back out to the others knowing that whatever happens, I won't be coming back here. Keith hits the horn again as I run through the lobby. I barge my way back out into the open and take a deep breath as soon as I'm outside, relieved to be out of that foul-smelling, claustrophobic hell-hole full of reminders of the person I used to be. I hear gunfire nearby, followed by a scream that could be either rage or pain. I throw my bag into the van, then climb in and slam the door.

'Any sign?' Paul asks.

'Nothing.'

Yet another helicopter hovers nearby, this one using a searchlight to illuminate the ground below.

'We're not going anywhere else for a while,' Keith announces as he start the engine and pulls away. 'This place is too bloody busy for my liking tonight. Anywhere close where we can hole up until it quietens down?'

All eyes are on me, and the pressure is unwelcome. The only thing I'm sure about is that I'm not going back into the flat. I try to think of other places nearby which might still be standing. Through a gap between two houses at the very bottom of Calder Grove I see the tall, dark outline of a tower block which looks reasonably intact. That'll do.

'Turn left at the bottom of the road,' I tell him. 'I know somewhere.'

12

Keith stops the van behind a row of overflowing waste bins, almost directly beneath the block of flats. We each grab our own bags of weapons and supplies and head for the shelter of the building. The front doors of the block are missing and the entrance foyer is as trashed as everywhere else. Like an idiot I instinctively press the button to call the lift. Old habits die hard.

'Don't think that's going to do anything, mate,' Paul whispers sarcastically. I push past him and follow Carol, who's already heading up the stairs, the glowing orange tip of another cigarette marking her route through the darkness. There's a woman's badly decomposed body at the very bottom of the first flight of steps. Her neck's been snapped and her decayed face is wedged against the wall. She was like us, and that immediately puts me on edge. I step over the corpse and start to climb, pointlessly wondering if she fell or if she was pushed.

For a few minutes we do nothing but climb, our footsteps echoing up and down along the entire length of this dark and otherwise silent stairwell. We move quickly, most of us climbing two steps at a time. It's hard work, but the pain is easy to ignore. It's a perverse reality of my situation: I eat scraps, survive out in the open and live from day to day, but I'm in better shape than I've ever been. The others are the same. Carol races ahead like a woman half her age. I feel strong and powerful, my body lean, toned and efficient. Makes me wonder, when everything was available to me on a plate and all I had to worry about was my family and my piss-easy job, how did I manage to fuck everything up so badly? The memory

71

of who and what I used to be is embarrassing. I wish this had happened to me years ago.

'How far?' Carol shouts down from several flights up.

'Just keep going,' I answer. We're more than halfway up now. The higher we go, the safer I think we'll be.

'Wait,' Keith yells. I stop climbing and turn back. He's still a floor below me. 'Look at this.'

'Look at what?' Paul grunts breathlessly as he pushes past and starts heading back down again. I follow him back to floor eight (of eleven or twelve, I think). This floor is different to the others. I passed it too quickly to notice, but the doors leading from the staircase to the rest of the building here have been boarded up. There's plenty of broken glass and other debris around, but it doesn't look like the barrier has been breached.

'This has been done from the inside,' Keith says, stating the blindingly obvious.

'So there might still be someone in there,' Carol adds, equally pointlessly.

'Must be Unchanged,' Paul says under his breath as he runs his hands over the large sheets of plywood which have been nailed to the inside of the door frame, pushing and prodding in different places, trying to find a weak spot. He finds one near the bottom right-hand corner, where the door frame is rotten. He kicks away shards of broken glass, then sits down on his backside and pushes the board with his boot. When it moves slightly he beckons for me to help him.

I position myself directly between him and the handrail of the staircase so he can't move backwards, then brace myself as he starts to kick at the wood. The noise is massively amplified by the confines of our surroundings, but in the moments of silence between each kick, everything else remains reassuringly quiet. He's barely forced open a wide enough gap when he turns around, drops his rucksack and scrambles through. Once on the other side he pulls at the plywood and manages to yank away a piece about a metre square. I slide his bag through then follow him.

We're standing on an empty, relatively uncluttered landing. There are three flats on this floor, two doors on one side of the landing, one on the other. Two of them are open. I quickly check one over. Its three main rooms are empty and fairly undamaged. There's even the stale, mould-covered remains of a final meal, untouched, on a table in front of a lifeless TV. The owner of the flat must have left (or been dragged out) in a hurry. Keith disappears into the other open flat and reappears on the landing after a few seconds.

'Nothing,' he says quietly, 'just a corpse on a bed.'

'On a bed?' Carol says, surprised.

'Someone's laid out their missus or their mother or something. Dressed her up nice and brushed her hair. Still looks fucking horrible.'

'Very touching,' Paul mumbles as he presses his ear against the closed door of the remaining apartment. He pushes it gently, but it doesn't move.

'Smash it?' I suggest, my axe ready in my hand. He thumps it uselessly, then nods his head and moves to one side. I lift the axe and thump it down, the clang of metal on metal filling the air as I mishit and catch the Yale lock. I lift my arm again.

Keith grabs my wrist before I can bring it down again. 'Listen.'

I do as he says, but I can't hear anything. I try to pull my hand free, but he tightens his grip and glares at me.

'I hear it,' Carol whispers. And then I do too: a muffled voice shouting at us from deep inside the flat.

'Not my . . .' it shouts, the third word unclear.

'Not my flat?' Keith suggests.

'Not my fault?' Paul offers, shrugging his shoulders. 'Get the door open, mate, and let's get him killed. It's just some nutter.'

I do as he asks, smashing the blade down again and again until the wood splinters and the lock gives. I kick it open and peer into the gloom. A well-timed explosion outside bathes everything in ice-white light like a camera flash for a fraction of a second, just long enough for me to see that there's some-one standing at the far end of a short hall on the other side of the door. I catch a glimpse of a motionless outline directly ahead. The door slowly swings shut again.

'How many?' Carol asks.

'Just one that I can see,' I answer. 'Pass us the torch, Keith.'

Keith switches on the torch, but, before he can pass it to me, the door flies open and the figure in the flat throws itself at me. The force of the sudden, unexpected attack takes me by surprise and I trip over my own feet as I stagger back. Before I know what's happening, I'm lying flat on my back with a foul-smelling fucker right on top of me. He grabs the collar of my coat and lowers his face until it's just centimetres from mine. His breath is so bad it's making me want to puke.

'Not my fight,' he shouts, peppering me with spittle. 'Not my fight . . .'

Keith smashes the side of his head with the torch, sending him reeling. 'Not my problem,' he sneers, laughing at his own joke.

The man who attacked me rolls over and gets up and stupidly starts walking back towards Keith again.

'Not my fight,' he says, blood running down his face. 'Leave me alone. It's not my fight. Get out of here . . .'

Keith lunges forward again, torch held ready to strike, sens-ing the kill.

'He's one of us, Keith,' Carol warns, but it's too late. He swings the torch around and smashes it into the man's face again and he drops to the ground, and this time he doesn't get up.

Keith shines the light down. Christ, Carol's right. He was one of ours. Keith looks at him with disdain, then steps over the corpse and goes into the flat.

The small, squalid apartment is like a cocoon. The door I broke down hadn't been opened for weeks. The air is musty and stale and the rooms are filled with boxes of supplies. On closer inspection, we find that almost all of the supplies have been used up. The dead man on the landing had scarcely any food left.

'He'd done well to last this long,' Paul says, watching me as I check through more empty cartons.

'If you ask me,' Keith says, wiping the torch clean on a floral curtain then opening a door into another room and glancing around it, 'people like that are as bad as the Unchanged. Not fighting with us is almost as bad as fighting against us. You don't have a choice whether or not you want to be a part of this war. There's no opt-out clause for anyone.'

'That was his wife, you know,' Paul says, following me out onto a small verandah which overlooks what's left of my home town. I've been out here for a while, just getting some air.

'What?'

'The guy Keith did in, that was his missus lying on the bed next door.'

'How d'you know?'

'Found a photo of the pair of them together. Lovely couple,' he murmurs sarcastically.

'Was she like us?'

'Nah, one of them.'

'But he couldn't let go?'

'Looks that way. Probably killed her, then regretted it. True love, eh?' he jokes. 'Never runs smooth.'

'You're not wrong. My other half was . . .'

'I know. Bad luck, mate.'

'What about you?'

'Good question.'

'What do you mean by that?'

'I'd been with my girlfriend for three years, then all this happened . . .'

'Was she Unchanged?'

'No, nothing like that. We stuck together for a while after the Change, then just drifted apart. We didn't need each other like we used to.'

I glance across at him. He's hanging his head out over the high balcony next to me, staring into the distance.

'I guess relationships and stuff like that have had to take a back seat with all this going on.'

'You're not wrong,' he sighs. 'You know, I was thinking the other day, I haven't had a hard-on for weeks.'

'Thanks for sharing.'

'I'm not complaining,' he says quickly, 'it just hadn't occurred to me before. I've stopped thinking about sex, stopped looking at women . . . hope to God this is just temporary.'

I'm the same, although I don't bother telling him. It's just a question of priorities, I expect. When the fighting's over, things will get back to normal again.

I look out at the city centre in the distance, glowing like the embers of a dying fire. There's a strange beauty to the devastation tonight. This place always seemed ugly and oppressive to me before, but these days, I see wonder and detail in things I used to look straight through. The Hate has opened my eyes. The area immediately around this tower block – the place I used to call home – is dark and largely silent, just a few small fires and the odd flash of movement visible through the early evening gloom. From up here tonight the world seems vast and never-ending. There are clouds looming on the horizon, swallowing up the stars. There's rain coming.

'What you thinking?' Paul asks after a couple of minutes have passed. 'Not still thinking about my dick, I hope!'

'Just how massive the world feels tonight,' I answer honestly as I watch a lone helicopter leading a distant convoy of Unchanged vehicles across their so-called exclusion zone. 'First time I've been back here in months. From up here I can see where I lived and where I worked and everything in-between. Can't believe I used to spend virtually all my time in the same few square miles of space. Kind of makes you feel insignificant, doesn't it?'

'The best thing about this life of ours now,' he tells me, 'is how open it's made everything. All the walls and barriers that used to hold us back have gone.'

'I've been thinking about my flat. It was only just bigger than this place, and there were five of us living there. Five of us! How the hell did we ever manage to cram that many lives into such a small space?'

'That wasn't living, that was just existing.'

'I can see it now, but when you're in the middle of it you just make do, don't you? You try and make the most of what you've got . . .'

Paul nudges my shoulder and I look across at him. He gestures out over the city. 'All of this, mate,' he says, 'is ours now.'

PART II

In a situation where everybody was either on one side or the other and there was no in-between, ascertaining who was who had become a priority. A DNA-based 'test of allegiance' had been developed early on, and from it the Central System had been born. It was little more than an electronic tick list – a massive summary of names cribbed from the electoral roll, voters' roll and births, deaths and marriages records. The details held on each person were sparse: name, sex, date of birth, last known address, whether they were dead or not and, most importantly, whether they were Hater or Unchanged.

Many records – no one knew exactly how many – were incomplete or inaccurate. Up-to-date information was increasingly hard to find. Data gathering had been carried out at cull sites, evacuation camps, temporary mortuaries, military checkpoints, and anywhere else there was a controlled flow of civilians. Within the first two months of the crisis, however, that flow had been reduced to a trickle, then a drip. The thousands of bodies lying rotting in their homes, in overgrown fields or on street corners remained unaccounted for. Should anyone enquire upon their names, blank records were returned.

The quality of data wasn't the only problem with the system. Administration, back-ups, integrity, access rights, security . . . the speed and chaotic nature of the Change meant that these, as with so many other aspects of development, were truncated, attempted half-heartedly, skimped, skipped over or simply abandoned altogether. But the ever-decreasing number of people still using the system continued to do what they could, believing that, eventually, their work would prove worthwhile.

Almost thirty-six hours since he'd been back to the hotel room. He'd managed to catch a few hours' sleep in the back of one of the empty food trucks this afternoon, but Mark was still exhausted. Volunteers were becoming increasingly hard to find, and they weren't about to let him go until they had to. He continued to do it because of the promise of extra rations (which had, so far, been fulfilled) and because he felt more secure being on the side of the people who had the biggest guns. The city streets were increasingly ugly and unsafe places. Better to walk them with the protection of a little body armour and a weapon, he thought, than without.

All that aside, Mark decided, when I get back to the hotel this time, I'm not coming out again.

Over the past few days he'd begun to sense a change in the air – a difficult situation becoming impossible, a slight risk becoming an almost-certainty. Things were deteriorating, and the rate of decline was accelerating. He hadn't completely given up hope of some semblance of normality eventually being restored, but he knew things were going to get a lot worse before they got any better.

Processing. Of all the jobs they had him do, he hated Processing the most. Maybe it was because, bizarrely, it reminded him of working in the call centre; perhaps it was just because it was so desperately sad. Those people who staggered into the military camp today, after months of trying to survive alone, well, they were little more than empty, traumatised shells.

Heavy rain lashed down onto the roof of the tent, clattering against the taut canvas. A steady *drip drip drip* hit the corner of his unsteady desk, each splash just wide enough to reach the edge of his papers. Hot days and generally clear skies frequently meant cold nights, and even though it was cloudy tonight, it was still damn cold. He warmed his hands around the gas lamp while he waited. Wouldn't be long now; he'd just had word that a food patrol had found another few stragglers hiding in a warehouse storeroom, drowning in their own filth. Kate had worked here when they'd first arrived in the city. Back then there'd been a steady stream of refugees coming through here twenty-four/seven. Now there were just a handful being processed every day.

'Should have seen him, Mark,' Gary Phillips said, sitting on the dry corner of the desk, 'he went fucking wild when we found him!'

Phillips had been out in many of the same convoys as Mark over the weeks. This afternoon he'd won the toss and had taken the last available seat, leaving Mark to fill the desk job. And now he was back, telling him in unnecessary detail how one of the survivors they'd found had lost the plot when they'd arrived at the warehouse. Mark wasn't sure if it was Phillips' way of coping with what he'd experienced, or whether he derived some sick pleasure from watching refugees suffer. Whatever the reason, he didn't tell him to shut up or piss off like he wanted to do. Instead he bit his lip and put up with his pointless drivel. Better that than to show any kind of reaction that might be misconstrued.

'It was just unbelievable, I tell you,' he continued, still pumped with adrenalin. 'There were six of them shut in this fucking storeroom smaller than this tent. They'd used up just about every scrap of food they had, but on the other side of the door there was a warehouse still half-full of stuff. Too fucking scared to put their heads out into the open.'

'Gets to us all in different ways, doesn't it?' Mark said quietly, drawing lines on a piece of paper with the longest ruler he could find and writing out the questions he needed to ask. All the photocopied forms had been used up weeks ago.

'I know, but this was a bit fucking extreme by anyone's standards. Anyway, the soldiers force the door open, not knowing what they're gonna find in there, and this guy comes charging out, convinced they're Haters. Fair play, they gave him a chance, which is more than I'd have done, but the dumb bastard wasn't listening. He just kept coming at them.'

'So what happened?'

'What do you think happened? Fucker didn't stand a chance. They put so many bullets in him I thought he was gonna— What's the matter?'

Mark was looking at the entrance to the tent. Phillips stopped talking and turned around. Behind him stood an elderly couple who, if you looked past the emaciation and their haunted, vacant stares, could have just stepped out of their house to go shopping together. Their surprisingly smart clothes, albeit drenched with rain and streaked with dirt, looked several sizes too big for them. Phillips jumped off the desk, feet splashing in a puddle of mud, grabbed a chair and placed it next to the one which was already opposite Mark.

'I'll leave you to it,' he said. 'See you around.' With that he was gone.

Mark gestured for the new arrivals to sit down. He hated doing this. It was hard, bloody hard. Too hard. He watched as the man sat his wife down, almost slipping in the greasy mud, then sat down next to her. Christ, after all they've probably been through, he's still managing to be a bloody gentleman. He'd probably been looking after his wife for so long that he was hard-wired to do it. She'd no doubt be the same, darning the holes in his clothes and checking he'd had enough to eat when both of them struggled to find any food at all and the world was falling apart around them. The couple huddled together for warmth, as the rain ran off their clothes and dripped from the ends of their noses. The woman was sobbing and shaking, her shoulders jerking forward again and again. Her husband wasn't able to console her – he tried, of course, but she wouldn't stop. He turned to Mark and stared at him, begging for help without saying a word, his eyes filled with tears.

'Okay, what are your—?' He stopped short when a low-flying jet tore through the air above the park, sounding like it was just metres above the roof of the tent. The gut-wrenching noise and blast of wind made the canvas walls shake, and the

84

woman wailed and screwed her eyes shut. Her husband took her hand in his and gripped it tight. Mark waited a few seconds for the jet to completely disappear before trying again.

'What are your names?' he asked.

Nothing.

'Do you have any identification papers with you?'

Nothing.

'Do you have any bank cards, letters – anything with your names on or an address . . . ?'

Nothing. Mark sighed and held his head in his hands, barely making any attempt to hide his frustration and fatigue. He looked up again, reached across the table and gently shook the old man's wet right arm. The old man reacted to his touch, shaking his head slightly as if he'd just been woken from a trance.

'Can you tell me your name?' Mark tried again.

'Graeme Reynolds,' the old man answered finally, his voice barely audible over the rain.

'Okay, Graeme,' he continued, looking down and scribbling the name at the top of the form he'd drawn up, 'and is this your wife?'

He nodded. Mark waited.

'What's her name?'

Another pause, almost as if he was having to dredge his memory for the answer.

'Mary.'

'Your date of birth?'

No answer. Graeme was looking past Mark now, gazing into space. Waste of fucking time, Mark thought to himself. He's gone again. What's the point?

'Wait there,' he told him, although he knew he wasn't going anywhere. He got up from his chair and walked across the dark tent to another table where he added the couple's names to a register, then entered the same names against the next available address in another file. He wrote out the details on a slip of paper and took it back, wondering if anyone was ever going to collect the files and update the Central System. When he and Kate had first started volunteering, the system had been updated religiously by a dedicated team tasked with keeping the information as accurate as was humanly possible. Now, whether it was because of a lack of functioning computers, a lack of trained operators or any one of a hundred possible other reasons, the system seemed to be falling apart as quickly as everything else.

Mark handed the slip of paper to Graeme Reynolds, who took it, but didn't look at it.

'Take that to the next tent,' he told him, unsure if there was anyone left working there tonight. 'Those are your billet details. The people next door will give you ration papers. When you're finished there, they'll send you to the food store. They'll give you something to eat, if there's anything left . . .'

He stopped speaking. Neither of them were listening; poor bastards were barely even conscious. They didn't know where they were, who he was, what he was doing, what he was trying to tell them . . . Graeme and Mary Reynolds didn't move. He looked long and hard into their empty, vacant faces and wondered, as he was doing with increasing and alarming regularity, why he was bothering. What was the point? When the fighting's over, he thought, will we ever return to any kind of normality? Or have we gone too far for that? Is this as good as it's ever going to get? All trust, all hope and faith, gone for ever . . . nothing left but fear and hate . . .

Mark stood up, took Graeme Reynolds' arm, waited as he helped his wife to get up, and then led them to the next tent. Without even stopping to see if there was anyone there, he grabbed his coat and the heavy wrench he always carried with him for self-defence and left. He went out into the rain and walked, determined not to stop again until he was back in the hotel room with Kate and the others.

13

I wake up stretched out on the threadbare living room carpet in the flat we broke into last night. I ache like hell, but I slept pretty well, considering. Our position midway up the tower block has kept us out of sight, separated by height from the rest of town. The flat is filled with dark shadows and the dull, blue-grey light of early morning. It's raining outside and the rain clatters against the glass like someone's throwing stones.

Paul's asleep in an armchair in the corner of the room, looking up at the ceiling with closed eyes, his head lolling back on his shoulders. Carol's curled up on the floor near his feet. I get up and stretch, seeing the dull room in daylight for the first time. The décor's badly dated and the entire flat's in a hell of a state as a result of its owner's self-imposed incarceration, but it still feels strangely complete and untouched – isolated to a surprising extent from everything that's happened outside. I glance at my monochrome reflection in a long-silent TV, then pick up a framed photograph that still sits on top of the set. It's a twenty- or thirty-year-old wedding day memory. The guy's just about recognisable as the man from last night. His bride is the corpse next door.

I find Keith in the kitchen with a map spread out on a small melamine-topped table.

'All right?' he asks as I trudge towards him, eyes still full of sleep.

'Fine. You?'

He nods and returns his attention to the map. 'We'll get moving in a while,' he announces. 'It's all quiet out there for now.'

I look down at the map with him and start trying to work

out the best route to Lizzie's sister's house. The same two circles representing the edge of the enemy encampment and their exclusion zone have been drawn on this map as on the one Preston showed me yesterday. Except I notice the lines are in slightly different positions on this map. According to this one, Lizzie's sister's house is just inside enemy territory. I point to roughly where the house is and look across at Keith. 'That's where we need to go.'

'That's where you *think* you need to go,' he answers quickly. 'That's where we're going to *try* to go, but I'm not promising anything. We're out here to find recruits. If we get your kid, it's a bonus.'

'I know, but . . .'

'But nothing. We'll head in that direction and see how far we get.'

'Is he still on about that bloody kid of his?' Carol says as she shuffles into the kitchen, bleary-eyed. She drags her feet across the sticky linoleum and lights up her first cigarette of the day.

'I've already told him,' Keith starts to say, trying (and failing) to stop her from getting involved.

'You've got to let her go,' she tells me, blowing smoke in my direction.

'No, I haven't . . .'

'Yes, you have. What's the point of looking for her? What are you going to do if you find her?'

'I just want to know that she's safe. I want her fighting alongside me.'

'And if you don't find her?'

'Then I guess I'll—'

'Assuming she's still alive, what'll happen if you don't find her?'

'She'll just carry on fighting wherever she is.'

'Exactly. So what difference does it make?'

'She needs me. She's only five.'

'I reckon you need her more than she needs you.'

'Bullshit!'

'Not bullshit,' she says, shaking her head and flicking ash into a sink filled with dirty plates and cups. 'I doubt she needs you at all.'

Stupid woman.

'Did you not hear me? She's five years old. I don't even know if she can fight—'

'Of course she can fight! We can all fight. It's instinctive.'

'Okay, but what about food? What about keeping warm in the winter and dry in the rain? What if she gets hurt?'

'She'll survive.'

'She'll survive? For Christ's sake, Carol, she can't even tie her own fucking shoelaces!'

Keith folds up his map and pushes his way between us, clearly fed up with being caught in the crossfire of our conversation. I shake my head in disbelief and follow him.

'You need to wake up and start living in the real world,' Carol shouts after me. There's no point arguing so I don't.

We're back in the van and ready to move within minutes of Paul waking up. The rain has eased, but the ground is still covered with puddles of dirty black rainwater which hide the potholes and debris and make it almost as difficult to follow the roads as it was in the dark last night. Keith manages to avoid most of the obstructions, but when he over-steers to avoid an overturned skip, one of the rear wheels clips something else. We carry on for a few metres further, then there's a sudden bang and hiss of air as a tyre blows out.

'Shit!' Keith curses, thumping the wheel in frustration.

'Got a spare?' I ask.

'No idea.'

He stops in the biggest patch of dry land we can find and I get out. Paul follows me out and opens the back. He rummages around and manages to find the jack and some other tools. The spare's underneath and he starts to get it out.

While I'm waiting I walk over to the other side of the road, to where the contents of someone's front room have been strewn across the pavement. Their flat-screen TV lies smashed in the gutter and an expensive-looking rain-soaked sofa hangs precariously out of the broken bay window. Before all this happened we each lived in relative privacy in individual brick-built boxes, what we did and how we did it hidden from view of the rest of the world by our walls, doors and windows. Strange how the physical worlds of so many people are now as dilapidated and ruined as their emotional state. There's no privacy any more, no boundaries. Everything we do now is in full view, completely exposed. There's no longer any—

'McCoyne!' Carol shouts at me from the van. 'Get out of the bloody way!'

I spin around quickly, but it's too late. Christ knows where he came from, but a powerful-looking man is running straight towards me. He's at least six foot tall and just as wide, and I can tell from the focus and intent in his wild, staring eyes that he's a Brute, like those I saw back at the cull site. Does he not know we're on the same side?

'Wait,' I shout to him, 'we're . . .'

His bulk belies his remarkable speed and before I can move he's grabbed hold of my arm. He spins me around and throws me over and slams me down onto my back. I'm already winded and gasping when he drops down onto my chest, and I cough violently as his knees force the air from my lungs. I try to shout for help, but there's no noise coming.

'Get off him, you fucking idiot,' I hear Paul say. I manage to turn my head to the side and watch as he starts hitting the Brute with part of the jack from the van. The Brute doesn't react; it looks like he barely even notices that he's being hit. He bears down on me, a bizarre mix of terror and excitement on his face.

'Like you,' I manage to squeak. 'I'm like you.'

Working together, Paul and Carol pull him away. They drag him back, drop him on his backside, then scatter like they've just lit the fuse on a stick of dynamite. I try to scramble away, moving back until I hit the wall of the house behind me. The

Brute springs up with a low, guttural warning growl and looks at each of us in turn. Then, painfully slowly, realisation seems to dawn. He looks from Paul to Carol to me and back again. Paul moves towards him with the jack, ready to attack. Carol pulls him back.

'Don't wind him up,' she hisses. 'Just drop it and walk away. He doesn't know what he's doing.'

Paul does as he's told, dropping the heavy metal tool, which clatters loudly on the ground. Carol stands motionless as the Brute looks her up and down, her back pressed up against the van. Then he slowly turns and slopes away. He's gone ten metres or so when something else catches his eye and he breaks into a slow, loping run.

'What the hell was that all about?' I ask as I pick myself up.

'No bloody idea,' Paul answers as he returns his attention to changing the spare wheel. I watch the Brute until he's disappeared from view. Did he think I was one of them, or was I just in the wrong place at the wrong time? Did he see me and think I was Unchanged? Are the Brutes really like us, or was he reacting to a difference between us? Should I start to be worried?

14

The heat and damp have combined to make the world stink more than ever this morning: the relentless, suffocating stench of decay combined with overflowing drains and Christ knows what else. Other than the noise of this tired old van, everything is generally quiet, but the fragile silence is frequently interrupted by sudden bursts of noise – the Unchanged military, moving and attacking, distant fighting, a scream as someone is hunted down and killed, the smashing of glass and the crumbling of collapsed buildings, the pained howl of a starving animal searching for food . . . The constant, smothering noise of the engine is unexpectedly welcome. It drowns out everything else.

I'm travelling in the front with Keith now, giving him directions. I'm trying to concentrate, but I'm distracted by the fact that a pub I used to drink in occasionally has disappeared – there's now just an unexpected gap and a pile of blackened rubble on the street where it used to be – and for a second I don't realise the significance of where we are. Then it dawns on me.

'Stop!'

'What's the problem?' he says, slowing down but not stopping.

'No problem. Take a left here.'

He does as I say.

Carol leans forward from the back.

'Trouble?'

'The kids' school,' I explain. 'They used to go to the school down here. My missus worked here too.'

'So?'

'So if I was in Ellis' shoes and I couldn't go back home, school might be the next best option.'

'Worth a look as we're here,' Keith reluctantly agrees. 'But if there's nothing we move on quick and so do you.'

The school is tucked away behind a church and a row of shops and offices. In the morning light everything looks a little more familiar than it did yesterday, but also a little more mutated and alien too. Windows are smashed, doors hang open and there's evidence of fighting almost everywhere I look.

The road ahead is blocked by the rusting wreck of a car which has mounted the pavement and crashed into a bus shelter. Its heavily decayed Unchanged driver has been thrown – or dragged – through the shattered windscreen. Looks like he was attacked as he tried to drive away. His body is sprawled out over the crumpled car bonnet, his blue-tinged skin slashed by jagged shards of glass. His right shoulder is a messy stump of ripped flesh and protruding bone. The rest of his arm is missing. Keith mounts the kerb and tries to steer the van gently through a narrow gap. He scrapes against a wall with a vile, high-pitched grating noise and I look down as we drive over another equally mutilated body. Whoever fought here was vicious. Probably more of those Brutes.

'Turn right here, down the alleyway next to the church.'

He does as I say, taking the narrow track which leads into the school grounds slowly. Over the low stone wall to my left I can see several more bodies in the church graveyard, none of them in one piece. Some are badly decayed, others relatively fresh. I hold my favoured knife tight in my hand, ready to attack or defend myself if the need arises. Even though I'm certain whoever did this was on our side, the brutality and savagery of these kills is remarkable. Keith drives through the empty teachers' car park and stops outside the main school gate.

'Bloody hell,' Paul says from the back. 'What happened here?'

He jumps out and walks over to the wire-mesh fence which

93

surrounds the small rectangular playground. I follow him and immediately see that the violence so apparent out on the streets has spread closer to the school too. The enclosed tarmac play area is completely covered with a patchwork quilt of body parts. I press my face against the tall fence which, bizarrely, makes the playground look like some kind of caged gladiatorial arena. I look down at the ground and, in the few clear spaces between the dead, I can still see brightly painted markings: hopscotch, snakes and ladders, oversized letters and numbers . . . I look up again and remember this place as it used to be, filled with a couple of hundred kids in their identical school uniforms, laughing and playing and—

'Brutes?' Keith shouts from the van, derailing my train of thought.

'Doubt it,' Paul answers quickly. 'Why would they be here? More to the point, why would *anyone* still be here?'

'Unchanged hideout?' I suggest. 'Think someone gatecrashed an evacuation?' I crouch down to look closer at some of the nearest corpses. It's impossible to be sure because of the extreme level of mutilation and deterioration, but all the dead faces I see here are Unchanged.

I push open the gate and we start walking towards the entrance to the school. We've left Carol and Keith guarding the van. The ground's much clearer here. In fact, it looks pretty much like it did when we used to walk the kids down to class. Paul nudges me. I look up and see a sudden flash of frantic movement up ahead as a small figure darts along the side of the building then jumps down off a low brick wall and disappears inside. I sprint down the path after them and shove the still-swinging door open. I push my way inside, then stop suddenly, recoiling at the obnoxious stench which immediately hits me. I can smell human waste, rotting food and other even worse odours.

I kick my way through the rubbish covering the floor of the small reception area. Directly in front of me is the door to the main assembly hall. To my left are what used to be the staff

94

rooms and offices and, to my right, a short flight of steps and a corridor which leads down to the classrooms. My eyes are slowly adjusting to the lack of light in here. What used to be a bright place full of noise, energy and life is now just as dark and dead as everywhere else; it's a stark contrast from what I remember. There's a display on the wall with photographs of the teachers and kids and I force myself not to look for Ellis, Edward and Lizzie's faces.

'There,' Paul whispers, pointing towards the classrooms. There's another shadowy blur of fleeting movement as something dashes from one room to another. I race to a classroom and push the door open, but I'm immediately sent flying back as something hurls itself at me with lightning speed and unexpected force.

I slide across the floor on my backside and struggle to fight off a fast-moving attacker who grabs hold of my neck and starts to squeeze. Can't tell if it's claws or teeth I feel digging into my flesh. I try to lift my knife and fight, but before I can even raise my arm another one of them dives on top of me and bites my hand until I drop the weapon. I feel the sharp pin-prick of another blade being forced up under my chin, almost breaking the skin, then I feel more small but savage hands grabbing both of my feet and my other arm and holding me down and then— And then they stop. One by one, Paul pulls them off me. My heart pounding, I scramble back across the floor, stopping only when I reach the wall and can't go any further back. I pick myself up and see there's a crowd of children, seven of them, of various sizes and ages, standing in front of me. They stare back, immediately losing interest when they realise we're all on the same side. They slowly scatter and trudge back into the classroom. Paul and I follow them at a cautious distance.

'None of these your daughter?'

'Can't see her,' I answer, still panting after the attack. I look around the room into a succession of pallid faces. Some of the children crawl away under desks, leaving only the biggest kids out in the open. They look like they've been here for some time, living in what used to be their class. Tables and chairs have been shoved to the sides of the room and the wood-tiled floor is now covered in litter and discarded clothing. Random scraps of material have been used as bedding and, in the far corner, wisps of smoke climb up from the ashes of a fire built from torn-up books. The room is in a horrendous condition. It smells like a toilet and feels like a slum, but if I look past the dirt, the bruises, the blood and the other stains and marks on the faces of these kids, they look completely fresh and alive. Their eyes are bright and full of life.

There's a lad who looks about the same age as my son Edward, squatting on top of what used to be the teacher's desk. If he came to this school they'd probably have been classmates, but I don't recognise him. He's digging into the wood with the tip of a fearsome-looking knife. I automatically go to tell him not to, but I stop myself – it doesn't matter, and he's not going to listen to me anyway. It's already clear that these kids do what they like, when they like. That's probably how they've managed to survive.

'I'm looking for my daughter,' I say to the boy.

He shrugs, but doesn't say anything.

'Are there any other children here?'

Still no answer.

'This is a waste of time,' Paul whispers. 'We should just get these kids into the van and get out of here.'

I'm not going anywhere until I've had some answers. 'Are there any adults here?'

The big kid sitting on the desk finally looks up. 'There was.'

'But not now?'

He shakes his head.

'So what happened to them?' Paul asks.

'They went.'

'You didn't go?'

'No point.'

'What about the war? The fighting?'

'What war?'

His answer surprises me. I take a step forward and accid-
ently kick an outstretched leg, which is immediately pulled
back out of sight. I crouch down and see a small girl curled
up under a desk on a bed of soiled cushions and pillows. She
doesn't react, but she watches me. She remains perfectly still,
her eyes following my every move. These children, I think to
myself, must have a strangely blinkered view of what's left of
the world. Like all kids, they're only interested in themselves. I
know they'd kill any Unchanged stupid enough to get too
close, but do they feel the same compulsion to go outside and
hunt them down as the rest of us do? As long as they're warm
and relatively comfortable and they've got a decent supply of
food, what more could they want? They're nesting here.

'I'm going to check the rest of the place out,' I tell Paul, keen
to keep looking for Ellis. I leave the classroom and work my
way back towards the main entrance, peering into the other
rooms as I pass them. They're all empty.

'There's no one else here,' a quiet voice says when I reach the
top of the stairs. I turn around quickly, but I can't see anyone.

A little girl cautiously steps out of the shadows and looks up
at me with huge, saucer-shaped eyes. I try to estimate her age,
but it's difficult. She appears completely innocent, but at the
same time strangely switched-on and knowing. She's a pitiful
sight: desperately thin, pale white skin, dirty and bedraggled,
her long hair tangled in knots. She's wearing pyjamas and her
feet are bare, muddy. Her clothing is bloodstained and, instinctively, I'm about to ask her if she's hurt herself. But then I
realise the blood is more than likely from someone else, and
that she more than likely killed them. I don't know what I'm
supposed to say.

We both stand there awkwardly, staring at each other in
silence, until something I see just over her shoulder catches my
eye. It's a line of metal coat hooks, hung on a long wooden rail
about a metre and a half off the ground. The name on the peg
directly behind her is Edward McCoyne. The girl suddenly

becomes invisible as I reach out and lift a small cloth bag off my son's peg.

'That's just old stuff,' she says. 'My bag's down there. Want to see it?'

'No, it's okay . . .' I open the bag and take out Edward's football shirt. His name's on the label inside the collar, written in pen in Lizzie's handwriting. I remember when we bought this for him. Christ, he nagged at us for months to get it because all the other kids had got one the same. The team changed their kit a couple of weeks later and the little shit stopped wearing it, complaining that he hadn't got the right one any more and . . . And what the hell am I doing? Got to stop thinking like this and get a grip. That life is gone now.

The girl brushes past me and leans against the assembly hall door.

'What's in there?' I ask, glad of the distraction.

'More stuff,' she answers nonchalantly, shrugging her shoulders. She pushes the door open and I follow her inside. I stop immediately, rooted to the spot. The entire floor of the large school hall is covered with bodies. Some of them are piled up, almost as if they're being stored here. There are bloody handprints on the walls, some of them too big to have been made by kids. The girl tiptoes through the carnage without a care and disappears out through a gaping hole in the outside wall where a fire exit used to be.

I follow at a distance, stepping over dismembered cadavers and swatting away buzzing flies. I'm distracted by an Unchanged woman's half-naked corpse at my feet. She's only a few days dead. She's face down with her arms stretched out, her fingers clawing the ground as if she died trying to get away. There are chunks missing out of the back of her naked thighs. Are those *bite* marks?

The overpowering stench in here is unbearable and it's making me gag. I follow the girl outside, desperate to get some fresher air. I find her at the edge of a murky, weed-filled pool. I don't know whether it's a deliberately dug pond or a crater left by a small explosion or other impact. Whatever, she's lying on her belly in the mud, thirstily lapping up the dirty green water.

It's a struggle to get the children rounded up and into the van. There were only the eight of them, but three managed to get away. Generally it's the older kids who understand what we're trying to do and why we want them to leave here. The promise of fighting and food is enough to persuade them to go.

'Good result,' Keith says. 'Job done. We'll get this lot back to the others. Preston can't complain about a catch like this.'

I knew that was coming. For the last half-hour they've been making noises about getting back to the people we left at the slaughterhouse. As far as they're concerned, it's Mission Accomplished. I know I should go with them, but I can't. Ellis is still out there somewhere . . .

'I'm not going back with you.'

'You soft bastard,' Carol snaps angrily. 'Don't be so bloody stupid.'

'We've got a van full of kids,' Keith argues.

'Yes, but we haven't got *my* kid.'

'We don't need *your* kid.'

'*I* do.'

'You don't. All you need is . . .'

'I'll find her and bring her back to the rest of you,' I shout over my shoulder as I start to walk away. 'I won't be far behind. Few hours at the most.'

I can hear them arguing, but it makes no difference.

'McCoyne, wait,' Paul shouts. I take a few more steps before stopping, against my better judgement, and turning around. 'He's right,' I hear him say to Carol and Keith. 'We've been told to find as many people to fight with us as we can, haven't we? It makes sense to split up. You deliver this lot; we'll keep looking for more. Okay?'

Keith thinks for a minute and eventually nods his head. 'Fair enough. Makes no difference to me.'

I start walking again, my rucksack on my back and my axe held ready in my hand.

'I'll go with him,' I hear Paul say. 'Julia told me to keep an eye on him.'

I speed up, more determined than ever to find Ellis. Seeing the kids in the school has made me feel more confident that she's survived, but at what cost? What condition is she in? If I don't find her and look after her, will she end up like the children we've found here?

'Hold on,' Paul shouts, but I just keep walking. I don't need him. I don't need any of them.

15

It seems that every couple of minutes, something I see catches me off-guard. This time it's a petrol station: an innocuous shell of a building that I normally wouldn't have given a second glance. I stop in the middle of the road and stare at it. The big, once brightly lit welcome sign lies on its side, blocking the way to the now lifeless fuel pumps. Metal grilles pointlessly protect long-since-smashed plate-glass windows. Inside, the shelves and displays have been stripped of everything of value . . .

'Problem?' Paul asks.

'Nothing,' I lie. 'Just thought I saw something.'

I take a couple of steps closer, wishing I was alone. There's nothing here, and he knows it. I just wanted to stop for a second and look and remember. It feels like five minutes, but it was probably about five months since I was last here. Lizzie took her dad to the hospital and I was left with the kids. I took them to see a film. We drove halfway across town and used half a tank of petrol to get to the cheapest cinema. They argued about what they wanted to see. Ed and I wanted to watch one thing, Ellis wanted to watch something else. Edward and I won the argument. Josh slept through the film and Ellis whined all the way through it.

We stopped here on the way back home to fill up the car and I bought Ellis some sweets just to shut her up. Then that started the other two moaning . . . If I half-close my eyes I can still see her in there. She took for ever to choose her sweets, dragging it out, trying to get as much out of me as she could.

It's the contrast that's taken me by surprise today. Everything was so trivial and unimportant back then. I walked into this shop with Ellis and I was just like any other dad trying to pacify his whingeing kid. Now look at me. A killer. A soldier (apparently, although I don't feel like one). Virtually unrecognisable from the man I used to be. Living from day to day and hour to hour . . . And if the war's had this much of an effect on me, what might it have done to Ellis? I wonder what the little girl who, on that day five months ago, had nothing more important to worry about other than what sweets she wanted, is doing now?

'Any time today would be fine,' Paul moans. 'Stop bloody daydreaming! It's dangerous out here, you know.'

'I wasn't daydreaming.'

'You were. For fuck's sake, get a grip.'

'I'm fine,' I say as I march past him.

'You were away with the bloody fairies again. You need to clear your head, mate. Get some focus.'

This guy never gives up. He's like a dog with a bone.

'I am focused,' I snap back at him.

'Focused on what? A bloody petrol station? Face it, McCoyne, you're drifting. You don't even have a proper plan.'

'Yes I do.'

'What, walk halfway across an enemy-occupied city to get to a house where you think your kid *might* have been? You're making it up as you go along, mate. Just give it up and move on. You've got to start putting the fight first and everything else second.'

'If it's such a bad idea, why did you come with me?'

'Like I said, to find more volunteers. Besides, I didn't fancy being shut in the back of that van with a load of feral kids.'

'*Volunteers* . . . is that what you're calling them now?'

'Well, what would you call them?'

'Conscripts? Lemmings?'

'So are you not bothered about this war any more then? Are you happy just to let the Unchanged carry on attacking us? You saw the gas chambers . . . you know what we're up against.'

'Nothing's changed, Paul. I still want to kill just as much as you do.'

'Start showing it, then. Listen, mate,' he sighs, 'I'm just trying to help you out. I understand what you're going through.'

'Understand! How the hell can you understand? My five-year-old daughter is out there on her own somewhere . . .'

For the first time in an age he's quiet. 'Do you really think you're the only one who's had it hard?' he finally says, his voice suddenly full of tension and previously suppressed emotion. 'Think you're the only one who's been dealt a shitty hand by all of this?'

'No, I—'

'Because I'll tell you, sunshine, you're not. We've *all* had it hard. What's happened has fucked everything up for every last one of us, and all we're trying to do is put things straight.'

'I'm not saying that I—'

'You've never once asked me about my family, have you? About what happened to me? What brought me here? And do you know why? I'll tell you, it's because you don't care – and you're right not to. It doesn't matter. It's not important, none of it is. What's done is done and all that matters now is what we do from here on in.'

'I get it, I do – but if I can find Ellis then I—'

I stop speaking because he's stopped walking again. I carry on for a few more paces then turn back to face him.

'It was a Wednesday night, about a quarter to ten, when it happened to me,' he says. 'It was all so bloody ordinary. I'd been watching the football on telly. My girlfriend had just gone to bed and I was on my own downstairs. I was just sat there, staring at the walls, when everything clicked into place and started to make sense. It was like someone had switched a bloody light on, you know? Like I could suddenly see everything clearly for the first time in years.'

'What are you on about?'

'So I sat there for a while,' he continues, ignoring me and wiping something away from the corner of his eye, 'then I went out to the garage and got myself a mallet and a saw, best things I could find. Then I went back inside, went upstairs and killed Sharon. After I'd finished with her, I did the same to Dylan. He was awake in his cot when I went into his room. He stood there, bouncing up and down on his mattress, grinning at me, but I did it just the same. I had to.'

'I'm sorry,' I mumble quietly, feeling like a total cunt and not knowing what else to say.

He walks on, trying unsuccessfully to hide his anger. 'Thing is, since I heard the things Preston's been saying, I can't help wondering what would've happened if I'd left him. Could I have made him like us?'

'Do you believe all that?'

'I don't know what I believe. All I know is that you've got no fucking right to question whether I understand what you're going through. You've got a kid who's probably still out there, fighting somewhere, and these days that's as much as anyone can hope for. Now shut up, wise up and get a fucking grip. Forget about her.'

16

We work our way along the outermost edge of the Unchanged exclusion zone, either just inside or just outside the boundary depending on whose map you're looking at. It's been uncomfortably quiet out here and we've seen only a handful of other fighters since splitting from the others back at the school. Here, though, things suddenly feel different. Paul and I make our way quickly through the ruins of a sprawling college campus, moving away from the battle-damaged buildings and climbing up a number of terraced football pitches, stacked like hugely oversized steps. From the furthest edge of the uppermost playing field we're able to look out over a huge swathe of the exclusion zone.

In the distance I can just about make out the area of town where Lizzie's sister lived, and I can see all the way across the wide stretch of no-man's land to the heart of the enemy refugee camp too. But it's what's directly below us which is of more immediate interest. We're overlooking what's left of St James' Hospital, and it's crawling with activity. Our fighters are all over it like ants over forgotten food.

'What do you reckon?'

Paul shrugs his shoulders. 'Got to be a reason for them being here,' he answers and, before I can speak again, he's crawling through a hole in a section of chain-link fence and starts running down a steep grassy slope towards the hospital. I try to resist for a second and force myself to concentrate on finding Ellis, but then I think about the fact that there must be Unchanged close by and the temptation becomes too strong to suppress. My mouth begins to water as I sprint down the hill after Paul, desperate to get down to the hospital and start killing. I hear gunfire as I start to run, a sure sign that the enemy are close. Suddenly all I can think about is satisfying my hunger to end Unchanged lives.

The main hospital entrance has been partially demolished, the automatic doors are stuck midway through opening, their metal frames buckled. As I catch up with Paul he's looking for a way around what's left of this part of the site. It sounds like most of the heavy fighting is concentrated around the car parks and the buildings at the far end of the complex.

'Cut straight through,' I suggest as I squeeze through the gap in the doors. He follows me as we head down a long corridor which has somehow remained surprisingly white and clean, and which even now still has the faintest tang of antiseptic in the air. The building feels vast and empty, and our footsteps echo as we run along the hard tiled floor towards the battle. A huge black zigzagging crack in one of the walls makes me momentarily question my decision to come this way, but it's too late now, and anyway, it's worth the risk. We're nearing the fighting. We're closing in on the enemy.

I burst through a set of swinging double doors and stop at a staircase. Instinct tells me to head down, but the way through is blocked by fallen rubble from a collapsed wall. Paul doesn't wait, deciding quickly to head up and work his way around whatever damage he finds up there. I follow him through more doors and along another, much shorter corridor which ends with a sharp right-hand turn.

We instinctively slow down when we enter a ward filled with corpses. I start to wonder whether these well-decayed people were just abandoned and forgotten when the war began, but a closer look at their injuries quickly tells me that wasn't the case. A skeletal woman, still dressed in her blood-stained nightgown, has been skewered with the metal support which once held her intravenous drip. Sitting on the floor to my left is the withered husk of an old man, slumped over with his legs apart. There's a vertical scar in the middle of his badly discoloured chest, running in almost a straight line down from just below the level of his sagging nipples. At the bottom of the scar, right where his navel would have been, the wound has been forced open and his innards pulled out. This guy's been disembowelled by someone with their bare hands. The ingenuity and brutality of whoever did this is breathtaking. But these bodies are old. Why are people still fighting here today?

A huge hole in the ceiling and a corresponding hole in the floor further down the ward force me to concentrate again. I follow Paul as he edges cautiously around the narrow ledge above the chasm. When I peer down I see a mass of rubble, beds and bodies directly below me. Looking up I see there are more holes above us, going through every floor all the way up to what's left of the roof.

At the end of the ward we reach another staircase. I look down through a large safety-glass window to a vast crowd of people battling outside. Our fighters are swarming around a collection of separate outbuildings right out on the furthest edge of the site. They look like they might have been store-rooms or boiler rooms once. Now there are enemy soldiers in every visible window and doorway, and more on the roof, all of them firing relentlessly and indiscriminately into the surging crowd. On the other side of the wrought-iron railings which surround the hospital grounds are their vehicles, ready for them to beat a hasty retreat if we get too close.

Paul's halfway down the stairs, but I stay at the window. Something's not right here.

'Come on!' he shouts.

'Wait—' I watch as another surge comes from deep within the crowd of fighters. People are jostling for position, trying to get closer to the enemy, using each other as human shields by default. A pair of Brutes almost get close enough to strike before they're driven back and brought down by another hail of bullets. Other fighters are immediately clamouring to take their places, trampling their fallen bodies, but the enemy seems to be managing to keep the crowd at bay.

'You fucking idiot!' Paul yells at me. 'They'll all be dead by the time you get down there!'

He disappears, but I don't move. On the face of it this looks like any one of a hundred battles I've witnessed or been a part of – but there's a subtle difference, and alarm bells are ringing. I sprint after Paul to try and stop him.

'Paul,' I yell, just managing to catch sight of the back of his head before he disappears out through an open door. 'Wait!'

'We'll tear them apart,' he shouts, glancing back at me. 'They're sitting ducks.'

'No, they're not!'

'What?'

'They could get out of here at any time. I saw it from up there. They're tight up against the perimeter and they've got vehicles on the other side, ready and waiting to take them out. They're playing us.'

'What?' he shouts again.

'It's a fucking set-up! Think about it . . . their secure area's just a mile or so from here, there's no way they've been cut off from the others, and they don't look like they're out here for supplies . . .'

'I don't care,' he says, thinking more about the kill than anything else, acting like a drug-starved junkie who's desperate for a hit.

'They're not waiting here to be evacuated,' I tell him. 'They're here to draw us out into the open.'

Paul looks at me, shakes his head as if he's disappointed, then turns and runs, charging deep into the sprawling, ever-growing crowd of fighters which is now almost completely filling the entire space between the main part of the hospital and the Unchanged-occupied buildings. Bullets shatter windows in the wall high above and jagged daggers of glass rain down around me.

Forced to move, I follow him outside, but I stay right at the very back of the crowd, using the mass of surging figures as cover as I try to squirm around the edge of the building and head back in the direction from which we had just come. Paul's already disappeared – just another face in the swollen crowd of bloodthirsty fighters, all of them desperate to kill. I don't know what's more terrifying, the fact that I think we're being set up, or how singularly focused this huge mass of people has become. It's like nothing else matters; the scent of blood is in the air and they're all behaving like Brutes, prepared to sacrifice anything for the thrill of the kill. The closeness of the enemy and their constant gunfire just seems to rile the hordes and make them even more aggressive. Maybe that's what they want?

I feel like I'm fighting against everyone else here now, and a moment of indecision and distraction costs me dear. Too busy watching what the bulk of the crowd are doing, I don't realise another group of fighters is approaching from behind until it's too late. They barge past me, shoving me out of the way and to the side, slamming me against a wall.

Before I know what's happening I'm on the ground, desperately trying to cover my head and scramble out of the way as people stampede all around me. The noise of the chaotic battle is muffled and distorted down here, increasing my disorientation. I try to follow the wall I just smacked into, still moving against the tide of people and hoping I'm heading in the right direction. I'm finally able pull myself back up onto my feet using a drainpipe for support. I haul myself up onto the top of a metal and glass smokers' shelter outside a blocked entrance door and look back over the heads of the crowd.

Almost all of the shooting has suddenly stopped and I see that our fighters have finally reached the small buildings. They're pouring inside, steamrolling anyone who gets in their way. I stand on the shelter and curse myself for overreacting. Maybe Paul was right. Did these stupid Unchanged bastards really just screw up and get themselves stranded out here?

I'm about to jump down when I hear something. The noise makes me stop and stare again. And then I see it – a line of armoured trucks and Jeeps heading away from the back of the buildings. A handful of fighters manage to make it over to the other side of the perimeter fence, but judging by the number of vehicles now racing across this part of the exclusion zone at speed, it looks like most, if not all, of the Unchanged soldiers have got away. More people scramble through the buildings and chase after the Unchanged, but they give up quickly and watch the enemy escape through clouds of dust.

Wait.

The sound of engines is getting louder.

The vehicles are almost of out sight, but the noise is continuing to increase in volume. It's vague, directionless, washing over us, then fading in and out before it starts to become stronger, more definite again. And then I realise that these engines are above us. I know what's coming next. The enemy's tactics are getting easier to predict.

I jump down off the shelter, going over on my ankle and accidentally taking out another couple of fighters in the process. There's an uncomfortable malaise about this place now. Only a few people on the frayed edges of the crowd are making any serious attempt to get away. Most of them are just standing there, some with their faces pressed against the railings, still watching the Unchanged flee. I'd do something about it if I could be bothered, but all I'm interested in now is getting myself out of here before it's too late.

I start running, pushing my way through crisscrossing bodies while trying to ignore the jabbing pain in my ankle. Above the roof of the hospital I catch a glimpse of a massive low-flying, slow-moving plane with an enormous wingspan and I'm willing myself to go faster and faster, even as I hear the high-pitched whistle of the first bombs beginning to fall. I'm away from the bulk of the crowd, but still nowhere near far enough to be safe. I keep trying to force my legs to work harder, but my muscles are burning with the effort and I think my ankle's going to give way at any second. *I can't keep moving.* I lean against a wall and half-hop, half-drag myself along, knowing that the building I'm holding onto is about to be obliterated. I can almost see the grassy hill Paul and I ran down now, but it's still too far away and I know I'll never get there. The piercing whine of the fast-falling munitions keeps increasing in volume until it's all I can hear. Then it stops.

Nothing.

A split second later and the air is filled with more noise than I can believe, the power of the blast forcing the air from my lungs. I drop down and cover my head, ready for the world around me to explode. The ground shakes violently and I curl myself up into the smallest shape possible, waiting for the remains of the hospital building to start falling. My guts churn with fear and I brace myself for what's coming next, knowing that the worst is yet to happen . . .

The noise starts to fade.

Everything sounds muffled, even the debris falling and the people in the distance who are screaming with pain and yelling for help.

Was that it?

I tell myself I'll count to thirty, and if nothing's happened I'll try to move. I only get to seven when I feel people starting to get up around me. Did all the bombs explode? Did the Unchanged pilot fuck up?

I cautiously stand up and turn around, not knowing what I'm going to see behind me. The air is filled with spewing clouds of dust, like a thick, dirty fog which is quickly settling, coating everything with grey. As it fades I realise I can still see the far end of the hospital building. It's intact. The out-buildings which were the focus of the fighting have gone, but the main campus is in much the same condition as it was before the attack.

The only other thing that's missing is the crowd of fighters and I realise that they were the target today, nothing else. Those Unchanged bastards have managed to wipe hundreds of us out, while leaving everything else relatively intact. I don't know whether it's the sight of the undamaged hospital building or the empty space where the crowds of fighters were standing which makes me hate them more.

As the haze settles, everything takes on a bizarrely calm, almost dreamlike state. Those who escaped the full force of the blast begin to stagger past me, some soaked with blood, others looking like white-faced ghosts, and all covered in powder-fine debris. Behind those who can walk I see others who've suffered far worse injuries. A woman, I think she might have been a Brute, is trying to drag herself along the ground. Both of her legs have been blown off below the knee and she's leaving an uneven snail-trail of glistening blood behind her. She manages to travel a couple of metres further before she dies. I shake my head clear and try to force myself into action as a man stumbles closer, walking like a drunk, carrying the lower part of his left arm in his right hand. He's asking me for help, I think, but I can't hear him. Is there something wrong with his voice? I try to answer, but I can't hear my own voice properly either. Everything sounds muffled and low and I realise the problem's with my ears. I nervously look from side to side, suddenly aware that if I can't hear properly, I'm wide open to attack. I need to get away from here and find somewhere safe so I can get my head together, then I need to get on with what I came back out here for. For half a second I wonder whether I should stop and look for Paul. It's a stupid idea, pointless. He's probably nothing more than a pile of blackened bone and ash at the bottom of the bomb crater now. He was no help, anyway. Stupid fucker didn't listen to a word I said.

Pull yourself together, I tell myself again as the shock and disorientation slowly start to fade and some clarity returns. I need to forget this place and get back on track. I need to keep moving towards Lizzie's sister's house. And I decide as I start to hobble away, my damaged ankle still hurting, that I need to do it on my own. I have to keep away from everybody else, because when we're together we become an easy target for the Unchanged to pick off from the sky. Cowardly bastards – they know they don't stand a chance face to face. Long-distance battles are the only ones they can win.

I start to run, slowly at first, until the pain in my ankle becomes slightly more bearable. I head back towards the entrance to the hospital I first came through, desperate to put some distance between me and everyone else.

I reach the bottom of the grassy slope below the college playing fields and this time I go right, moving towards the ruins of a housing estate, hoping that the closely packed terraced houses on either side of the road will provide me with some temporary cover. I tuck in tight against the buildings on my right, hiding in their shadows. As I move past a succession of grim, crumbling façades, I start to think maybe I should stay here for a while. The enemy have already hit this place – what would they gain from striking here again? And now that I've made the decision that I'll only travel alone, maybe it would be better to wait until dark?

But then I think about Ellis and the kids at the school and I know I have to keep moving.

Shit, there's someone in the road up ahead. I crouch down behind a low stone wall in the front yard of one of the houses and watch. Don't think he's seen me, but he's coming this way. He's Unchanged: I can tell by the way he moves, from his slow, cautious movements and lack of confidence.

So why the hell am I cowering like this? Stay calm and consider the options, I tell myself. He's alone, and if he is one of them, I'll just kill him. I must still be shaken up from the bombing because my heart's pounding and I'm suddenly sweating like a pig. I need to face this fucker head-on, whoever and whatever he is. I try to focus on the euphoria I know I'll feel when I end his miserable life.

I grab my axe, then stand up and run at him. When he sees me he immediately reaches for his belt and I curse my stupidity, certain that he's about to draw a gun and fire. But he doesn't, he backs away, running from me faster than I'm moving towards him, screaming into a handheld radio. Now

I'm sure he's Unchanged, and I know I can't let him live. He accelerates, moving with a frantic speed that I can't match. It's a struggle for me even to keep up, but I can't let him go. Have to kill him—

He turns a blind corner and I follow, then stop dead in my tracks. There are three more of them racing down the road ahead towards me, one on a motorbike in full leathers. It's four against one and I'm fucked. But I can't let it end like this. Do I go out fighting or—? The bike rider lifts what looks like a riot baton and accelerates and that's my decision made. Like a fucking coward I turn and run, not even bothering to attack, with the screaming sound of the bike's engine ringing in my ears.

I run through the open door of the nearest house and slam it shut behind me. That should slow the bastards down. Rather than risk heading upstairs and getting trapped in this ruin I start running through a ransacked living room and jumping over the outstretched legs of the corpse of a woman leaning up against an empty fireplace. She looks like she's praying. The kitchen of the house is filled with rubble and there's a gaping hole where a window used to be.

I scramble up onto an unsteady draining board and jump out through the gap, landing in a concrete yard on my injured ankle. I bite my lip hard, refusing to shout out, and breathe through the pain. In the brief moment of quiet I listen to the echoing sound of the motorbike as it fades and swirls and seems to move away.

Then I hear the Unchanged enter the front of the house and I force myself forward again. I run down a narrow path in the middle of an overgrown lawn, heading towards a high brick wall at the back of the garden. There's a water butt in the corner and I use it to climb up onto the top of the wall, then kick it over to stop anyone from following. It was half-full, by the look of the scummy water.

I'm down the other side, and I find myself standing in an open space in the middle of a block of six lock-up garages, three on either side. I can either hide here and wait to be found or make a break for it. Apart from going back over the wall there's only one way out. I sprint forward, but I stop when the bastard on the bike appears from nowhere and cuts me off, swerving the bike around so that it blocks the road. I manage to weave around his back tyre and get past, but I've taken only a few steps further when I hear him accelerate again. I look back over my shoulder as he rears up, riot baton held ready. I try to change direction again, try to wrong-foot him, but my ankle gives way and I stumble, barely managing to keep upright and moving. I feel sudden, searing pain as the baton cracks against the back of my legs and I hit the tarmac hard and roll over in agony.

More of them are coming, their Unchanged faces hidden by motorcycle helmets, face masks, visors and scarves. I try to stand up, but one of them slams me back down, pinning my arms to the ground. Another one holds my legs. I struggle, but they're too strong. There're too many of them.

'Just do it,' I yell at them, 'fucking do it! Kill me now and get it over with!'

Yet another one appears, looming over me, and I can see this one's face. He looks me up and down then pulls the plastic stopper off the tip of a hypodermic needle with his teeth and spits it out. I arch my back, trying to break their grip and get away, but I can't do anything to stop the fucker thumping the needle hard into my chest.

PART III

Within weeks the mechanism for the ongoing distribution of food and medical aid to the population of the refugee camp had begun to falter and fail. In retrospect it had looked like a large-scale but reasonably straightforward undertaking, but as what had originally been envisaged as a short-term operation dragged into its fourth month with no end in sight, the situation continued to rapidly deteriorate.

The initial ground rules and hastily cobbled together official procedures had been simple. Under military control, all resources were to be coordinated via the City Arena – a vast, cavernous, ten-thousand-seat concert venue. Its football-pitch-sized concrete floor had been cleared and all rations, supplies, emergency aid and 'collected' foodstuffs were held there under armed guard. Lorries full of provisions were shipped out to ten nominated distribution centres within the huge camp on a daily basis: a cinema complex, the Town Hall, two sports centres and a number of other similar-sized public buildings. From these centres food was distributed to the city's population, all of whom carried ration books with their identification papers.

By the beginning of the second month, supplies had already dwindled to dangerously low levels, the authorities having severely underestimated both the number of refugees requiring rations and the duration of their enforced incarceration. Similarly, they'd overestimated their ability to source and replenish food stocks. Officially acquired (looted) food continued to enter the city on a daily basis as a result of frequent military excursions, but it was nowhere near enough. More importantly, no more food was being produced. No crops were being grown and harvested, no factories were operating, every transportation and distribution system had been rendered unusable.

By midway through the second month, supplies had fallen to such a low level that the daily restocking of the ten distribution centres was reduced to every other day. By the beginning of the third month, deliveries were being made weekly.

A black market emerged on the streets and for a short while it thrived and flourished. Also in Month Two, a militia unit known colloquially as the Milkmen, because of the herd of stolen cows they kept penned in on the pitch of a heavily guarded local football club, assumed control of two of the distribution centres. The irony of small-time criminals dealing in milk and occasionally beef alongside the usual staples of drugs and weapons was not lost on either the military who tolerated their activities (it took some of the pressure off them) or the poor bastards forced to trade with them.

Business boomed temporarily, until the basic economic principle of supply and demand could no longer be applied. Food, water and medicines became both the commodities and the currency. The demand was inexhaustible, the supply non-existent. Trade stopped. The militia units closed their doors, emerging only to attack and raid other distribution centres to continue to feed and water themselves. When even the black-marketeers could no longer source enough food and water for their own needs, infighting took hold and their previously untouchable operations imploded.

As the end of Month Three approached, the City Arena was all but empty and eight of the distribution centres (including those previously run by the militia) had ceased to function. Of the three remaining sites, the Arena was now being run by the military purely for the benefit of the military. One of the distribution centres housed in an old market hall continued to be maintained by a rapidly dwindling group of do-gooders who were stupid enough to still believe in helping other people. They dutifully handed out almost microscopic portions to the ever-growing crowds who queued outside the building twenty-four hours a day, seven days a week. Truth was, the only reason they were still in business was because they drip-fed provisions, a mouthful at a time. Perversely, the sheer mass of desperate refugees both protected the distribution centre from the threat of militia attack and isolated it from the military authorities and supply routes.

This morning, the last functioning distribution centre, housed in a long-empty factory building, collapsed. The food supplies had finally run dry and the news, predictably, caused a riot. The military commander responsible for overseeing the centre from a safe distance wasted no time in locking the site down and ordering the execution of the three hundred or so rioting civilians trapped inside. The public had to be controlled, what-ever the cost. Disorder like that couldn't be allowed to spread. The implications were unthinkable.

Three-quarters of an hour ago Mark had left the cramped hotel room for the first time since returning from his final shift as a volunteer. Kate had pleaded with him not to go, but what choice had he had? He had a duty to provide for her and his unborn child, not to mention the other family members they'd found themselves unwillingly imprisoned alongside.

Walking the streets was a bizarre and frankly terrifying experience, and he quickly realised how much he missed the security of travelling with the military. Even being surrounded by Haters felt safer than this. He desperately tried to keep himself to himself, looking at the ground whenever he passed anyone else, or looking over the heads of the crowds he was walking through. He didn't know where he was going or what he was hoping to achieve, but he had to keep trying. He couldn't just sit there with the rest of them and wait for some-thing to happen. They were starving, cold and frightened, and he begrudgingly felt responsible for all of them.

Mark made his way in the general direction of the factory building where he, Kate and the others had collected their rations in the past. He walked via Leftbank Place, an area of waste ground which had been earmarked for redevelopment for years. That was never going to happen now. He struggled to see through the never-ending mass of temporary shelters which blanketed the ground, making it look more like a third world slum than anything else. The remains of entire families sat huddled together under polythene sheets, desperately clinging on to their last few belongings and each other. For a while it made him almost feel grateful for the relative comfort and security of the hotel room where he and the others had been billeted.

It was obvious as soon as he got near the distribution centre that it had closed down. Where he'd expected to find uneasy, virtually silent queues of people he now saw only an empty site – and as any space was at a premium now, the fact that people were completely avoiding the area was a bad sign in itself.

He'd already decided to turn around and head back to the hotel when he saw bodies being dragged away and a plume of hazy grey smoke drifting up from behind the large building. He recognised it as the smoke from a funeral pyre – a typical military clean-up operation. They burnt all dead bodies now, to stop, or at least slow, the spread of disease.

He changed direction gradually, feeling acutely self-conscious, and so afraid of everyone else that he didn't dare make any sudden alterations to his route. He felt – being paranoid, maybe – that people were watching him. He found himself at the base of the McIver Tower, the place where he used to work, and he allowed himself to look up, just for a moment, and remember.

Up there, on the seventh floor, surrounded by a hundred and fifty co-workers, all sitting in front of identical computers, wearing identical headsets and working towards identical targets: that was how he'd spent endless hours before all of this had happened. He'd sold insurance, dealt with people's claims. Those were the days, he thought, almost daring to smile, when a burst pipe or a broken window was considered an emergency . . . It all seemed so trivial and unimportant now, but it had mattered then, not just to him, but to everyone. He'd struggled with the monotony of the job at times, but he'd have given anything to be able to return to the boredom and routine of his former life now.

He stopped by a telephone box, an excuse to look a little longer, and tried not to look suspicious, avoiding eye-contact with the man who was sitting on the floor inside it, his back pressed against the door to prevent anyone else from getting in. Mark counted up to floor seven of the office block, then worked his way along to the window nearest to where he used to sit. There were people living up there now – he could see them, even from down here. Hundreds of them were packed in together, desperate for space. Around the base of the building, in a low-walled, rectangular area which had once been an exclusive car park reserved for company executives and senior managers, was an enormous pile of redundant computer equipment. Hundreds of unneeded screens, keyboards and tower units had been chucked out as the floors above had been emptied to make room.

Mark looked down at the man in the phone box again. He hadn't moved. Was he just sleeping? He casually tapped the glass with his knuckles, but the man didn't react so he did it again. Then, moving slowly, he shook the door. Still no reaction. Was he dead? Whatever it was that was wrong with him, Mark saw that he had a carrier bag tucked inside his filthy raincoat. It had to be food. Other than weapons and drugs, food was the only thing worth hiding now. He kicked the glass again, this time cringing inwardly as a couple of other people either turned around or glanced up before remembering themselves and looking away again.

The appearance of a small boy walking along the wall around the base of his old work building distracted him. The poor kid looked hopelessly lost and exhausted, all life and energy drained out of him. It said something about this crisis that even the kids were affected to such an extent. He'd seen movies of children playing resiliently around the ruins of their homes in World War II bombsites before now, and footage of kids laughing and running through disease-ridden subcontinent slums, but this . . . this was different. Even the most innocent and naïve members of society knew how dire this situation was becoming. The boy shouldn't have been on his own. Who was he with? Was he lost? Abandoned, or orphaned? He'd adopted the same emotionless, almost vacant gaze as everyone else, trying to separate himself from the rest of the world, but he was unable to escape its close confines. Mark was worried that he had no way of knowing if this kid was okay or if he was sick or—

He forced himself to stop. He had to look away and block him out. He couldn't afford to care.

This morning, before he'd left the hotel, Mark had argued with Kate. Neither of them had meant for it to happen, but once they'd started shouting, weeks of pent-up frustrations meant neither of them could stop. Kate was becoming increasingly claustrophobic in the hotel room and the lack of privacy was driving her insane.

'What am I supposed to do?' he'd said to her. 'Until things change, this is all we've got. There are no hospitals or clinics.'

'So what happens when the baby comes?'

'We deal with it.'

'How?'

'I don't know . . . we get some towels and water like they said and—'

'What towels? Where's the water going to come from? Christ, Mark, I won't even be able to wash the kid. We don't have enough water to drink, let alone—'

'Calm down, Katie, you're just—'

'Calm down! Jesus Christ, why should I? I'm fucking terrified and you're expecting me to give birth to our baby on the floor of a hotel room in front of my parents.'

'It's months away yet – four months. Think how much might change in another four months—'

'Think how much worse it might get.'

'Now you're just being stupid.'

'I'm scared.'

'We're all scared.'

'I'm scared about the baby.'

'Millions of women give birth every year, don't they? And they used to manage before hospitals and—'

'It's not that—'

'What then?'

She whispered, 'I'm scared about what our baby might be. What if it's not like us? What if it's one of them and it . . . ?'

'Don't be stupid. I'm normal and you're normal. Our baby will be normal too.'

'But what if it isn't? You don't know that for sure, do you? No one knows why we're like we are and why they're different . . .'

She was right, of course, but he kept on trying to persuade her that everything would be okay, doing his best to keep up the bullshit because it was all he could do.

A sudden noise nearby diverted Mark's attention back to the present. There was a disturbance deep in a crowd of people on the other side of the road. He couldn't clearly see what was happening. It looked like a fight – someone had probably cracked under the strain of this impossible situation that they – and everyone else – found themselves in. The sudden, un-expected outpouring of long-suppressed emotions provoked a range of reactions from the other refugees nearby. Some ran. Some did all that they could to pretend it wasn't happening. Others forgot where they were and all that they'd been through and responded with the most basic, natural of reactions. They fought.

Mark didn't give a damn what was happening or why. Taking full advantage of the situation, and the distraction it was causing, he shoved the door of the phone box, hard. When the motionless man on the ground still didn't react, he pushed the door again until there was a wide enough gap for him to squeeze his arm through. He grabbed the man's carrier bag, shoved it inside his coat and walked back towards the hotel.

17

Jesus, my head hurts.

Where the hell am I? It's dark, pitch-black almost. I'm lying flat on my back on a narrow bed, naked but for a T-shirt and shorts. I try to move, but my ankles and wrists have been chained to the corners of the metal bed frame. There's no slack and I can't even lift my hands up off the mattress. The harder I try, the tighter the chains seem to get. I attempt to move my head, but there's some kind of strap right across my forehead, keeping me down. When he comes back I'll kill the fucker who's done this.

My eyes are getting used to the lack of light in here, but there's not a lot to see. It's a narrow, rectangular room with this bed against one wall and a chair opposite. There's nothing on the walls except for a lopsided crucifix just to the side of the solid wooden door. I stretch my neck back as far as I can. There's a small boarded-up window behind me with the faintest crack of light showing round the edges.

How long have I been here? Have I just woken up, or have I been out cold for days? I feel myself starting to panic and I make myself breathe slowly and work my way back through what I remember . . . The children at the school, travelling with Paul, the fighting at the hospital, the Unchanged in the streets who chased me down and drugged me . . . We were set up, and the bastards who did it must be the ones who brought me here. I pull on my chains again, but I still can't move. I don't understand this – it doesn't make sense. If they really were Unchanged, why didn't they just kill me? Why bring me here, wherever *here* is?

Someone screams. Can't tell where the noise is coming from.

Don't know if they're screaming for help or crying in pain – is this a torture chamber? A place where sick, perverted Unchanged fuckers tie us up and make us suffer? Bastards could come in here any second and start on me and there'd be nothing I could do. Maybe they're experimenting, trying to find out what makes us better and stronger than them by cutting us up? How many others before they get to me? Is it my turn next?

Concentrate.

Calm.

Focus.

I think about killing to keep me strong. I think about all the Unchanged I've massacred over the months, all the pointless lives I've ended, and I think about how easy it was, and will be again.

Ellis.

Just for a second, from out of nowhere, I think about Ellis, and everything comes crashing down again. The chains feel tighter and the darkness closes in and I can't move a fucking muscle. I've failed her. She's on her own somewhere while I'm locked up here like a fucking animal. Every minute she's alone out there increases the chance of her ending up like the kids in the school.

I try and move again, pulling as hard as I can. For a second I think that I can break the chains and get out of here, but nothing happens and the ties just get tighter. I feel like I'm in the queue outside the cull site again, all lined up and waiting to die. And just like then, there's nothing I can do about it.

My arms hurt. They feel heavy, numb. Shoulders are burning with pain. Got an itch on the side of my right leg, just above the knee, and all I want to do is scratch it. I try to ignore it, but it won't go. Now it's all I can think about, and the more I think about it, the worse it gets. Now it's like someone's dragging the point of a needle up and down across my skin and it's driving me fucking crazy.

Good.

Focus.

Concentrate on the pain and block everything else out.

18

Have I been asleep? I can't see the window when I tilt my head back and look behind me. Is it dark outside? Is it even an outside window? Am I in the same room, or did they move me while I was asleep – if I was asleep? Maybe I've been awake all the time. I could have been lying here for hours. Might be longer. Might have been here for days.

Everything's quiet except for a slow drip in the corner of the room. Sounds like a leaking pipe. It's constant, steady . . . I count to eight between each drip.

Throat's dry. Need water. Want to call out, but I can't. Don't know who's listening. Won't lower myself to speak to Unchanged even if . . .

'How are you feeling?'

The voice from the darkness scares the shit out of me. The only thing I can move is my eyes, and all I see is nothing, whichever way I look. Did I imagine it? My heart's thumping in my chest like I've run ten miles. I try and move, but I'm still held tight. Someone's next to me. I can hear their breathing. Can't see him, but I know he's close. I feel him brush against my hand and my whole body stiffens. The door opens inwards a fraction, just enough to let a narrow wedge of dull yellow light trickle into the room.

'Didn't mean to startle you,' the deep voice continues. It's an African-sounding accent. 'I've been watching you for a while. Just wanted to make sure you were all right.'

The man stops speaking and stands over me. I can see his short but broad frame outlined by the light from outside. Is he waiting for a response? He'll be waiting a long time 'cause I'm not speaking to anyone until I know who and what they are and why I'm here.

What's he doing now? He crouches down and I can hear him messing with something on the floor beside the bed.

'You might want to close your eyes. I've got a lamp here.'

I try to keep my eyes wide open, but they shut involuntarily when he strikes a match and lights a bright gas lamp. I force myself to open them again, ignoring the pain, desperate to see as much of my surroundings as possible after what feels like hours – days, even – of darkness. The brilliant light burns my eyes. All I can see is the mantle of the lamp, glowing white-hot. The roar of the burning gas jet fills the room, incredibly loud after so much silence.

The intense glare of the light begins to fade as my eyes get used to the brightness. The man puts the lamp on a chair opposite the bed. He turns back around and I get my first proper look at his face. The bastard is Unchanged and I can't help but react. I try and lunge forward, but the chains are still holding me down. I arch my back and try to break free, but I can hardly move. He shuffles back into the corner of the room, too scared to get too close. *Need to kill him.* I need to get rid of him, but I can't. Losing control. All I can do is spit. The spittle hits the wall and starts to drip down. Mouth's too dry to make any more . . .

'Finished?' he asks. Bastard. I relax my aching muscles, feeling searing pain in my shoulders, wrists, legs and neck. Can't stand being this close to one of the Unchanged and not trying to kill them. My guts are in knots. Can't think straight. Can't move. Can't do anything. Need to kill him, but it's physically impossible. Bastard. Haven't even got enough strength to spit again.

The dark-skinned Unchanged man picks the lamp up off the chair and puts it on the floor. He sits down next to me. I manage to turn my head to the side slightly and I stare at him. Won't take my eyes off the fucker. I'd kill him in a heartbeat if it wasn't for these chains. He's – what? five-five, five-six at the most, and he's overweight, as round as he is tall. The whites of his eyes are bright and clear. I imagine them bulging as I wrap these chains around his neck and pull them tight . . .

'Take it easy,' he says. 'Calm yourself down.'

He's unarmed. He's sitting casually in the chair and he's grinning at me with a look in his dark, staring eyes that is cold and evil. His legs are spread, arms uncrossed, palms open and facing upwards. Textbook body language. Does he think I'm stupid? Fucker's doing all he can to appear open and non-confrontational, but I don't buy it. Inside he's terrified, scared shitless, because he knows what I'll do to him when I get free. Can't stand being this close to him, breathing the same air . . .

'Bet you've got more than a few questions to ask,' he says. He's right, I have a hundred questions ready. He knows I won't ask any, but he still waits for me to speak. Wish he was close enough to kill. If I just had one hand free I'd have wrapped these chains around his throat and garrotted him before he'd known what was happening. If I could I'd smash his head into the wall, or burn him with the lamp or smash the glass and grind it into his face or . . .

'My name's Joseph Mallon,' he says, his heavily accented voice sounding composed, calm and unhurried. 'I'll be working with you while you're here.'

Working with me? What the hell's he on about?

'Not many got away from the hospital, by all accounts,' he continues. 'Now that says to me you were either incredibly lucky or very smart. I'm hoping it's the latter. You look like you've lasted well out there. You're in good shape . . .'

Does he want to kill me or fuck me?

'I'll tell you what I know about you, just to get us started . . .'

He pauses, and in the gap between his words I almost forget myself and speak. But at the last second I remember what he is and I stay silent, feeling my body tensing up again.

'I've been through your stuff,' he says. 'It's all safe, by the way. I know your name's Danny McCoyne. It's funny how we still carry things like wallets around. I guess it's just habit, isn't it? Even someone like you, someone who's so desperate not to be anything like the person he was before, you still had your wallet kicking around at the bottom of your bag. Couldn't bring yourself to get rid of it, eh? You've got no use for it, but there it was, full of useless bank notes, credit cards you'll never use again, pictures of your family. Lovely looking kids, by the way—'

At the mention of my family I automatically try to move, pulling against my chains again. He grins. That was exactly what he wanted. I curse myself for being so transparent.

'That touched a nerve, didn't it?' he laughs, looking pleased with himself. 'Might explain why a big, hard man like you is carrying a doll and kid's clothing around in his bag. Were you looking for someone?'

I look away, deliberately breaking eye-contact and staring up at the ceiling. Undeterred, Mallon gets up and leans over me. I arch my back again, trying to get closer so I can freak the fucker out, but this time he stands his ground. The light shining up from the lamp on the floor casts strange shadows over his foul face. He grins and leans closer, staying just out of reach. I can feel his breath on me.

'Just relax. You're going nowhere, Danny McCoyne.'

There's a noise outside which distracts him, the dull, muffled thump and rumble of a distant explosion. He walks to the window and pulls the board away slightly to look outside. He doesn't say anything about what he sees, but the fact that he's able to look outside and I can't reminds me again that I don't even know where I am. I don't know where this place is. And add to that the fact that I don't know how long I was unconscious for . . . Jesus, I could be anywhere.

'Questions,' Mallon suddenly announces, carefully replacing the board and sitting down again. 'If you're not going to talk to me, let me see if I can hazard a guess at some of the questions you're too proud to ask. We'll start with the basics, shall we? Who am I? Where are you? What are you doing here? How come you're still alive? How long will you stay alive? What are we going to do to you? Tell me, Danny, am I on the right lines?'

He's right: I do need to know all of that and more, but I still won't answer him. Won't even look at him. I *can't* answer. I clench my fists, tense my muscles and grind my teeth while I stare up at the ceiling, doing all I can not to give him the satisfaction of a response. He shakes his head and sucks his teeth. If I stay quiet for long enough, maybe he'll tell me anyway? Bastard seems to like the sound of his own voice.

'You not going to talk to me at all this evening?'

Don't react. He wants you to react. He's trying to antagonise you.

'You know I can keep you here as long as I like, don't you?'

Ignore him.

'I'm thinking you're uncomfortable lying there like that. If I leave you all night it's going to get pretty bloody painful.'

He won't undo these chains whatever I do. More bullshit.

'And you're gonna get mighty hungry. How long's it been since you've eaten? A day? Longer? And water, too . . . your throat must be burning . . .'

Fucker's playing mind-games. Don't bite.

He waits. Watching me. Trying to out-psych me.

'Danny McCoyne,' he sighs, voice full of mock disappointment, picking up the lamp and leaning closer, 'you need to spend some time thinking about your predicament. You've lost all control, sunshine. What happens to you now is totally up to me.'

He stares down at me for a moment longer. I meet his gaze, determined not to be the one who'll crack. After a few seconds which feel like minutes he stands up straight and moves back towards the door.

'Well, I'm not wasting any more time on you tonight. I'm hungry. We've got good supplies here, better than most. Going to fetch myself something to drink and some food, then I'll get some sleep. It's been good talking to you.'

With that he leaves, taking the lamp with him. He pulls the door shut with a loud thud, and locks it. I hear his footsteps walking away, then nothing. The quiet is deafening, interrupted only by the fading sound of a far-off helicopter or plane and the steady drip of the water in the corner.

The room is pitch-black, no light at all: the kind of dark your eyes won't ever get used to.

Who the hell is Joseph Mallon? Is he on his own here, just a lone crackpot trying to make a stand, or is he part of something bigger?

My gut begins to rumble with hunger again and the itch by my right knee returns. Wish I could scratch it. That's all it'd take, just a few seconds scratching, then it would go. Feels like someone's digging a nail into my flesh.

19

I hear a scream in the darkness, but I can't tell whether it's coming from somewhere inside this building or outside. In the smothering darkness everything has lost definition. I have no concept of time, or how long I've been here. I tried counting the drips, but my tired brain can't keep track and now the noise each drip makes is like a hammer-blow to the head. I can't stay still, but I can't move, either. Every time I pull on my chains it feels like they're getting even tighter.

I don't know how long it's been since I last drank anything, but my bladder's been filling steadily. I won't shout out. That would put me at the mercy of Joseph Mallon, or any other Unchanged scum that might be here. That's what he wants. He's trying to get me to break under pressure by starving me and keeping me chained up and in the dark. I'm better than him. I won't let him get to me. But at the same time I can't stop my body from doing what it's supposed to. So I pissed myself. What else could I do? It was either that or shout for Mallon. Now I'm soaked with stinking urine. It was warm, but my bare legs are freezing now and I stink. That bastard has reduced me to this, but I won't let him beat me.

My body aches. My legs and arms are numb. Never thought not moving could hurt so much. Just wish I could get up and walk around. And God, I'm so fucking hungry. My empty stomach keeps cramping so bad it feels like it's turning itself inside out. Don't know what I'm going to do when I need to shit. Not even going to think about that until it happens. Have to try and keep myself distracted, but it's impossible when I can't see or hear anything and when I can't move and when

I don't know where I am or why or how long I'm going to be here . . .

Stop.

Focus.

This is what he wants. He's trying to push me over the edge. It won't work. *I won't let it work.*

Leg's itching again, worse than before.

Helicopter . . . long way off . . .

How long before you go crazy in the dark? A kid at school – long, long time ago – once told me it was just hours if there was absolutely no light at all. Pointless thinking about time because I don't know how long I've been lying here. Part of me is starting to wish Joseph Mallon would come back, just to break the monotony. Never thought I'd actually look forward to seeing one of the Unchanged, but staring at that evil piece of shit's face would be better than lying here staring at nothing, just thinking. Don't like being able to think like this. Makes me question things I have always known are right. Makes me start to doubt myself. Makes me think stupid, crazy thoughts about Ellis – how close I might have got to her, and how far I am from her now. I was within a couple of miles of Lizzie's sister's house and now I could be anywhere.

What's my little girl doing? Is she fighting? Is she already dead? Is she in another room in this building? Is she in the room next door? What if Mallon doesn't come back? What if I've fucked up and blown my chance with him? What if he leaves me here to starve to death, strapped to a piss-soaked bed?

What a fucking failure. All that noise and fighting and bullshit – four months of it – and I've let myself get beaten by an overweight Unchanged who looks like he couldn't fight his way out of a paper bag. He can't be the only one running this place. There were at least four of them got me out on the street, and none of them were as fat and out of shape as Mallon.

Thinking about the street makes me think about the hospital and how I criticised Paul for running head first into a one-sided fight that I thought was a set-up. At least he went out fighting. For all I know he might still be out there, still fighting, while I'm stuck here . . .

I'm starting to get scared.

The dripping noise is getting louder, faster.

Thought I felt something moving on the bed.

Thought I saw a flash of light.

Am I hallucinating now?

Am I going out of my fucking mind? Going crazy in the dark? Need to keep focused, so I try and remember Ellis' face, but the harder I concentrate, the less I see. I'm scared I'll forget what she looks like. The face I see now isn't her, it's a combination of the faces of the feral kids we found in the school this morning . . . or yesterday morning . . . or whenever the hell that was.

Leg hurts.

Just want to scratch that fucking itch.

20

The door flies open and Mallon barges into the room. He's carrying something in both hands, holding the light beneath it. The combination of searing light and dark shadows stops me from seeing anything. He doesn't look at me, must be focused on whatever it is he's going to do to me. He turns his back and puts something down on the chair, then he puts the lamp on the floor in the corner of the room.

What's that smell? Christ, it's beautiful. Smells like hot food . . . some kind of stew or soup, I think. But it can't be, can it? Can you imagine a smell? Is this another trick my tired mind's playing on me? Mallon turns around and moves closer. He's left a tray on the chair. There's a bowl on it with steam snaking up and next to it is a plastic bottle full of water. My stomach starts to growl.

'You must be damn hungry,' he says, his deep voice filling the room. I stop myself, the words on the very tip of my tongue, remembering at the last second what he is and what his kind have done to people like me. 'You look hungry. You must be starving.'

He leans over me and I instinctively strain against my chains to get to him. Maybe this time I'll reach him . . .

My arms and legs hurt too much and I quickly drop back down. Bastard doesn't even flinch. He knows I'm not going anywhere.

'You smell of piss,' he says, laughing at me. 'You're in a bad way, big man! Lost, all alone, chained up and soaked with piss!'

I can't help trying to lunge forward again, but the pain's intense and this time I hardly move. He looks me in the eye and raises his hand. I screw my eyes shut and tense up, ready for him to hit me. But the pain doesn't come. I feel him tugging on the wide strap across my forehead. He loosens it slightly, then steps back. I still can't lift my head up, but at least I've got more side to side movement now. That little freedom is bliss.

Mallon picks up the tray and sits down on the chair opposite. He sniffs the soup or stew or whatever it is then takes a spoonful and holds it up to his lips. He stops just before he eats it.

'You want some of this?'

Fucker knows how much I want it. He's playing games with me again and I have to resist. I won't give him the satisfaction of a response. Won't lower myself to speak to him. I watch his every move as he blows on it again, then takes a mouthful. He closes his eyes and shakes his head with pleasure, deliberately overdoing it for effect.

'Oh, that's *good* . . . You know, Danny, it's getting harder and harder to find food like this these days. I'm betting it's been a long time since you've tasted anything as good as this soup.'

He eats more. I want him to stop. Please don't eat it all . . .

'It's chicken, you know. It's out of a can, of course, but man, you can still taste the meat. I don't even know if it really is meat, but oh, this is damn fine soup.'

He puts down the spoon and opens the bottle of water. My mouth and throat are dry. My tongue feels ten times its normal size, like it's too big. He takes a huge swig of water, gasping with overstated pleasure when he's done. My eyes are fixed on him and he knows it. My stomach churns noisily.

He gets up and brings the tray over. I stare at the steam coming off the soup and watch it disappear into the air, trying to imagine what it tastes like. I can't remember the last time I ate hot food . . .

'You can have this,' he tells me, putting the tray down on my chest. I watch it going up and down with my fast, nervous breathing. I feel the heat from the soup on my body. 'You can have all this and more; you just have to do one thing. Do you know what that is?'

I don't react. Don't know and I don't want to know. I don't have anything this sick fucker could want. But if there is something, something I've not thought about which matters, then I know he'll keep pushing. And the longer I act dumb, the harder he'll have to push. If I stay silent long enough he'll have to tell me something to keep this bullshit interrogation moving along. He clears his throat to speak again. Predictable bastard.

'All you have to do, Danny,' he says, leaning closer, 'is talk to me. We don't even have to have a proper conversation. You can just tell me to piss off if you like; all I want is to hear your voice. I just want you to respond to me . . .'

I won't do it. I'd rather starve. He waits, looking at me hopefully. Keep waiting, fucker.

And he does.

'Seems strange to me,' he eventually whispers after he's been watching for a couple of minutes, 'that someone like you who's obviously so hungry and thirsty can't bring himself to do one small thing to get what you need so badly. No one else is going to know about it, Danny. No one's watching . . .'

Stay focused. I look up at the ceiling and count the cracks.

'You really are strange, strange people. If I had the time and inclination to wait and watch, I think you really would lie there until you die rather than drop your guard. Crazy behaviour . . .'

He leans over me until his face is all I can see. I start to tense my body again, but he gently pushes me back down with one hand and I know there's nothing I can do. I make eye-contact and refuse to break it. I'll kill him when I get out of here. I'll rip his damn body apart, smash his face into the wall . . .

Mallon sighs. He shakes his head with feigned disappointment, then picks up the tray and puts it back on the chair. I stare at the bottle of water, still three-quarters full, and watch the last few wisps of steam rising up from the soup. He stands in the open doorway with the lamp.

'All you have to do is talk to me. Just say something . . . anything . . .'

Another pause, then he leaves. He slams and locks the door and the room is plunged back into total darkness.

PART IV

The ramifications of the Hate were vast and incalculable. While the impact was predominantly felt by the surviving population – those remaining on both sides of the Change – its effects reached much, much further.

The very nature of the Change, which had split the human race in two unequal parts, had caused irreparable damage to every area of life where two or more people were expected to work together. Basic services had faltered and collapsed with in a matter of days, and what followed was a frantic period of reprioritisation as the remaining Unchanged resources were diverted to the maintenance of defence and vital services. Within weeks, even the most basic of public services had either fallen apart or been brought to their knees. A govern-ment of sorts (with a civilian mouthpiece, but under military control) continued to try to coordinate what remained of the country's infrastructure. City and district councils collapsed or were dissolved. All schools were closed. The hospitals and the health service were overwhelmed and couldn't cope. What was left of the police force and fire brigade were absorbed into the military.

Water, gas and electricity supplies failed with astonishing speed as power stations, pumps and pipelines were abandoned, destroyed or disabled. Every single person without exception was dragged into the war, so the installations which remained operational longest were those that could function unmanned.

The concentration of huge masses of Unchanged refugees in hopelessly unprepared locations – they were evacuated into the city centres – also presented enormous, virtually insurmount-able logistical and practical problems, not least the lack of food, shelter and basic medical care. The military managed to maintain extremely limited utility supplies for themselves: fuck the civilians, there's a war to be won.

Without adequate clean water and medical supplies the refugee camps quickly became breeding grounds for disease as previously minor ailments rapidly became killers, and small outbreaks of sickness metamorphosed into fatal epidemics. Where possible dead bodies were collected up and burnt, but scores of corpses inevitably remained undetected, and together with the vast piles of untreated and uncollected garbage contributed to the proliferation of disease.

Rats and other vermin benefited from suddenly plentiful supplies of food, and those drains and sewers which had not been damaged by the fighting instead became blocked with debris.

In late May, an increase in temperature combined with frequent heavy downpours of rain to further accelerate the decline in conditions.

Every available scrap of indoor space had been utilised to house the displaced, but, inevitably, demand far outweighed availability and huge numbers of Unchanged were left outside, housed in tents, caravans and Portakabins, or making do with temporary shelters constructed from whatever materials they could find. More than thirty per cent of the total population of the refugee camp, hundreds of thousands of exhausted, vulnerable, malnourished people, were forced to live outdoors at the mercy of the elements.

'Block it up!' Mark yelled as water poured in through the broken top-floor hotel window. The room was almost pitch-black, the rising sun completely hidden by the swollen storm clouds. Rain had been pounding down for more than fifteen minutes already, and it showed no signs of abating. The guttering and drainpipes serving the dilapidated old building couldn't cope with the sheer amount of water flushing through them; a blocked section of gutter had overflowed and the water had

146

seeped behind a rotting fascia board, then flooded through the window frame. More water was coming through a broken pane of glass.

'Block it with what?' Kate shouted, using a bucket, a bin, cups and whatever else she could find to catch the water.

'I don't know! Stay there; I'll go and find something.'

'Don't go outside,' she pleaded, struggling to turn around and physically stop him. 'Please, Mark—'

'Just to the end of the landing, okay?'

He didn't give her time to answer, but weaved his way around the bottom of the double bed where Kate's traumatised parents were lying, cold and wet, and terrified, then ran past the permanently locked bathroom door. He unbolted the main door, took off the security chain and put his head outside. Just a handful of people on the landing – a rain-soaked woman from the room next door (who obviously had similar problems) and the Chinese guy with his three kids who slept in the broken lift. Mark looked up and down, then spied a wooden hatch on the wall between two of the opposite rooms. The fire hose which used to be hidden behind the small square door was missing. He pulled at the hatch, then pushed down on it from above until he felt the hinges begin to weaken. A few seconds of violent pushing and pulling and he was able to yank it free with an almighty splintering crack. He ran back to room 33 with it, stopping only to pull the one remaining curtain down from the side of the large gallery window that overlooked the street below. Jesus Christ, things looked bad down there. Crowds of people were pressed up against the sides of the buildings, desperate for whatever shelter they could find, woken without warning by the early morning deluge of ice-cold rain. The main Arley Road itself, a wide, relatively straight and gently sloping thoroughfare, looked more like a river as a fast-moving, debris-carrying torrent of rainwater surged down it towards the centre of town.

Back in the hotel room, Mark threw the curtain to Kate,

who started mopping up the water which was still cascading down the glass and over the windowsill, soaking the carpet.

'Who's that?' Kate's elderly, confused father yelled in panic, lifting his head off the pillow for the first time in hours. 'Is it one of them?'

Next to him, her mother lay on her side, sobbing, the dirty bedclothes pulled up tight under her chin.

'It's just Mark, Dad,' Kate shouted.

'It's me, Joe,' Mark said, leaning closer to the old man so he could see his face. He'd lost his glasses weeks ago. He didn't know whether Joe recognised him or not.

Mark leant the hatch door against the window over the broken glass and used what was left of a telephone directory to wedge and hold it in place.

'Save the water,' he said to Kate.

'What?'

'The rainwater . . . save it!'

'Where?'

'In the bath.'

The flow of water into the room temporarily plugged, Kate carried the half-full bucket across the room, her bare feet squelching on the damp carpet. She knocked on the bathroom door.

'Let me in.'

There was a brief pause, then the latch clicked and the door opened. Another adult refugee appeared, her face drawn and haggard-looking.

'Everything okay?' she asked. Kate nodded.

'Mark said we should try and save the water in the bath.'

The woman nodded and took the bucket from her. Mark passed her several water-filled cups which he'd collected from the window ledge.

'Makes sense to try and hoard as much as we can,' he said, taking back the empty bucket. She nodded, but didn't answer.

The floodwater temporarily stemmed, Kate sat down, ex-hausted, on a rain-splashed chair next to her parents. Her mother continued to sob, but she couldn't face trying to comfort her. Instead she closed her eyes and ran her hands over her swollen stomach.

The rain was finally easing. Mark picked up the last pot of water and carried it to the bathroom. The woman in the shadows took it from him and emptied it into the bath.

'Thanks, Lizzie,' he said.

21

I can't stand much more of this. It must be hours since Mallon left me. Can't smell the food any more, but I know it's still there and I want it. My guts feel like they're somersaulting one minute and being ripped open the next. The pain's unbearable, almost like my body's eating itself from the inside out. I try to put the hunger out of my mind, but frustration takes its place. The frustration turns into confusion then the confusion turns into fear. The fear makes my aching shoulders, arms and legs feel a thousand times worse. I try to lie still; even the slightest movement is agony.

What the hell was that? Something's moving over me. It feels like there's insects crawling over my itching leg. Maybe there are? I haven't looked at my legs since I woke up strapped to this bed. Who's to say that itch isn't an open untreated wound? Who's to say I haven't got some kind of infection, that there aren't maggots and worms and Christ knows what else feeding on my flesh? I can feel them wriggling and squirming inside the cut, digging deep into me, boring through my skin—

Then it stops again.

Am I just imagining things? Or was it something bigger? A mouse or a rat?

The dripping is the only distraction. It's constant now, almost like machine-gun fire, and it never bloody stops.

I could end this. All I have to do is talk, he said. Just give him that one small victory and I'll have some light and food and water. Christ, I need to drink something so badly . . .

I open my mouth to shout for help, then stop myself. What the hell am I thinking? Have I forgotten what Joseph Mallon is and what his people did (and are still doing) to my kind?

They're the reason all of this happened. If it wasn't for them, we wouldn't have had to kill, and my family would still be together. We had to kill them for *protection*. This whole war has been fought in self-defence . . . that's the only reason. They *made* us do it. And to think I was about to beg one of them for mercy . . . Christ, what kind of a person would that make me? I'd be pissing on the memory of all those who've already died in the fighting.

But why not?

Why shouldn't I talk?

No one's going to know, and what are my options? Do I lie here and starve to death or swallow my pride and cooperate?

No . . . no way . . . they almost had me then. That's exactly what they want me to think. They're trying to get me to crack under pressure and submit – but why should I? I'm stronger than all of them. I'll outsmart them and outlast them. *I'll* break *them*, not the other way around. When all of this is done, *they'll* be the ones lying broken on the ground, not me. I'll be standing over them, their blood on my hands.

Except right now I can't stand up. Right now I can't move. Right now I can't do anything without that fucker Mallon's say-so. For Christ's sake, I'm lying in a bed, in my own filth, and I can hardly think straight. I don't know what time of day it is, where I am, who's holding me here . . . and none of that's going to change unless someone gives way. They've got nothing to lose. Unless Mallon gets some twisted kick out of doing this, if I die it's just one less of us for them to worry about. But what really happens if I keep refusing to cooperate and fade away to nothing in the endless darkness here? I'll never see Ellis again. Chances are I won't find her anyway, but the fact of the matter is I'll definitely never see her as long as I'm locked up in here.

The hunger hurts. I need to eat and drink.

Going to do it.

I clear my throat, then stop myself – more indecision. But bottom line: what use am I to Ellis like this?

Someone has to give way.

I try and shout, but my voice is hoarse and hardly any sound comes out, just a pathetic, strangled whine. For a second I'm relieved, then I tell myself I have to do it. But now I can't even build up enough spit in my mouth to make a decent noise. Frustrated, I try again, this time a little louder. I manage something that's half a word and half a cough and immediately wish I hadn't. I feel like a traitor, colluding with the enemy. Maybe that's it? Could this place be run by Chris Ankin's people? Are they testing my loyalty?

I wait and listen hopefully. Over the dripping of water I can hear distant fighting, the occasional burst of gunfire and shelling, a jet scorching through the sky. But the rest of this building is silent, quieter than ever. Am I on my own here? For all I know this might be the last occupied room in a crumbling ruin. Joseph Mallon might be long gone . . .

One more shout, this time so loud it feels like it's ripping the inside of my throat apart.

I lie back on the bed, freezing cold, smelling of piss and feeling pathetic. Am I really so naïve, desperate enough to believe that Mallon's going to come back and feed me? I yell again, this time more in frustration than anything else, then stop. Did I just hear something? It's so faint that I convince myself I'm imagining it. But there it is again . . . the definite sound of approaching footsteps. I feel relief and fear in equal measure.

Joseph Mallon marches into the room, carrying a torch. He shines the light into my face. 'Did you say something?'

I'm immediately gagged by my emotions again, too angry and full of hate to respond. He waves the torch towards the food on the chair. It's cold now, but I still want it. The light makes the water sparkle, looking clear and pure.

He walks up to the window behind me, looks outside for a second, then turns around and shines the torch back at me again. 'I thought I heard you say something?'

Still can't speak. The words are stuck in my throat, choking me. It's like the strap across my forehead has slipped down across my windpipe, stopping me from speaking. I want to, but I can't . . .

'My mistake,' Mallon sighs. 'Sorry to have disturbed you.'

He steps back out through the door.

'Don't . . .'

My voice stops him. He turns back around to face me. The weak yellow light from the torch makes him look tired, old beyond his years, but slowly his expression changes from a scowl to a smile which becomes a broad grin.

'Good man! I knew you'd do it!'

He doesn't say anything else. He doesn't try to get me to talk like I thought he would. He doesn't try more of his stupid mind-games. Instead he just picks up the plastic bottle of water and squirts it into my mouth. It tastes so good . . . it's stale and warm but so refreshing. I swallow, and feel it running down the sides of my throat. Thank God . . .

The bottle empty, Mallon does the same with the cold soup, ladling it spoonful by spoonful into my mouth. I almost gag on it; it's cold and lumpy, with a gristly texture, but I force it down, knowing that every mouthful helps replace the nutrients and energy I've lost since being held here. As I finish eating he loosens the chains on my wrists slightly. They're still attached to the bed, but at least now I have some limited freedom of movement. The relief I feel when I can finally move my shoulders and arms is indescribable.

'Didn't hurt, did it?' he grins before he leaves and locks the door.

22

I open my eyes again and this time the narrow room is full of long shadows. Rain is hammering against the window and the water in the corner is trickling constantly now, no longer just dripping. I tilt my head back as far as it will go and see that the board over the glass has been moved. Mallon must have done it when he was last here. It's only been shifted slightly, but it's enough to let dull shards of light slope across the opposite wall, stretching almost halfway from the window over to the lopsided crucifix. I must have been asleep.

Wish I'd never spoken. I feel like a traitor, like I've betrayed myself and my kind, like I'm somehow now less of a man because I spoke to Mallon . . . But if I hadn't done it, I'd still be in total darkness, with my ankles and wrists bound tight and my stomach even emptier. I tell myself that I didn't give anything away (not that I have anything to tell) and I haven't compromised anyone but myself. It's down to survival of the fittest now, and if I stay like this, trapped, I'll be fucked when the next fight begins. And there will be another fight . . .

I can hear something happening outside, someone moving on the other side of the door, and suddenly it's thrown open and Mallon barges in. The loud noise startles me and I curse myself for not concentrating, not realising he was close. *Can't afford to let my guard down like that.* Lying here I'm vulnerable and exposed: if he decides to turn on me I'm dead.

He locks the door, then puts a fresh bottle of water down on the chair. 'How are you this morning, Danny?'

I won't answer. He leans over me and looks into my face. Instinctively I try to attack, forgetting the chains which still hold me down. My arms are yanked back down, my already aching shoulders feeling like they've been pulled out of their sockets. Mallon, standing a little further back, is unfazed. Fucker. I want to see fear and hate on his face, but there's nothing. More games. More fucking mind-games.

'Let's get some proper light in here so we can see each other,' he says, walking over to the window. He moves the board completely and for the first time I can see every corner of the small room where I've been held captive properly. It's grubby and well used, with dirty handprints all over the door like someone's been hammering to get out. And the walls are pink, for Christ's sake! God knows what this place really is – I know it's not a prison (there are no bars on the window) but pink walls apart, this room is definitely a cell.

Watching me with caution, Mallon crouches down at the side of the bed and reaches underneath it. He's pulling on the chains, probably tightening them again. He gets up and moves away and I find that I can now move my left hand with a little more freedom than before. He tosses me the water. I'm just about able to catch it. I open the lid with my teeth, hold it to my lips and drain it dry. I crush the empty bottle and throw it back at him with a flick of my still-restricted wrist. Smug bastard just smiles.

Mallon moves the chair marginally closer, carefully position-ing it as if there's a specific mark on the floor at the point where he's safe. He sits down and looks long and hard into my face. I hold his gaze, determined that I won't be the first one to break. He makes it easy for me when he's the one who looks away.

'You've been here for almost two days now, Danny,' he says, 'and you've not had any answers to those questions of yours, have you? I'm also betting that if you're anything like the rest of your people I've gone through this with, you're probably not ready to start asking yet. In fact, if I were to loosen your chains just a little bit more, I know you'd try to get off that bed and kill me.'

Damn right – there's nothing I want to do more than wrap these chains around his windpipe and choke the life out of this pathetic bastard. But I know it's not going to happen. Not yet, anyway.

'Now, what I want this morning,' he continues, his voice low and infuriatingly calm, 'is just for you to lie still and listen to me. I want to tell you my story. It won't be nothing you haven't heard a hundred times already. Well, maybe you won't have heard a story like this, but I'm betting you've seen plenty of similar things. Hell, I'm sure you've *done* worse things yourself than what I'm going to tell you. You see, Danny, you and your kind ripped a hole in my life. I lost everything because of you. You tore my world apart . . .'

What the hell's he expecting from me? Pity? An apology? It makes me feel good to know that we've made him suffer. I want to hear more. I want every detail. I want to know exactly how we hurt him, what we did.

'Picture the scene, Danny,' he begins, his voice almost too calm. 'It's a Friday night and I've just got home from work. I won't bore you with the details about where I lived and what I used to do for a living before all this because, if I'm being honest, it *was* boring. Thing is, it was *my* life and *my* routine and I was happy with it. And you and your kind took it all away from me.'

He remains composed but I sense raw emotion bubbling just under the surface. Is he going to crack? I want to see this bastard's pain, want to see him hurt.

He stops speaking, closes his eyes, takes a breath and then continues, 'It was pretty early on, I suppose. You remember what it was like in the early days, when we thought there wasn't really a problem and that the streets were full of copy-cat vigilantes fighting just because everyone else was? Before we knew that people like you were actually changing, back in the days before we all got too scared to even look at each other? Remember then?'

He automatically looks at me for a response but he doesn't get one.

'Anyway, like I said, it was a Friday night. We'd just finished eating and I was watching the news on TV, hearing about how bad everything was starting to get. My wife was in the kitchen, arguing with Keisha, our seventeen-year-old, about going out. She was going through the whole "protective mother" routine, you know? Telling her how she didn't like her going into town at the weekend anyway, but especially not then with all the trouble going on . . . you get the picture. Now I'm sitting there with my feet up, trying to block out the noise and concentrate on the TV, but it's getting louder and louder in there. Keisha's shouting at Jess, Jess is shouting at Keisha, then Keisha's shouting back again, and I'm just staring at the screen, wishing they'd both shut up . . .'

His voice trails off again and in the sudden silence I remember all the TV- and kid-orientated arguments that used to grind me down in my own dead-end former life. I check myself quickly. Am I identifying with this fucker? Maybe that's what he wants? This is probably just more calculated bullshit to try and get me onside.

'The shouting gets louder and louder,' he says, 'and I hear the back door swing open and slam shut and I think, that's it, that's Keisha storming out, but I can still hear both their voices. Then I hear a crash and one of them starts screaming, then a thump and another crash. And then all the screaming stops.'

He looks straight at me. There are tears rolling down his cheeks. He wipes them away with his sleeve.

'I get up and start walking towards the kitchen and there's this guy just standing there in the middle of the room with his back to me. Both my girls are lying at his feet. I know they're dead as soon as I see them. He's got a baseball bat in his hand and there's blood dripping off the end of it. I can only see Keisha's legs, but Jess is lying on her back, her head just a metre or so from where I'm standing, and her face . . . Christ, there's nothing left of it, her whole skull's been caved in and there's just a dark, bloody hole where that beautiful face used to be . . .

'Now our house was just a small, modest place . . . narrow, mid-terrace, you know the type? I start backing away from the kitchen, praying the killer's not gonna see me. I'm halfway across the living room when he starts to move. We had a cupboard under the stairs with one of those slatted louvre doors, you know? I drop down to my hands and knees, crawl behind the sofa to the cupboard, shut myself inside. And the worst thing is, when I get in there I've still got a clear view of everything. I see the man step over my wife's body and walk into the living room. Bastard was crying like a baby. I can't even remember what he looked like now, I just remember him wailing and sobbing, like it was him just found his family dead. I reckon the Change had just hit him, you know? It was like he was regretting what he'd done, like he was trying to work out what he was, come to terms with it. Tell me, Danny, was it like that for you?'

I think about the nervous panic and confusion I felt immediately after killing Harry but I don't say anything.

Mallon wipes his eyes again and goes on, 'Anyway, after a while he started to calm down. He sat down in my seat like he owned the place and watched my TV. Even helped himself to a couple cans of my beer from the fridge. He stayed there for hours, and I stayed shut in the cupboard, just like you're stuck in here now. Except you don't have to look at the battered bodies of the people you loved most in the world, do you?'

A trace of bitterness has crept into his voice but I still don't react. I'm just wondering how long this pathetic sob story's going on for.

'Eventually he just got up and left. Didn't even look around the rest of the house. He just upped and went, and I didn't have the balls to stop him, or to try and fight back. I wanted to stay there with my family, but I couldn't, not when I saw what he'd done to them both.'

If they were Unchanged, they had to die. Simple as that. I'm on the verge of telling him as much when he starts speaking again.

'Like I said,' he continues, a little more composed again, 'it's nothing you haven't heard before. But after it happened I decided you lot weren't going to get away with it and I went out looking for revenge. Hard to believe when you look at me, but I was on the streets, looking for trouble – wasn't long before I realised it wasn't working. Got myself mixed up in all kinds of nasty business. I never killed anyone, but I came close to dying a few times . . . you can imagine what it was like.

'I latched onto a group of vigilantes. A couple of times things got really bad, and you know why? Because people thought we were like you! They saw us trying to take a stand and fight back, and they thought we were the Haters! And then after a couple of weeks I stopped and took a step back from it all and I realised they were right. There was hardly any difference between us and people like you. And I thought about the man who killed my girls and how he cried and I understood. He didn't *want* to kill them. He thought he *had* to do it.'

Mallon gets up from his seat and crosses over to the window, making sure he stays well out of my limited reach. He stands on tiptoe and looks down.

'And that leads me to the main part of my sermon this morning,' he grins. 'Pay attention, Danny, you need to listen carefully to this bit. You see, when I stopped trying to fight, life started to get better again. That might sound like bullshit to you, but it's true. I was already resigned to the fact that things were never going to be easy again, and that nothing I could do would bring Jess and Keisha back, but I realised that revenge wasn't the answer. You can't fight fire with fire, you know what I'm saying?'

He moves away from the window and paces the length of the short room.

'Then I found the people here, people who'd all reached the same conclusion as me. And I realised that it doesn't matter what made any of this happen, all that's important now is putting a stop to it before it's too late. So that's what we're doing. We're trying to end the cycle. I think of us like a firebreak, you know what I mean? When they're trying to stop a forest fire spreading, they sometimes burn a strip of land further ahead. Then, when the fire reaches it, there's nothing left to burn and it dies out. We're like that. We've all done our share of fighting. Our battles have been fought. So when people like you reach us with your hate, there's nothing left to burn. We're putting the fire out. Stopping things from getting any worse.'

He sits down again and stares straight at me. What's he thinking? Does he actually believe any of the crap he's just been spouting? I look back into his dark brown eyes and all I can think is that I want him dead like I've wanted all the rest of them dead.

But there is a slight difference here. All the others I've killed looked back at me with hate in *their* eyes – but not Mallon. There *is* something different about him. Is there any truth in any of what he's just said, or is it total bullshit? Is he just preying on me? Wearing me down and fucking with my mind before he goes in for the kill? He's probably trying to catch me off-guard. As soon as I lower my defences, he'll attack.

He starts speaking again. 'Doesn't matter who you are or what side you're on, everybody is conditioned to react to the Hate in the same way. It's all about self-preservation at the expense of everyone and everything else. Everybody fights. Everybody wants to survive. That's why everything fell apart so quickly – at the first sign of trouble we all turned on each other, to protect ourselves. And despite all the noise and bullshit that was thrown around at the start, do you know which side was worst of all?'

Instinctively I shake my head, still held down by the wide strap.

'We were,' he says, answering his own question. 'And we still are. Did you see anything of the massacres we carried out? Gas chambers, for crying out loud! We spend years educating generation after generation about the Holocaust and how we can't ever let it happen again. Then, when it suits us and we're the ones facing the threat, we forget everything we've always believed in and resort to genocide. Thousands upon thousands of men, women and children slaughtered . . . I tell you, Danny, it makes me feel ashamed to be human.'

Christ, could there actually be some substance to what this guy's saying? Don't be stupid, I tell myself, he's Unchanged. In the sudden silence I try to concentrate on the dripping water in the corner again, doing all I can not to let myself be suckered in by Mallon and his mind-games.

'Question for you,' he suddenly announces. 'What's going to happen if we just let things run their course?'

He waits expectantly for an answer, knowing full well I won't give him one. More to the point, I can't. The future is something I've only dared to think about in my quietest, darkest moments. Until recently the virtually constant adrenalin rush of fight after fight after fight has been enough of a distraction. Surviving today has been more important than thinking about tomorrow.

'What happens if we don't break the cycle? Where's this all going to end? If I trusted you enough to take off your chains and let you walk outside, all you'd see would be rubble and ruin. We're not safe here – no one is any more – but we're in a better position than most. The world's falling apart but the people here are getting stronger. We've been sifting through the debris looking for people like you, Danny, to rehabilitate. We're going to form that firebreak and stop the pain and hate from spreading.'

He gets up quickly, as if he's just remembered he's supposed to be somewhere else. He moves closer to the bed as he pushes the chair back, and his sudden proximity makes me react. I quickly reach out for him with my left hand, but the chain snaps my wrist back when it reaches full stretch. Mallon doesn't flinch, but I can see him watching me over his shoulder. He did that on purpose to see if I'd bite. I watch him intently as he moves towards the door and try to maintain my aggression. I've been forgetting myself.

'That's enough for now. I might bring you some more food

and water in a while. Until then, just try and relax. Build your strength up; you'll need it later.'

What the hell did he mean by that? He quickly crosses the room again and replaces the board over the window. The impenetrable blackness returns. Can't stand it like this. Don't leave me in the dark again, please. He stands in the doorway, looking at me, waiting for a reaction. He starts to close the door.

'Wait . . .' I say, surprising myself with the sound of my own voice, but it's too late. The door's shut and Mallon's gone and all I can hear is the dripping in the corner.

23

It feels like an eternity has passed before he comes back again. He enters the room hurriedly and doesn't look at me, or speak. Unusually, he leaves the door open. I can see two other Unchanged men waiting outside and my pulse starts to quicken. Is this my execution party? But that goes against everything he said earlier. I don't know what to think. I've lost track of what's bullshit and what's fact.

Mallon removes the strap across my forehead, then lies on the floor and does something to the chains holding my arms and legs down. I try to lift my head and look, but I can't see anything. He's out of sight under the bed for a couple of minutes, doing Christ knows what, then he scrambles back up and brushes himself down. He stands on the other side of the room and looks at me.

'There you go, you can . . .'

Before he's even finished his sentence I've realised the shackles have been detached from the bed frame. I swing myself around in a sudden single, painful movement and use my weight to throw myself forward and stand up. My legs and arms are cold, numb, they feel heavy and unresponsive, but I know this is my chance to kill him. I raise my aching arms and stretch a length of chain between them, ready to wrap it around the fucker's filthy neck and squeeze the life out of him. I lunge, but he sidesteps easily, then sticks out a foot and trips me up. I fall quickly, too fast to put my hands out and stop myself. My left shoulder clips the edge of the chair and my head smacks against the wall. I roll over onto my back in agony, my head spinning, my vision blurred.

Mallon stands over me. He looks down, shakes his head and tuts. 'Do you think I'm stupid?'

He moves the chair out of the way and sighs with disappointment. 'Honestly, Danny, were you not listening to anything I said earlier? Haven't you worked it out yet? The more you struggle and fight, the less you're going to achieve.'

In the confusion of my pathetic, fumbled attempt to attack, I managed to kick the door shut. It opens again and Mallon gestures for the two men outside to come in. One of them, a huge, evil-looking bastard, grabs the chains hanging from my wrists and hauls me up onto my unsteady feet with worrying ease. If he'd have been like us, I think to myself, he'd have been a Brute. He grips my arms tight and it feels like I'm being squeezed in a vice. There's nothing I can do about it. The other man walks towards me and puts something over my head. It's a pillowcase, I think, thin enough for me to be able to breathe through, but thick enough to block out the light and stop me from seeing. The chains around my ankles are padlocked together. The floor is cold and wet under my bare feet.

'Stay calm and keep your temper in check and you'll be okay,' Mallon says. 'Fight back and you'll regret it.'

Is that a threat, or just a warning to play by his rules? Whatever, the slight glimmer of hope I'd been feeling since Mallon's earlier visit has gone now and has been replaced by fear. What are they going to do to me? I'm completely at the mercy of these foul bastards and there's nothing I can do about it. I feel like a failure; ashamed that I've been beaten by the Unchanged. Even if I did manage to fight them off, I'm still bound and chained. I'd never get away.

'Move,' the huge man standing behind me grunts in my ear, his deep voice emotionless. He shoves me squarely in the middle of my back and I fly forward, barely managing to stay upright. I almost trip over the chains between my feet, but one of the men – it might even be Mallon – catches me and keeps me upright.

Head bowed, all I can see are my dirty, shackled feet. My

legs feel leaden with pain and weak with nerves as I realise this could be my final walk. All that crap about not fighting fire with fire and trying to break the cycle . . . it was all lies – a cheap, pathetic ruse to keep me occupied and catch me off-guard. And the worst thing of all is how easily I fell for it. I should have seen through the bullshit. They were just trying to keep me pacified, to make it easier for them to kill me when they're ready. What am I walking towards? A firing squad? A stoning? The room where I'll be given my lethal injection?

I try to stop, try to turn around and fight my way out of this, but the fuckers surrounding me are having none of it. They restrain me, but they don't strike back, not even allowing me the satisfaction of going down fighting. When I stop struggling again they relax their grip and let me walk on alone. The journey to my final destination feels endless. I think about Ellis, and then about Lizzie, Josh and Edward, and the pain and frustration is too much to stand. I start crying like a bloody baby, all pathetic sobbing and shaking.

We turn right and I trip through another doorway, stubbing my toe on a low step. This must be it. I'm led across a wide open space and then we stop and I stand there, still, exposed, feeling vulnerable. I feel tugging on my chains, then someone's removing the shackles from my feet and I hear the clink of metal on metal as another chain is wrapped tight around my waist then attached to something behind me.

I wait and listen as he walks away again, heading back in the direction from which we just came. I'm left here alone, sway-ing slightly, wrists still bound, my heavy legs still stiff and aching after endless hours of inactivity. I lean forward until the slack is taken up and the chains become tight enough to support my weight. I look down at my bare feet and the grubby old carpet, and now I'm crying pathetic tears of anger and desperation which soak into the carpet. What will I see when they uncover my head? Will they even bother? Maybe they'll just shoot me blind. I picture the two men standing at the other end of the room, either side of Mallon, both of them holding guns aimed in my direction. They could fire at any second. These might be my last few seconds of life. My legs feel like they're about to give way, but I'm determined to stand proud and defiant and face this like a man. But this wasn't how it was supposed to end . . .

The pillowcase is whipped off my head and dropped on the floor. I close my eyes for a split second, then open them wide again and look up. Mallon is backing away from me. He's the only other person here. I'm standing alone in a large, open room, chained to the back wall by an industrial-strength bracket. The fear starts to lessen and uneasy, tentative relief takes its place, but I know it's not over. Just because he hasn't killed me yet doesn't mean he's not still going to. The room is bright and cold. There are windows along one wall but they're too far away and too high to see through. I can see the very tops of distant trees and the squally, rain-filled sky, nothing else.

Mallon watches me intently, then turns and leaves. The temporary relief immediately disappears with him. What happens next? Is this another gas chamber? There's no pipe-work or exhaust fans that I can see, but there are red and brown stains on the grubby wall behind me – blood, shit and Christ knows what else. There are two filthy buckets over to my right, one of them full of water. Waterboarding? Torture? But I don't have any secrets or restricted information, so what can they hope to get from me? Or is it worse than that – is Mallon about to start playing masochistic games with me? Whatever he decides, there's nothing I can do about it, but when it happens I'll fight the fucker until either he's dead or I am.

He's back, this time carrying more food and a pile of clothes. My last supper?

'Move back,' he says, watching me carefully. 'Right up against the wall.'

I do as he says, shuffling backwards but not risking turning around. Mallon edges forward to the spot where I was standing, watching me constantly. He puts down the clothes and the food, then moves back again. He sits down a safe distance away.

'Help yourself.'

Stunned, I can't help speaking.

'What?'

'I said help yourself. The food tastes like shit today, but it's warm and it's better than nothing. And the clothes are from a dead man, I'm afraid. But hey, they don't stink of piss like yours do!'

I don't move. He gestures for me to come closer and I slowly start to edge forward, moving like a bear circling a bloody lump of fresh meat in the middle of a trap. Is the food I'm about to shovel into my mouth poisoned? It wasn't before. I sit down cross-legged and start eating, too hungry to care. I can't tell what it is I'm eating, and he's right, it does taste like shit, but that doesn't matter – it's food. It's finished too soon and I wash it down with another bottle of stale lukewarm water.

'Better?' Mallon asks, stretching out on the floor and looking surprisingly relaxed. 'I'll get you some more later. There's soap and water for you to wash with in one of those buckets over there. Scrub yourself down, Danny. Get rid of the stink and try and make yourself feel human again.'

I don't argue. I get up and move over to the buckets. They're just inside the reach of the chains. I take off my soiled shorts and rip off my shirt (the shackles on my wrists prevent me taking it off any other way), then I start to wash. There's an inch of disinfectant at the bottom of the other bucket and its purpose is obvious. I drag it closer to the wall, turn my back on Mallon and squat and shit. I wipe myself clean on the torn clothes I've just discarded.

I wash myself as best I can, then dry off with a blanket which Mallon throws over to me. I pull on a pair of trousers which just about fit, then wrap the blanket around my shoulders to keep warm. I walk towards Mallon until the chains are at full stretch. Bastard just sits there and looks up at me. He knows I can't reach him.

But then – to my complete amazement and disbelief – he throws a bunch of keys and some other stuff out of reach and stands up. He waits, as if psyching himself up, then he walks closer, so close we're almost touching.

'All we need . . .' he starts to say but I shut the fucker up. I grab his collar, spin him around and slam him down on the floor. He tries to fight me off, but I brush him aside. He's had this coming for too long. I drag him nearer to the back wall, his stumpy, pathetic limbs flailing, then I take up the slack from the chain around my right wrist and wrap it around his neck. He splutters, showering me with foul Unchanged spittle, and his already bulging eyes grow wider still. I pull tighter, feeling his life slipping away, focusing on the image of him lying dead at my feet.

'Kill me,' he says, his breath a hissing, choked whisper, 'and you've lost everything.'

I pull harder, feeling the chain digging into his neck, constricting his windpipe and cutting off his air supply.

Then I stop. What did he say? Is he right . . . ?

He flops over onto his front, gasping for breath, and starts to crawl away. He's barely gone a metre when I snap myself out of this stupid malaise. I reach out, grab his leg and drag him back, feeling myself getting stronger by the second. I roll him over and form my hand into a chain-wrapped fist.

I'm ready to smash it into his face when he speaks again.

'Break the cycle.'

I punch him, just catching his jaw as he turns his head away. I straddle his out-of-shape body, a knee on either side to stop him moving, ready to end his miserable life. My left leg is wet. He's pissed himself with fear.

'Now who stinks of piss?' I lift my fist again and he raises his arms to cover his face.

'Please, Danny. Show some control. Kill me now and they'll leave you chained up here to rot.'

I pull my fist back even further. When I hit him this time I know I'll finish him.

'Think about your family. Think about what you could do if you got out of here.'

Bullshit.

Is it?

He's right about one thing – I'm still chained to the wall and I can't escape this room. And I know he only mentioned my family for effect, but how can I do anything to help Ellis if I'm stuck here and left to starve? I can see the keys on the floor, well out of reach.

Against my better judgement – against everything I feel and believe – I stand up and step back. Mallon scrambles to safety, holding his mouth and spitting blood onto the floor. Is the fucker going to leave me here now? He staggers away, then stops. Still rubbing his jaw, he turns around and grins, blood covering his yellow-white teeth.

'You did it! I knew you could!'

'What?'

'You did it, Danny. Or rather, more to the point, you didn't do it.'

I don't understand. He sits down, exhausted, breathing heavily. I walk as far as the chains will let me.

'I gave you a chance to kill me, and you didn't take it. You almost did, but you stopped yourself. You held the Hate.'

'Only because . . .' I start to explain.

He holds up his hand to stop me talking, and washes out his mouth with water from my bottle. One of us must have kicked it across the room in the fight. He spits red-tinged water out onto the dirty carpet.

'Doesn't matter why,' he says, 'fact is you did it. Takes a person of intelligence to do that. Someone who can look beyond all this hatred and fighting and see what's really important.'

Patronising bastard.

'I made a mistake and you got lucky.'

He shakes his head. 'I don't think so.'

'I do.'

'No,' he says, his voice suddenly more serious, 'you're

wrong. This is what happened – I gave you an opportunity to kill me, which you instinctively tried to take. But, before you could do it, you stopped and weighed up the pros and cons. And you realised your choice was pretty stark: kill me and rot here, or let me go and survive.'

Bastard. He's right.

'What's important,' he continues, 'is the fact that you over-ruled your instincts. Like I said, you held the Hate.'

I can't argue. I want to, but I can't. I sit down opposite him. I should have killed him, but I didn't. What does that make me? I feel strangely dirty and defiled, as if I've just made the most embarrassing, basic mistake, like a teenage boy caught wanking by his mum. In the distance I can hear the muffled thumps and bangs of explosions: the fighting continues else-where, and it should have continued in here too. I should reach across, grab hold of him and kill him now. But I don't.

'So how did it happen to you?' he asks, mouth still bleeding. 'I've told you my story, Danny, what your people did to my family. Now you tell me yours.'

I say nothing.

'Come on . . . what have you got to lose by talking to me? Face facts: I could have had you killed when you first arrived here, but I didn't. I could have done it myself, but instead I've fed you, watered you, I haven't tortured you . . . You don't have any information I want, no top secret plans of attack . . . There's no need for you not to speak now. You've already done the hard part, now finish the job. Break the cycle. Talk to me like the rational human being I know you really are. It's up to you . . .'

I can see the frustration in his face. Truth is, I'm not trying to be defiant now. I'm thinking about what he said. Either he's right, and I've got nothing left to lose, or it's too late, and I've already lost it all. Or is my sudden pathetic weakness just a result of the physical and emotional stress of captivity? Have I just lost the ability to think straight?

'Back in your room yesterday,' he continues, 'you flinched

when I mentioned your family. Those things I found in your bag, the doll and the clothes . . . do you want to start there? Are they trophies or reminders?'

I try hard to hide it, but my reaction when he mentions my family is disappointingly obvious. He immediately picks up on it.

'So what happened? Were you with them when you changed? Are you carrying around some kind of guilt because you killed the people you used to love?'

Can't help myself. He's hit a nerve. 'My only guilt is that I didn't kill them.' My voice sounds loud and over-amplified, alien and strange.

'Tell me more.'

'I was confused, disorientated,' I tell him, my words sounding angry, strangled by emotion. 'Should have killed them, but I didn't. They caught me off-guard.'

'Partner?'

I nod my head.

'Kids?'

'Three. One like me, two like you.'

He looks confused. 'One like you?'

'Ellis, my daughter.'

'What happened to her?'

I'm about to tell him, but I stop myself, suddenly remembering that I'm talking to one of the Unchanged. Don't want him to know she's the reason I came back to the city.

'Her mother took her,' I answer, spitting out the words. He nods slowly, trying to make it look like he understands.

'Must be hard to deal with,' he says. 'I mean, I thought I'd had it bad, but at least I know what happened to my family. I know they're both dead and I've had closure, but you, you don't have a clue where any of them are, or even if they're still alive . . .'

'I should have killed them,' I say again.

'I can't begin to imagine what you've been through. The

realisation you were a killer must have been hard enough. How did they get away?'

'I was disorientated. I'd kill them in a heartbeat if they were here now.'

'You didn't kill me.'

'No, but I—'

'You're from around here, right?' he interrupts.

'Depends where "here" is.'

'What about the other two kids?'

'Two boys. One older, one younger than my girl.'

'Really tough,' he says quietly, shaking his head and rinsing his bloody mouth out again. 'So how have you coped?'

Is he taking the piss now? 'I've killed as many of you fuckers as I've been able to find,' I answer, feeling my body start to tense up again.

'Except me.'

'There's still time . . .'

'Okay,' he says quickly, leaning back and looking up at the ceiling, 'but has it actually helped? Has it got you any closer to getting your daughter back? I presume that's what you were heading back to the city for?'

Christ, I have to give him his due, he's good. That one came from out of nowhere. 'I'll find her if it's the last thing I do.'

'That's good.'

'Is it?'

He nods his head vigorously.

'Of course it is. It shows there's more to you than just wanting to fight and kill all the time. You still give a damn about your daughter, and that means you've still got a chance. Honestly, Danny, most of the people like you who come through here are complete no-hopers, only interested in killing. You, you're different. You're thinking further ahead than the next battle.'

'Doesn't mean I won't fight. Doesn't mean I won't still kill you.'

'Of course not, but from where I'm sitting, killing me would be the worst thing you could do. How would it help? Like you said earlier, you'd just be fighting fire with fire. Just stop for a second and work your way back, Danny. Think about everything that's happened to you to bring you to this point. The Hate has taken everything you ever had. It's stripped you of your soul and your identity. It's stopped you functioning as a human being.'

'It hasn't. I know exactly . . .'

'You've lost *everything* because of it: your family, your home, your daughter. If it wasn't for the Hate you might be with her now. Christ, man, it's even cost you your dignity and your freedom. You've spent the last two days lying in your own piss, tied up and caged like an animal. And at this precise moment in time, you're close to losing control of your future too. If I wanted, I could walk out of here right now and not look back. I could leave you here alone to starve and die. You don't know where you are, how many other people are here, what's on the other side of the door to this room . . . Face it, Danny, right now all you have is me.'

He stops talking and waits for me to respond, but I can't. All I can do is stare back at his barely human face. Is he right?

He shuffles forward until he's just within reach.

Is he taunting me? Testing me?

'People tell me I'm wasting my time with your type. They tell me you're no better than animals, that you've got dog blood running through your veins and you should be rounded up and shot.'

'I don't care what they—'

'You know what I tell them? I tell them they're wrong. But you're the only one who can really decide who's right. If the boot was on the other foot and I was your prisoner, Danny, what would you do now?'

'I'd—'

'Stupid question. We'd have never got to this stage. You'd already have killed me. You could do it now if you want to, but I think you're better than that.'

He moves forward again. I move to scratch the stabbing itch by my right knee which has just returned and he flinches. He's trembling. Is this just part of the act, or is his fear genuine?

'Cooperate with me and prove the rest of them wrong. Show me you can control your emotions and I'll help you. I can get access to records. I could try and find out what happened to your daughter . . .'

That doesn't ring true at all. It smacks of desperation, and he knows it.

'Bullshit.'

He shrugs his shoulders.

'It might be, but what have I got to gain? More to the point, what have you got to lose?'

Head's spinning. Can't take all this in. Can't think straight. My heart says kill, but something's telling me to wait because he's right, fighting has got me nowhere. And if there's even the slightest chance he'll be able to help me, shouldn't I take it? He leans back and picks up the keys. He takes one of the keys off the ring and throws it over to me.

'For the chains around your wrists,' he says. 'Take them off and finish getting dressed.'

I do as he says, stretching my arms and flexing my muscles. The freedom feels good after endless hours of being wrapped in chains. I walk back across the room to the pile of clothes. All the time, Joseph stays sitting on the floor. He's within the reach of the chains around my waist. We both know I could kill him if I wanted to. He's terrified, I can see it in his eyes, and that gives me strength to hold my nerve. I hold the Hate.

Maybe I'll give him a chance. If he lets me down, I'll kill him.

PART V

Weather forecasts were a long-forgotten luxury, so the torrential rains were unexpected. The flash floods wreaked unprecedented destruction on the city centre refugee camp and its densely packed population. Those living out on the streets bore the brunt of the pain as almost a month's worth of rain fell in less than two hours, literally washing away scores of people and their few remaining belongings. Blocked and broken drains stopped the water from draining away, transforming many streets and pavements into stagnant lakes. Countless buildings were flooded, with basements, cellars and ground floors under water. Almost half of the military base in the municipal park was washed away, a huge number of refugee-occupied tents lost. And then, to add insult to injury, as quickly as the rains came, they disappeared and though, thankfully, the sun remained hidden behind a layer of heavy cloud for most of the day, the summer heat and a few sharp bursts of sunlight were enough to dry out and bake the bedraggled world below. Every outdoor surface was caked in a layer of foul-smelling mud, with grubby tidemarks on building walls a grim reminder of how high the floodwaters had climbed. Huge mountains of rain-soaked garbage and waste began to ferment, and the insect population feeding multiplied by the hour.

Constant helicopter patrols continued to police the border and the exclusion zone. All scheduled missions outside the city were temporarily abandoned as, for once, the already severely depleted military forces turned their attention to the thousands of people already supposedly in their care. Their orders were simple: get as many people off the streets as possible (living or dead), then clear the major routes through town.

Ahead of the motley collection of vehicles which crawled slowly along the Arley Road, groups of soldiers on foot moved from building to building through the early evening darkness. One of the snowplough-fitted trucks was used to clear a route through, pushing tons of sodden waste towards the gutter and leaving a noxious drift of garbage in its wake. Hazard-suited soldiers followed behind on the freshly scraped tarmac, pulling corpses from the metres-high piles and loading them into the backs of the yellow refuse and recycling trucks which had been recently commandeered from the now-dissolved city council.

A group of three soldiers emerged from an office building which had once been a large house. By torchlight, one of them spray-painted the brick wall beside the door, a message for those who followed:

37 INSIDE
6 DEAD
20 MORE

Ignoring the countless frightened questions and the grabbing hands of the refugees who surrounded them, the soldiers moved on to the next building. Thirty-seven survivors, six bodies to remove, space for twenty more inside.

There was a sudden loud thump on the door of room 33. Mark jumped up from the space on the damp floor where he'd been trying to sleep and ran to the door, tripping over Kate's father's leg which was hanging out of the bed. He pressed his eye to the spy-hole.

'Who is it?' Kate asked, standing close behind him.

'Soldiers.'

'Don't let them in.'

'I have to.'

The lead soldier thumped the door again and yelled for them to open up.

'Don't . . .' Kate pleaded.

'If I don't open it they'll batter the bloody thing down.' Before she could protest he pulled the door open and three soldiers barged through, pushing him to the side. They stood in the middle of the room, each of them shining their torches around, exposing every corner of the small, cramped space.

'What's going on?' Mark asked, positioning himself directly in one of the beams of light.

'Assessing space,' the soldier replied, looking around him, his voice devoid of interest or emotion. 'How many you got here?'

'Five of us. And five's more than enough. There's barely enough room as it is. We can't fit anyone else in!'

'Who?'

'What?'

'Who's here?'

'Me, my girlfriend, her parents and my cousin's wife. And my girlfriend's pregnant. Like I said, there's no room for anyone else—'

One of the other soldiers made a note on a clipboard. The others continued to look around. Kate forced her way between them, stopping one of them from getting around the side of the double bed. She stood in front of him, thrusting out her pregnant belly for maximum effect.

'He told you. There's no more space here.'

The soldier ignored her, moving her out of the way, then ducking down and looking under the bed. He shone his torch onto the bed's occupants, the two starving elderly refugees shaking in fear under the sheets like characters from a Roald Dahl story.

'Your parents?'

She nodded. He spun around. Lizzie sat on a chair in front of the bathroom door, her legs drawn up beneath her, nervously chewing on her nails. She kept her eyes down, refusing to look up. Mark tried diplomatically to coax the soldiers back out.

'My cousin's partner,' he explained, keeping his voice low so she couldn't hear him. 'He was, you know . . . one of them?

She lost her kids and it's really fucked her up. Honestly, mate, it's not a good idea to put anyone else in here with us. What with the baby coming and . . .'

'Not my decision, pal,' the soldier said.

'But I've been a volunteer,' he protested. 'I've been outside the city with you. I've been—'

'Not my decision,' he said again, and the soldiers left the room. Mark slammed the door shut and leant against it, staying there until he was sure he'd heard the door to the next room opening.

He started to walk back to the others but Kate stopped him.

'We can't go on like this,' she whispered. 'We should find somewhere else for her. It's not safe here.'

'And where exactly *is* safe these days?' he sighed, leaning back against the door again.

'But she's—'

'She's family. They all are. Your family, my family – *our* family. We stick together and that's all there is to it.'

'But Mark—'

'Would I ask you to throw your parents out?'

'That's different—'

'Is it? I'm not talking about this again, Kate. It's a pointless conversation. She's family and she stays. No one's going anywhere.'

24

Back in the cell. I cooperated and let them bring me back here. Thought the silence and darkness would help me work things out but the longer I've been left, the more uncertain I've become again. Don't know who or what I believe any more. I can't understand why I didn't kill Mallon when I had the chance, but at the same time I know that while I'm here, he really is my best – my only – hope. He hasn't screwed me over so far. But if he does, now he thinks I trust him, I'll kill him before he even realises I've turned.

I'm still chained to the bed, but now the shackles are only loosely anchored to the metal bed frame and I'm able to move around. I've been able to shift the board and look outside for the first time, but the view is disappointingly limited. All I can see from this window are the red-brick walls of other parts of this building and the grey slate roof of another section below. I can see a few other windows and I've been watching them, hoping to catch sight of other people like me. I haven't seen anyone else yet. It's dark now. Maybe I'll see more tomorrow.

My head is spinning. Still can't think straight enough to work this out. The lines between what I feel and what I know are blurring to the point where I can't make sense of anything any more. I keep swinging between feeling anger and frustration that I didn't kill Mallon, then wanting him to come back again so we can talk some more. I want him to tell me what he knows about Ellis, but at the same time I know he won't have found anything out. I don't even think he has the means to find out, but I can't rule out the fact that he might. Maybe I'll just kill him when he next comes into this room and put an end to all this pointless pissing about.

I sit back on the bed (I've turned the mattress but it's still damp) and look up at the ceiling, tracing the familiar patterns in the yellowed paint again. If I killed Mallon (and I know I could) what would it achieve? I still don't know where I am. For all I know I could be surrounded by hundreds of Unchanged, all of them armed to the teeth. I could be dead before Mallon's body is cold. No, as hard as it is to swallow this decision, right now he's all I've got.

But what does he really want from me? Ignoring all the bullshit, why is he doing this? He's already made it clear I don't have anything he wants, so is he still playing mind-games just for the hell of it, or does he think he can house-train me like a pet? When you consider all the options, other than looking for a 'cure' or resorting to extermination, trying to learn how to tame or control us is probably the only viable option the Unchanged think they have left.

So what do I do?

I'm daydreaming now, imagining walking around this place unchained, mixing freely with the Unchanged. I picture myself in a crowded room, surrounded by them but not yet killing, forcing myself to swallow down the fear and hold the Hate. I look into their faces, their stupid, evil, ignorant faces, and none of them knows who or what I am. They need their DNA tests and records and the strength of our reactions to be able to see what we are. But we, on the other hand, simply *sense* them. We know what they are without a word being spoken . . .

Fuck. The penny drops.

The enormity of today suddenly hits me like a hammer blow. Does Mallon even realise what he's done?

Today I resisted the temptation to kill! Regardless of the reasons why, I stayed in control and didn't fight. And if I truly can hold the Hate, then in time I could do exactly what I've just been imagining: I could walk among the Unchanged undetected. Imagine the power and advantage that would give me . . . I could stand shoulder to shoulder with the enemy unseen. I could go anywhere, do anything, kill anyone . . .

But can I do it? Can I really choose to hold the Hate at will? Or did Mallon just catch me at my weakest ebb?

I think back to that moment earlier today when I could have killed him but didn't. I wanted to do it, but I stopped myself. And it wasn't Mallon's words that stopped me . . . *I stopped myself*. I could do it again, I know I could.

It doesn't matter what I believe, whether or not I subscribe to Mallon's bullshit theories of breaking the cycle and not fighting fire with fire; the fact is, he's handed control back to me and I have to take advantage of it.

25

'Food,' Mallon announces as he barges into the room, waking me up. It's late and he's carrying his lamp. The familiar urge to kill fills me as soon as I see his face, but I force myself not to attack. I swallow it down like unspewed vomit, the nauseous unease sitting heavy in my gut. I get up and stand opposite him, and although he tries to hide it, I can see the nervousness in his eyes. The longer we remain facing each other, the more confident he slowly begins to become. But I can still feel his fear. I can almost taste it.

'You, my man,' he says, as I take the tray from him and sit back down on the bed and start to eat, 'have done incredibly well.'

'Thanks,' I mumble, my mouth full. Truth is, I don't give a shit what he thinks. I'm just relieved, excited almost, that I managed not to attack. It's hard, very hard, but I force myself to keep control. I try and concentrate on the food to distract myself, but the urge to kill him refuses to fade and I am struggling to keep it in check. I almost drop the tray and lunge at him when he moves, but I manage to regain my focus at the last second. This is almost impossible. It's a constant fight, almost like I'm having to remember to breathe.

'I'm really pleased,' Mallon continues, the sound of his voice making my guts twist with agitation. 'You've really understood what we're trying to do here. You know, most people take a few more days to get to this stage but you, you've got brains. You've worked it out in no time.'

'Not a lot to work out really, is there?' I say, trying to keep up the illusion. 'It's like you said, the more you fight, the less you get.'

'Exactly.'

He watches me a while longer as I polish off the rest of the tasteless food, like a proud parent, and it dawns on me that he really does believe all the bullshit he's been spinning. I feel vastly superior to this idiot. He thinks he's the one in the driving seat, but I'm in control. The mental advantage I have now makes it easier to cope.

'So what next?' I ask, feeling calmer and more assured. I decide to hedge my bets and see how far I can push him.

'What do you mean?'

'What's your plan? Do you just want to keep me locked up here for ever? Is this some kind of rehabilitation programme you've started? Or are you going to start experimenting on me and cutting me up into little pieces?'

Smug bastard starts laughing. 'You're good! No, to tell you the truth, Danny, what happens next isn't up to me.'

'So who decides?'

'Two people.'

'Who?'

'You, for one . . .'

'And . . . ?'

'And Sahota.'

'Sahota? Who the hell's Sahota?'

'You'll find out tomorrow.' He starts moving towards the door. Suddenly this is a conversation he doesn't want to have.

'You can't just walk out now. . . Who is Sahota?'

I stand up again and move towards him, but all that does is make him move faster. He stops midway out of the door – just beyond the reach of my chains – and turns back to face me.

'The boss man,' he says simply. Now he's definitely playing games again, feeding me just enough detail to keep my interest, then clamming up and leaving me dangling. It's all he's got left. Other than these physical chains, information is the only advantage remaining. If he was any closer I'd rip his fucking throat out.

He pulls the door shut but then stops and opens it again. 'Wait. There's something I forgot to tell you.'

'What?'

'Your daughter—'

'You found her?' I can't hide my sudden interest and emotion. Please tell me something.

'No,' he says, 'you've got to understand, Danny, information's hard to come by these days. You learn more from what you're not told than from what you're told. The Central System is creaking under the weight of what's happened and—'

'Tell me!'

He sighs and takes a deep breath, drawing it out as long as he can. 'There's good and bad news—'

'Give me both!'

'The bad news is there are no records of her anywhere.'

'So how can there be any good news?'

'Can't you see, that *is* the good news. It means she might not be dead.'

'She might not be dead . . . that's all you can tell me?'

'Be thankful for small mercies, Danny. As far as I know, *my* daughter's still lying on the kitchen floor with a bloody hole where her face used to be. I could have been telling you the date your girl died and where they burnt her body. As it is, you've still got some hope. What you do with it is up to you.'

He slams the door shut and locks it.

PART VI

Six a.m. Sandwiched between two heavily armed military Jeeps and chaperoned by columns of soldiers and militia fighters, several hundred displaced refugees were led out along the Arley Road. With no regard for personal preferences, friendships, partners or relatives, specified numbers of individuals were filtered off towards each building. No one resisted or complained. They were too tired and too scared to show any defiance or opposition to what they were being told to do. Their choices were stark: put up with it or fuck off and take your chances on your own. And anyone who dared show any resistance to the military would be on the street with a bullet in their head. Public order *had* to be maintained.

'But there's no more room in here,' Mark protested, blocking the door of room 33. 'I told them last night . . .'

The soldier, completely uninterested in his point of view, barged him aside and forced his way in.

'What's the problem?' Kate asked, getting up from the end of the bed and standing in his way, instinctively wrapping her arms around her pregnant belly, cradling and protecting her unborn child.

'There's no problem,' he answered quickly, his tired, gruff voice muffled by his face mask. 'New roommate for you, that's all.'

'But that's crazy! We don't have enough space as it is. How are we supposed to—?'

The soldier put his hands on her shoulders and pushed her back down onto the bed, then turned and walked back towards the door again, pausing only to sidestep Mark. Mark knew there was no point trying to argue; at best he'd be ignored, at worst he could be accused of being a Hater and 'removed'. Kate chased after the officer, far less concerned about the potential repercussions. Behind her, her parents sat up to try and see what was happening.

Her father, weakened by age, fear and malnutrition, simply lay back again when he couldn't see anything, too tired to care.

Her mother, once an intelligent, gentle woman, balanced on the end of the bed half-naked, screaming like a banshee. 'There's enough of them in here already. We don't want more. You take them and find somewhere else for them to go. You can't—'

Kate ran back to silence her, leaving Mark at the door to placate the soldier.

'Gurmit Singh,' the trooper announced as he shoved an elderly Asian man into the room. Gurmit Singh was protesting in high-volume, high-speed Punjabi, which was neither understood nor acknowledged by anyone. A battered leather holdall containing the sum total of his worldly possessions was thrown into the room after him. He tripped over the bag, almost losing his orange turban in the process, and turned around and continued his vociferous tirade. When the soldier pulled the door shut in his face he simply turned again without pausing for breath and started unloading at Mark, who shook his head.

'Don't understand,' he said, desperate to shut the man up. 'Speak English.'

'No English,' Singh snapped back, and continued his Punjabi rant.

'He can't stay here,' Kate's mother screamed from the bed, 'we can't have his type here—'

Singh pointed at her, or was it at the bed? He rubbed the small of his back and thumped his hand on the mattress. He raised his voice ever louder.

Mark tried reasoning with him, desperate for him to be quiet, but Singh ignored him. He picked up his holdall and angrily sat down in the armchair in the corner of the room, still yelling furiously and pointing at the bed.

Kate stood by the hotel room door, her hands over her ears, desperately trying to block out the endless screeching coming from her mother and Gurmit Singh. Mark went over and tried to hold her, but she pulled away from him, recoiling from his touch.

'I can't stand this,' she sobbed. 'Either they go, or I go.'

'None of us can go anywhere – for Christ's sake, Katie, that's the problem! *There is nowhere else to go.*'

'I don't care,' she cried, 'kick them out – throw them out on the street if you have to.'

'Who are you talking about now?'

'You know exactly who I mean. It's too dangerous. We've got to think about ourselves and the baby and just screw the rest of them—'

'I can't, Katie. You know I can't . . .'

'Then I will. I mean it, Mark, if you don't get rid of them, I'll leave.'

'Katie, there's nowhere for them to go. Please, sweetheart, just calm down and—'

'Don't fucking patronise me! Don't bloody tell me to calm down! How the fuck can I calm down when—?'

'Shh,' he begged, putting his hand up to her mouth, 'please don't shout, Katie; they'll hear us. Don't do anything that'll give them any reason to come back in here. You know what'll happen if they do . . .'

'Maybe I should,' she said, pushing him away. 'Maybe that's exactly what I should do. Maybe if they knew what was going on here they'd help. They'd come up here and get rid of—'

'Shut up!' he hissed angrily, covering her mouth again.

Gurmit Singh, who had just started to quieten down, suddenly exploded into life again, startled by the appearance of Lizzie, who emerged from the bathroom.

'Who the hell's this?'

'Mr Singh,' Mark answered. 'He's just been delivered.'

'But we don't have any space . . .'

'We can't have his kind here,' Kate's mother yelled, reaching out and grabbing hold of Lizzie's arm and pulling her closer. Lizzie shrugged her off.

'Too many here,' Singh yelled back, suddenly switching to English. 'Back bad. Need bed.'

'Oh, you can do the language when it suits you then,' Kate sneered at him.

'What's going on, Mark?' Lizzie asked.

'Nothing we can do about it,' he began. 'We don't have any say in—'

'We can't go on like this,' Kate interrupted, desperate tears welling up in her eyes again.

'We have to . . .' Mark started.

'So tell me what I'm supposed to do then, Kate?' Lizzie snapped angrily. 'I heard what you were saying. I know what you want—'

'Then do something about it!'

'Where else am I supposed to go? What exactly do you want me to do?'

Their argument was interrupted by another outburst from Singh, who got up from his seat and barged his way between them, still gesturing furiously at the bed.

Lizzie, furious, shoved him back down again. 'Back off!' she spat before turning to face Kate again. 'Put yourself in my shoes, Katie, what would you do?'

'She can't stay here. It's not safe. You're putting all of us at risk.'

'Look around: we're already at risk. Everyone who's left alive is at risk, for Christ's sake.'

'Calm down, both of you,' Mark whispered, trying unsuccessfully to separate the two women, worried that their noise would bring the soldiers back.

'I'm not going to calm down,' Kate yelled, throwing open the bathroom door and pointing inside. 'That thing in there is evil.'

'That thing in there is my daughter.'

'She killed your sons!'

'I know, but she's still my daughter.' Lizzie knelt down in the doorway. Curled up on the floor in front of her, gagged and bound and heavily sedated and chained to the sink pedestal, lay Ellis. She stroked her hair and ran her hand gently down the side of her tranquillised face.

'She could kill you, Lizzie. She could kill all of us.'

'I know, but I can't let her go. Try and understand—'

'There's nothing to understand.'

'Yes there is. What if your baby turns out to be like this? Will things be different then? Could you imagine giving your baby up?'

'No . . .'

'She's my daughter, Katie, and no matter what she is, what she's done or what she might still do, she's my responsibility. I'll protect her and fight for her until the bitter end.'

'If we carry on like this,' Kate warned, 'that will be sooner than you think.'

26

The morning I thought would never come is finally here. I lay on the bed for hours, but I couldn't sleep. It reminded me of being back in the flat with Ellis, when we shut ourselves off from the others and slept on Edward's top bunk. I kept thinking about her wide, innocent eyes. Oblivious to all that was happening around her, she curled up alongside me, full of love and complete, unspoken trust.

Barefoot and cold, I've spent most of the last few hours looking out of the small window, watching the darkness turn to grey as the sun rose over the roof of this bizarre prison. I've stood here for hours trying to work out who this Sahota might be, and what he wants from me. I've taken some reassurance from the fact that I'm sure Joseph Mallon's naïve trust in me is genuine – he put his life on the line several times yesterday, and all the Unchanged have left now is their lives. He's either supremely confident and brave, stupidly optimistic or, and this seems most likely, he genuinely believes all the crap he's been pedalling. So will Sahota be the same? I've been trying to work out my tactics, deciding how I should play my showdown with Boss Man. But how can I prepare for a meeting in a place I don't know with a person I've never met?

It's all irrelevant.

The only thing that matters now is getting out and looking for Ellis. The war – us and them, taking sides – all of that has to be relegated to second place from now on. I'll play along with Mallon and his hippy/pacifist/conscientious-objector bullshit for as long as it takes until I get out of here. Unless, of course, they don't intend letting me out. Then I'll resort to my back-up plan – my Plan B which used to be Plan A – start fighting and don't stop until every last one of the fuckers is lying dead at my feet.

The door finally opens and Mallon strides in. About time. There's no tray of food, no small talk or niceties this morning. It's like he's just got a job to do. Is he abandoning me and moving on to a new pet? Or is he just unable to look me in the eye because he knows what's coming next? I want to attack him but I don't, forcing myself to swallow the Hate back down like poisonous bile.

'What's going to happen?' I ask, instantly regretting having spoken. Christ, how far I've fallen. It's bad enough that I'm being held captive by the Unchanged, now I'm begging them for information too. Pathetic.

'I told you last night. You're going to see Sahota.'

'Yes, but . . .'

Mallon stands up straight and looks at me, still on his guard, but allowing himself to relax slightly. He puts a hand on my shoulder and I resist the temptation to shrug it off. 'Have faith, Danny. Sahota is a good man. The kind of man who could bring an end to this war.'

That doesn't make me feel any better. 'But who is he? What does he want to see me for?'

My questions obviously sound as desperate as I suddenly feel.

Mallon manages half a smile. 'You'll find out.'

He bends down and takes the shackles off my feet. Now the only chains left are those which bind my hands together. I could kill him now, but that would be a mistake. If I'm going to kill anyone this morning, it should be the main man, not one of his minions.

Mallon leads me out into a wide corridor. There's no security this time, no bag over my head, and I get my first proper look at the building I'm being held in. It's an odd-looking place, nothing like the prison I'd imagined. The walls are bare, their light yellow paint faded and peeling, and the air is cold. There are traces of religious paraphernalia lying around, like the crucifix in my room: a painting of some serene-looking woman at the top of a staircase, some unfathomable ancient slogan scrawled across another wall, enough crucifixes to ward off a whole army of vampires . . .

We reach a T-junction at the end of the long corridor, walking under an unrepaired hole in the roof where rainwater has poured in and soaked the carpet. To my left the corridor continues towards another long staircase. To my right there's a short, narrow landing, then three steps leading up to an ominous-looking door. Is this my Room 101? Is this the very end of my journey? All the fears and uncertainties I'd managed to dismiss suddenly manifest themselves again. My pulse is racing and my throat's dry. My body tenses. I stop and turn towards Mallon. The urge to kill him is strong, almost too strong . . .

'Don't, Danny,' he pleads pathetically, my intent obviously clear, 'please don't. You're so close now—'

He moves past me quickly, climbs the steps and opens the door. He pushes it wide open and I edge a little closer, trying to look past him and see inside. It looks bizarrely like a doctor's waiting room, more like another short corridor than a room: clean, a door at either end, light flooding in through a skylight, a low table and a row of three chairs against one wall. I take a step closer, my curiosity and nerves getting the better of me. Mallon stands there, blocking my way, and it's like he's somehow taunting me. *Can't stand this.* This bullshit has gone on for too long. I don't think there's anyone else in this damn building. I'll kill him, then fight my way out of here.

I run at the fucker, but he sidesteps and pushes me into the other room. I spin around as he slams the door in my face.

'Don't blow it,' he shouts as it shuts. I hear a bolt slide across, then hear his muffled voice still talking to me. 'Keep the faith Danny, you're almost there. Remember everything you've learnt . . .'

I hammer on the door, but it's no use – it's locked and he's gone. How could I have been so fucking dumb to walk into a simple trap like this?

I'll wait for Sahota to show his face now.

I'm ready to fight. Bastard won't know what's hit him.

27

Silence. Absolute, total fucking silence. I stand and watch the other door, waiting for it to open, ready to attack. No one's coming. Is this another set-up? More stupid games, making me wait and trying to get me to panic and crack? Too late for that now.

Both doors are locked, but the skylight above is open slightly. I climb up onto one of the chairs, my hands still bound together, and try to haul myself up. The rattling chains are heavy around my wrists and the frame of the skylight doesn't feel strong enough to support my weight. I'll pull it down before I—

'Going somewhere?'

I drop, spin around and throw myself at the figure standing in the other door. I swing my chain-wrapped hands at his head, hard enough to decapitate him. He manages to somehow duck out of the way then shoves me in the gut. I trip over the chair I was just standing on, falling back and cracking my head hard against the floor. I roll over and try to get up, but this bastard's fast. He pushes me back down and plants a boot right between my shoulder blades, stopping me from moving. I brace myself for his next strike, but it doesn't come and he lifts his foot off.

I look back and watch him walk away. Confused, I drag myself up using another chair for support, suck in a deep breath of air, and turn around to face him.

What? How can he—?

'You must be Danny McCoyne,' he says, but I can't answer. 'I'm Sahota.'

Standing in front of me, wearing a smart, if a little crumpled, pinstripe suit and a remarkably clean white shirt, is one of our people. He's not Unchanged. I do a double-take, but I know I'm right: this man is a friend and an ally, and I immediately know we're on the same side. He's short and his build is slight, but he stands tall with confidence and composure. The surprise and confusion he obviously sees on my face is clearly not unexpected.

'Apologies for all the subterfuge and bullshit over the last few days,' he says, gesturing for me to follow him through into the next room. He stops just inside the room as if he's remembered something important. He checks his trouser pockets, then pulls out a key and undoes the chains around my wrists. He throws them out into the waiting area and closes the door behind us.

All I can do is stand and stare at Sahota. I don't know what I was expecting, but he isn't it, in any way, shape or form. He's a good foot and a half shorter than me, dark-skinned, with close-cropped dark hair, greying at the temples. He has a neatly trimmed moustache and wears a pair of wire-framed glasses. For the first time in months I'm suddenly conscious of my shabby appearance: dead man's trousers and shirt, no shoes, hair long and shaggy, face covered in bristles.

'Come in and sit down,' he says, ushering me further into the room. It's a wide, spacious and relatively clean office-cum-living area. In one corner is a metal-framed bed, similar to the one in my cell, but with clean bedding folded back with military precision. Along one wall are several huge, mostly intact windows (only one pane of glass has been boarded up) and, in front of me, a large wooden desk with a single chair on either side. Sahota locks the door and sits down at the desk with his back to the window. He beckons for me to sit opposite.

'Where do you want to start?' he asks in a clipped, well-educated accent as he pours me a drink and slides it across the table.

'Don't know,' I mumble pathetically between thirsty gulps

of water. Truth is, I've got so many questions to ask I'm struggling to make sense of any of them.

'Don't worry,' he says with a grin, 'it's not unusual. You've been through a lot.'

'I don't even know what I've been through.'

He grins again. 'We wouldn't have done it this way if there'd been any alternative.'

'So what exactly have you done?'

'Which one of them looked after you? Selena, Joseph or Simon?'

'Looked after me? That's not how I'd put it.'

'Which one?'

'Joseph.'

'And what did he tell you?'

'Lots of bullshit about breaking the cycle, not fighting fire with fire, holding the Hate . . . He said the more I fought, the harder it would get.'

'Did you believe any of it?'

I shrug my shoulders. Truth be told, I'm still not sure what I believe. 'Bits of it made sense.'

'Well, some of what he said must have had an effect on you because you're here and he's still alive. You'd have killed him otherwise.'

'He said I was only locked up here because of the Hate. He said the more we fight, the less we get.'

'And what do you think about that, Danny?'

'I'm not sure what I think,' I repeated.

'But you must have some kind of opinion? You can't tell me an intelligent man like you lay there alone in the darkness for hours and didn't think about what he'd been told?'

'I think he was right when he said we were stuck in a vicious circle and that things are only going to get worse.'

'Go on.'

'But I don't understand what difference that makes? What else are we supposed to do? We can't live with the Unchanged. We have to kill them.'

'You're absolutely right.'

'So how do we win a war without fighting?'

Sahota stands, picks up his drink and walks over to the window. He looks out, choosing his next words with care and consideration. 'There is an alternative.'

'Is there? I can't see one.'

'That's because you're looking in the wrong place. You need to change your perspective, Danny, and that's what this place is all about. That's why we're here. Tell me, before we brought you here, did you ever hear anything of Chris Ankin and his plans?'

'I heard his messages when the war started, and I was with a group for a couple of days. They said they were trying to build an army.'

He turns back to face me. 'And what did you think of that?'

'Gut reaction?'

'Yes.'

'As soon as we start grouping together in large numbers, the enemy will blow the shit out of us.'

'Exactly right. We're still outnumbered, and they still have a structured military with a just-about operational chain of command. We'd only be able to take the fight to them on limited fronts, and yes, they'd probably blow us out of the water. While we're concentrating on one of their cities, the others would still be standing strong. They've already shown they're willing to sacrifice thousands of their own to try and wipe us out. You've only got to look at how they lost London—'

'What *did* happen to London?'

'You didn't hear?'

'Not really, only a few details.'

'It was early on, before these refugee camps were set up. It wasn't something we planned, rather, it was something they couldn't prevent. The capital was too big for them to defend, too sprawling. Really, London showed us what we could achieve. The fighting on the streets must have been incredible – I almost wish I could have been there. There were hardly any of us in comparison to them, but the panic we caused was beyond anything we could have hoped for. They reached critical mass—'

'Critical mass? I don't understand.'

'The point of no return. The point where it was impossible for them to regain any order, where the number of individual battles was so high and the fighting so intense that they could no longer separate *them* from *us*. They didn't know who was who any more. The only option left to them was to destroy everything.'

'*They destroyed London?*'

'The whole city, and everyone in it. Wiped out thousands of our people, but they took hundreds of thousands of their own with them.'

We're digressing and I'm confused. 'I still don't understand – so what's that got to do with you holding me here?'

'In the end it was their confusion and panic which destroyed London, simple as that. But if we'd attacked with an army, they'd have seen us coming and wiped us out before we'd even got close.'

'You said I was looking in the wrong place—'

'That's right, and so were they.'

'Look, I'm sorry, you've spent days fucking with my brain and I'm tired. Stop talking in riddles and just explain.'

'Have you ever heard of a text called *The Art of War*?'

'I've heard the title. Don't know anything about it though; never read it.'

'It's a Chinese guide to warfare, written by Sun Tzu more than two thousand years ago.'

'And? What did he know about us and the Unchanged?'

'Nothing at all! But even though this war is unique, some of Sun Tzu's tactics for fighting remain as valid today as they were in ancient China. He said that all warfare is based on deception. We have to fool our enemy, make them believe we're weak when we're strong, make them think we're miles away when we're next to them. "Hold out baits to entice the enemy. Feign disorder, and crush him." '

Sahota recites the script perfectly from memory. He waits for a reaction from me, but my head's still spinning and I can't make sense of anything. He senses my confusion and explains, 'They're expecting us to fight head-on. As far as they can see, our only tactic is to fight and keep fighting until we're the only ones left standing. When you get deeper into the city you'll see how that stops them from interacting—'

'Wait a second,' I interrupt, 'what do you mean, when I get deeper into the city?'

Sahota grins and pours me another glass of water. 'They're expecting us to run straight at them with fists flying, screaming in their faces. What they're *not* expecting is for us to be standing beside them and alongside them. We're going to go deep into their cities to stir up trouble and cause them to panic. Then, when they're too busy tearing themselves apart to notice, Ankin's army will come into play. We're going to make them destroy themselves from the inside out.'

'But how are we supposed to do that? Get within a few metres of any of them and all we'll be able to do is fight—'

'Is that right? Didn't you learn anything from your time with Joseph?'

It finally makes sense. *That's* what this place is about. 'Holding the Hate.'

'That's exactly it,' he says, sitting down again and leaning towards me. 'Thing is, this is the only way to teach someone how to do it. If you're not held or restricted in some way, you'll kill them before you realise what you're doing.'

'But Joseph . . . ?'

'Joseph and the others are just puppets. They have no idea. They genuinely believe what they tell you, but it's all just bullshit in the end. Joseph's the best – or the worst – depending how you look at it. Some days it's all I can do not to kill him myself.'

'Incredible . . .'

Sahota's eyes are wide with excitement. 'Think of the advantage this gives us, Danny. *We* know who *they* are, but they can't tell us apart until we start fighting. They won't even know we're there until it's too late.'

'Jesus Christ!'

'We're having to move fast. For various reasons things are deteriorating rapidly in the city. Normally we'd have given you a few more days here, to make sure you understand, to make sure you can hold the Hate, but time's a luxury we no longer have. This is the perfect moment for us to do this. Think you're up to it?'

Talk about being put on the spot. I fumble for an answer for a second, before realising that there's only one thing I can say. 'Yes.'

'Good man! That's the spirit! As soon as they told me about you I knew you'd be a good candidate . . .'

'What do you mean by that? Who told you . . . ?'

'We send people out looking for battles. They wait on the outskirts of the fighting, watching out for people like you who manage to demonstrate some degree of control and don't just attack. Let's face it; we'd be wasting our time trying to teach this stuff to Brutes, wouldn't we? No, we need people like you who are able to take a step back and consider the options before committing to an attack. People who use the Hate and control it, rather than letting it control them.'

He looks me straight in the eye. 'Tell me, do you remember when you first stood next to Joseph and didn't attack?'

'I remember.'

'And what were you thinking at the time, Danny? Were you thinking what he was saying was right, or were you just toeing the line to get the best out of a bad situation?'

The memory of the last few days is filled with confusion and uncertainty, the distinction between 'us' and 'them' suddenly unclear. But now I'm away from my cell and Sahota has put his question so simply, the answer's clear and unequivocal. Everything has been brought back into sharp focus.

'I was playing with him, stringing him along. Doing what he wanted me to do just to get food and freedom . . .'

'Exactly! A perfect answer! From the moment you decided not to kill him, you were in control.'

This is too much to take in.

Sahota watches me intently and I'm uncomfortable under his constant gaze. I try to look anywhere but back at him. The sun momentarily breaks through the heavy grey cloud cover and streams in through the dirty window. Christ, I've been so preoccupied with this bizarre conversation that I'd forgotten my newfound freedom – in the back of my mind I still think I'm chained to the spot. I get up and walk around the side of the desk.

'You local?' Sahota asks.

'Don't know yet,' I answer. 'That depends where local is. Where exactly are we?'

'Not far from the hospital where we picked you up. A couple of miles maybe.'

'A couple of miles in which direction? Further away from the city centre or . . . ?' My words trail away to nothing as soon as I look out of the window. I know this place.

Sahota's office overlooks a narrow car park. Beyond that, the overgrown back gardens of a row of once well-appointed but now derelict houses stretch away. Beyond the houses is a small, sloping, oddly shaped patch of parkland, the brightly painted swings and slides of a children's play area looking strangely at odds with the chaos of everything else I can see. A narrow track between two of the houses connects the car park to the road and a huge, wrought-iron gate prevents anyone unwanted from either getting in or getting out.

'Is this—?' I start to ask.

'Holy Sisters of the Poor, to give it its original title,' he explains, standing beside me and looking down. 'Strange place, this was.'

'Strange?'

'Part convent, part nursing home. Ideal for us.'

He's not wrong. The huge Victorian brick complex is like a fortress. Built in the middle of what used to be a fairly affluent area and hidden from view by houses on all sides, it's set back off the road and surrounded by walls tall enough to keep even the most determined intruder out. Most people wouldn't even have known it was here at all. From what I remember, this started as a convent, and became a church-run, community-funded rest home. I'm sure Lizzie's dad Harry had a friend living here for a while . . .

'This is Highwell, isn't it?'

'We're on the border between Highwell and Steply, to be precise, about two miles from the centre of town.'

'Yes, so we're—'

'Already in the city, yes. Right on the innermost edge of their exclusion zone.'

'Christ! How many people like us are here?'

'Not many. Just me and a couple of others at any one time. Apart from me this place is almost exclusively staffed by my team of idiot Unchanged pacifists who think they're saving the world. As soon as people like you have learnt how to control their emotions I send them out into the city. Like I said, the situation's deteriorating rapidly out there. We don't have a lot of time to waste.'

For a moment all I can do is stand in silence and stare out of the window. Beyond the car park and the houses, everything is still, looking completely lifeless. There are the usual tell-tale signs of battle, and everything's even more overgrown and wild than I remember, but the world otherwise just seems abandoned, empty.

The longer I look, though, the more I see. In the distance a single helicopter flies towards the city centre, visible only in the gaps between the tops of trees. There's a pile of corpses in the park, dumped in a flowerbed. Closer, in the shadows of the car park directly below, several Unchanged are carrying bags of supplies between one building and another, constantly looking over their shoulders for fear of attack. Coming along the road on the far right is a battered car, slowly approaching. It enters the complex through another gate and stops in the shadow of the tall perimeter wall and as I watch two Unchanged deliver another fighter like me, his arms and legs already tightly bound. The irony of what's happening here is beautiful: these fools think they're working towards some kind of salvation, but all they're doing is training their own assassins.

'I've set up a number of sleeper cells right in the heart of the city,' Sahota is saying. 'I want you to join one of them.'

'Okay.' I answer quickly and without thinking through any implications. It'll get me out of here, and right now that's the most important thing.

'I'll get your stuff brought up, and I'll give you directions, contact information and some supplies. Get out there, get used to being neck-deep in the enemy, then find your cell.'

'And then?'

'And then you sit and wait for the signal. When the time's right, the cells will be instructed to take up pre-planned positions deep in the heart of the city. At the signal, each cell will start fighting, causing as much panic as possible. Just imagine it, Danny: sudden swells of violence in random locations, all happening at the same time – and for no apparent reason? The enemy won't know what's going on; they won't even see us there. They'll look straight through us and turn on each other, and it'll be beautiful, like dropping a match into the petrol tank of a car. Before you know it, the whole city will be tearing itself apart. Think of us less like terrorist cells, more like cancer cells.'

It sounds magnificent, and all too easy. 'So all we have to do—'

'All *you* have to do,' he interrupts, correcting me, 'is get in there, wait until we're ready, then cause as much mayhem and carnage as you can.'

28

A couple of hours ago I thought I was a dead man. And now here I am with a rucksack full of weapons and supplies, and Ellis' things returned to me, walking through the dead ruins of the city I used to call home, ready to help bring the enemy down. This new world order is fickle and unpredictable; one minute you're down, the next you're on top again.

The roads around Sahota's building were reassuringly quiet and I was feeling confident and strong – but the moment I saw the first of the Unchanged I began to doubt myself again.

There were three of them, huddled together in the doorway of a partially collapsed building, barely visible from the street. I just caught sight of their eyes, staring out from the darkness. Even after all I've been through, my instinct was still to kill. No one would have been any the wiser, and with my knives and axe hanging from my belt again, I was sure I could have got rid of all three of them without even breaking sweat. But I was scared – scared that if I started killing out here I wouldn't be able to stop again.

I forced myself to relax, to overcome the temptation and keep walking. The foul fuckers watched me like hawks as I passed them, but two thoughts kept me moving forward: first, if I actually make it into the city there's a chance, however slight, that I might be able to find information about what happened to Ellis. And second, the longer I last without killing, and the deeper I manage to get into town, the more casualties there'll be when the fighting starts up again. It was easier letting those three live (if you could call that living) knowing that it would bring me closer to killing thousands of their kind.

Unexpectedly, the more Unchanged I've subsequently seen,

the easier being around them has become. I still have to fight to control myself each time I see one of them, but their vast numbers act as a constant reminder that to start killing now would be suicidal. Or maybe it's just that seeing them like this, crammed together and on their knees in such desperately appalling conditions, reinforces my comparative strength and superiority. These people are *nothing*.

Christ, I'm cold. I run my hand over my freshly shaved head and chin as I catch a glimpse of my reflection in a grubby shop window. I look like a new man, like I've been reborn out of the mind-fuck of the last few days. It was something Sahota suggested – something I'd never even considered until now. He told me to try and blend in with the Unchanged masses. I'd been content to wear the same fighting clothes day after day, until they wore out, but some of the Unchanged, incredibly, still care about their appearance. Sure, standards have slipped, and there are no high street stores selling the latest fashions any more, but, to a surprising number of them, how they look still matters. It's all about being accepted, he told me, blending in and being part of the crowd. I saw a woman a minute ago who was still wearing make-up. What's the fucking point of that? Stupid bitch – it's not going to matter what she looks like when she dies . . .

Concentrate on breathing, that's my technique. I force myself to keep my breathing low and level, to move slowly, keep to a steady, deliberate pace. If I start thinking about killing and fighting, I try distracting myself with trivialities, counting lampposts, avoiding cracks in the pavement, trying to remember the names and the faces of people I used to know. It's the weirdest sensation – I imagine this is how a recovering alcoholic must feel. As long as I'm not killing, I'm fine. But if I were to attack just one of them, I'd be just like the alcoholic falling off the wagon and having his first drink; I know I wouldn't be able to stop. I remember Mallon's catchphrase: the more you fight, the less you get. He was right. If I cause any trouble out here on my own I'll be completely screwed. So I will stay calm, and I will have a chance.

My surroundings are bizarre, not at all what I expected. The streets and buildings on the inside of the enemy cordon look different. Beyond the city limits, outside their exclusion zone, everything has been pounded into ruin by weeks and weeks of fighting. Over the weeks and months the Unchanged military attacked us with relentless ferocity and unchallenged explosive force, reducing much of the outside world to a ruined wasteland. Some villages and small towns I've seen have been hit so badly that they've simply ceased to exist – mounds of overgrown rubble are all that's left. Here the basic structures are still largely intact, but they look like they're slowly decaying. Everything is covered in a thick layer of detritus and grime.

Ahead of me is a slagheap of uncollected waste, some of it in ripped black sacks, most of it loose. Rats and other vermin scavenge through the mountain of garbage in broad daylight, suddenly cocksure and confident, no longer afraid of man. Birds are pecking at the bodies, and there's a steady trickle of stagnant, foul-smelling water running away from the huge decaying mound. It's pooled in the gutter and spread out into the road, a black lake, because the drains are blocked. The gentle breeze is making its surface ripple, and bits of rubbish are floating like odd-shaped boats.

The address Sahota gave me is a place not far west of here, on the inner border of the exclusion zone. He warned me to stick to main routes and to stay out in the open, no matter how strong the temptation might be to try and disappear. I can already see the logic in his advice. It's like the population here is in a bizarre, almost trance-like state of 'false calm'. For the most part they line the sides of the streets, cramming themselves into the shadows, each trying to squeeze into as small a space as possible, almost as if they want to disappear. Some hide in the dark gaps between buildings, others sit behind the wheels of useless, abandoned cars which are never going anywhere again. From time to time I glance up at the windows of the places I pass and see pale faces pressed against the glass. Not a single scrap of space has been left unclaimed. Around me is an apparently never-ending succession of lost, haunted individuals, alone or sometimes in twos and threes, most of them looking down at the ground, too afraid to make eye-contact with anyone other than their few remaining trusted friends or relatives. The instinctive urge to kill them is un-diminished, but these people aren't even worth the effort. They are empty shells, and they are as good as dead already.

There are other people moving along the road, many of them going in the same direction as me, some walking aimlessly the other way. None of them seem to have any purpose. They're just drifting, and I do my best to match their slow, purposeless gait. It's hard, like being forced to hold your hand in a bowl of boiling water. I want to run to get through this part of town, but I don't dare do anything that's going to draw attention to me, or mark me out as different. There's an unspoken tension here; fear is bubbling just under the surface and everyone, me included, is being forced to keep their emotions suppressed, terrified by the prospect of what might happen if anyone lets their true feelings show. As much as the thought of comparing myself to the enemy is abhorrent, I realise that everyone here, me included, is doing exactly the same thing. We're all pre-tending to be something we're not.

Apart from the odd military vehicle, the constant buzz of helicopters scurrying through the air above me and the occa-sional rumble of distant, directionless fighting, everywhere else remains unnaturally quiet. I walk along a road which runs parallel with the side of the City Arena, a huge, soulless con-cert venue I could never afford to go to. There are blockades around the perimeter of the vast building for as far as I can see, and a heavy military presence around the doors and exits. There are scores of empty trucks parked in its various car parks. Was this some kind of feeding centre? Whatever it was, it looks like it's been decommissioned now, but there are still huge numbers of civilians camped around its outskirts.

Maybe they're waiting silently for supplies which will never come. In another fenced-off area nearby is a still-smoking mound of corpses. Must be hundreds of bodies there.

I'm so distracted by the grim sights all around me that I collide head-on with someone coming the other way who's obviously paying as little attention to the human traffic on the road as me. The unexpected impact catches me off-guard. In a sudden, uncontrollable blind panic, I spring forward and grab the dishevelled-looking man by his lapels. I spin him around and slam him down onto the tarmac and reach for my knife before—

Before I remember where I am and who I am. I let him go immediately and walk on, terrified that I've been seen and that my sudden violent overreaction will give me away. I look back and see him scramble away, getting up quickly and sprinting until there's a decent distance between us. He puts his head down and keeps walking, trying not to panic, frequently looking back over his shoulder. I glance from side to side. There are plenty of people watching me, but thankfully they're all too scared to get involved.

Fucking idiot. Can't afford to make mistakes like that.

I know exactly where I am now. Around the next corner is the PFP – the Parking Fines Processing Centre where I used to work. When I see the building I'm immediately filled with a mass of conflicting emotions: disgust that I wasted so much of my miserable former life here, relief that those days are long gone and, catching me off-guard, a painful nostalgia when I remember all that I've lost and left behind. It all feels like forever ago, like the memories belong to someone else. Coming here, remembering this place and all that happened here, it's like watching a TV movie of someone else's life. Christ, there are people living in the building now! I can see them looking out of the same windows I used to spend hours staring from – could there be a worse existence than that?

Without realising it, I've stopped right outside the PFP and

I'm standing in the middle of the street like a dumb sightseer, suddenly oblivious to everything else around me. The noise of a fast-approaching engine snaps me out of my dangerous stupor. I turn around and see a Jeep driving up the middle of the road towards me, flanked by several heavily armed soldiers on either side, their impenetrable face masks hiding their intent. Are they looking for me? The Jeep moves forward quickly, the driver making no attempt to dodge or weave through the masses of drifting refugees who're littering the street. They jump for cover, staying well back until the military have passed by. Preoccupied by my irrational fear and not knowing whether I should do nothing or fight, I'm slow to react. A soldier shoves me to one side and it's all I can do not to kill him. I stand firm and square up to him, stupidly defiant, my face reflected back at me in his visor.

'Problem?' he yells, his ugly face just inches from mine. I can feel bile rising in my throat, a noxious, nauseous terror building up inside me, and I don't know if I can keep it down. Can I stand to let him live? When all I want to do is kill, doing nothing is almost impossible. But I force myself to remember being back in the cell with Joseph Mallon, and remembering the fact that I was so easily able to fool him gives me much-needed strength. Act dumb, I plead with myself. Let this one go. You'll kill thousands more when it's time . . .

'No problem,' I answer and I back down and slope away, trying to mimic the behaviour of the countless other cowards milling around me. I feel his eyes burning into me, but I don't allow myself to look back. I keep walking . . .

Ten seconds and nothing's happened.

Don't look back.

Another ten seconds. Have they moved on?

I turn the corner and I know I'm safe.

Millennium Square. Last time I was here I got caught in the crossfire between groups of armed police officers who suddenly found themselves on opposing sides. I ran for cover along with hundreds of other people, each person as scared and confused as the next. That was the day, I recall, when everything really changed: that was the day the Hate took over. Strange how what was such a terrifying experience now seems, with hindsight, like nothing much out of the ordinary. I'm harder now, stronger – back then I was just one of the crowd, trying to blend in with the masses and not be noticed. Today I'm here to kill them.

This vast public square is no longer the underused empty space it always used to be. For as far as I can see the ground is covered with a sea of temporary shelters of endless different colours, shapes and sizes. I can't help looking into a few as I pass, and I see the same thing inside every one: refugees, desperately hoping that their flimsy structures of canvas or cardboard, wood or polythene will keep them safe inside and everyone else out. The middle-aged occupants of one shelter are both dead, their green-tinged corpses lying together motionless, entwined and unnoticed. The stale air inside the small space is thick with flies.

Squatters have taken over the public toilets and moved in. The loos used to get vandalised every other week; they were more a pick-up point for gay men than anything else. There's a man and a woman, sitting on plastic lawn chairs in the dark doorway, looking like a king and queen surveying their particularly grim kingdom. A fierce-looking dog tied up with rope is keeping everyone else at bay.

There's a patch of land up ahead which is unexpectedly empty. As I get closer I see that the road there is covered with puddles of drying mud, making it look like a dried-up riverbed. It looks like the rains have washed away huge numbers of these improvised tents, leaving this muddy paved expanse visible. I can see weeds sprouting in the gaps between the concrete slabs. The council used to spend a bloody fortune on this place – I remember hearing someone from another department bitching about it – and now it's just as godforsaken as everywhere else. Incredibly, though, a street clock and calendar I walk past is still working. It says it's coming up to three p.m. and it's a Thursday, and for a fraction of a second I feel an instinctive swell of relief because the weekend's coming. Christ, how stupid is that? It makes me realise that no matter how much everything has changed, the effects of years of conditioning are going to take more than a few months to disappear. Has the clock been maintained purposely for precisely that reason? Does it help the Unchanged masses cope if they know where they are in relation to their old routines?

Something on the far side of the square catches my eye. Virtually the full width of two adjacent buildings are covered with what looks like hundreds of posters, from the ground to some two metres high. As I get closer, I see it's a huge collage of photographs of people, pinned, nailed and stapled to the massive sheets of plywood that were used to board up the buildings. I move nearer, figuring it's safe to do so because there are other Unchanged milling around here too. I've seen similar displays in films and on TV before: shattered populations coming together to share their grief and build an improvised shrine to remember the friends and family they've lost. Maybe Lizzie's picture is here somewhere? I start to look along the rain-blurred and sun-bleached pictures.

I stop and stare at a random face, one of hundreds, no more or less remarkable than any of those above, below or around it. It's a man in his late forties with a mop of curly dark hair, a short beard and dark, angular glasses. There's writing in the space below his face. It says 'James Jenkins. Killed his wife Louise and daughter Claire'. There's a similar scrawled message on the next picture: 'Marie Yates. Murdered everyone who mattered to me'. These aren't the faces of victims, I realise: these are their killers. Christ, is my face up here somewhere? I panic and start quickly scanning the display, suddenly self-conscious, hoping I'll find my picture before anyone else does. I wish I hadn't shaved my head like Sahota told me to; I should have stayed hidden beneath that layer of stubble and shaggy hair. And then, bizarrely, I find myself making a sudden

U-turn, hoping that I actually do manage to find my photograph because that, I tell myself, would be proof positive that Lizzie's been here.

But here or not, it won't make any difference.

I force myself to move on, knowing that I can't afford to waste time. Somewhere in this stinking, unhygienic, over-crowded wreck of a city, the woman I used to share my life with might still be hiding. And if I can track her down, she'll be able to tell me what happened to my daughter.

29

I must be getting close now. I thought I knew the address Sahota gave me, but it all looks so very different to how I remember. I'm back out on the furthest edge of the refugee camp, heading for the border with the exclusion zone. As I've moved away from the centre of the city again, so the number of Unchanged around me has quickly diminished. It's a relief not to be surrounded by them, and not to have to constantly struggle to keep myself under control. There are more empty buildings here than there are occupied. There are one or two Unchanged almost always in sight, but they make every effort to ignore me, sliding into the shadows whenever I approach.

I stop outside a fortified house which has metal grilles and bars covering its windows and doors. The houses on either side have been destroyed, but this one looks like it's managed to escape the fighting pretty much undamaged. Curious, I walk down a narrow passageway between the house and the rubble remains of its nearest neighbour. The badly decomposed body of an Unchanged man is lying face-down in the middle of an overgrown lawn, military fatigues flapping in the wind around his skeletal limbs. He's been dead for several weeks at least. Was he the owner of this place? The back door's been prised off its hinges and I go inside. Most of the furniture has been used to blockade each room, leaving just a chair, a small table and a bed in an upstairs bedroom. The remains of boxes and boxes of supplies cover the floors and the walls have been daubed with pointless, empty slogans: DEATH TO THE HATERS and KILL THEM BEFORE THEY KILL YOU. There's nothing of value left here. I leave the house, shaking my head and laughing to myself at the pathetic Unchanged who clearly spent so long trying to defend and protect what was his. Total waste of effort. He'd have been better off taking his chances in the centre of town with the rest of them.

The wreck of a truck blocks the road ahead. It's over on its side like a beached whale, the contents of the upturned skip it was carrying now scattered across the entire width of the road. I clamber through the mess and continue down a sloping ramp towards what was once a busy local shopping precinct. My footsteps echo around the drab little plaza. Half of the open space is submerged under a shallow pool of filthy black water. At its deepest point the booted foot of a dead body sticks up above the rippling surface like a shark's fin.

Around me are abandoned and looted shops: a book-maker's, with signs in the window advertising odds on an international football match which never took place, a fish and chip shop, a takeaway pizza joint, a hairdresser's, a gen-eral housewares store . . . I don't waste time looking in any of them. If there ever was anything useful I reckon it's long since been taken, or destroyed by the mindless vandals who've been through the place.

I cross the plaza diagonally, feeling increasingly uncomfort-able and exposed as I skirt around the edge of the lapping lake of dirty rainwater. I'm a Hater deep in Unchanged territory. Are they watching me? Keen to get under cover, I quicken my pace and cut between two more deserted buildings. Then I finally see the place Sahota sent me to find: the Risemore Conservative Members Club. It's as ugly as everything else around here – a squat red-brick social club that looks like it might actually have benefited from having a bomb dropped on it. I used to do all I could to avoid places like this in the days before the war.

When I was little, before he walked out on us, my dad used to drag me out to his drinking club some weekends. I'd sit there with him, bored out of my mind, having to make one can of Coke last for hours while he got drunk, smoked, read the paper, argued with his equally drunk mates or sat and watched piss-poor comics, singers and variety acts who, by rights, should have been banned from ever performing in public. As I edge closer to the club I automatically build up a mental image of what it's going to be like inside: loud, stale, musty, with a heavy fug of cigarette smoke hanging in the air, grubby, sticky carpets, uncomfortable plastic-covered seating with the stuffing hanging out . . .

There's an impassable mound of fallen masonry blocking the door, so I can't get in that way. I go around to the back to look for another entrance, cursing my naïveté. I was never supposed to get in through the front. You don't want just anyone to be able to stroll up and knock on your front door if you're trying to coordinate a terrorist cell, do you? Is that what I am now, a terrorist? A suicide-bomber without the bomb? Or am *I* the bomb?

A narrow, brick-walled passageway runs from the front of the building straight through to the back, opening out into an enclosed but largely empty car park. Can't see anyone around here, or even any evidence that anyone's been here for a while. There's a fire exit, a strong, metal doorway. I hammer on it with my fist and wait for an answer, starting to doubt whether I'm at the right place. A mangy tabby cat darts out from under a hedge behind me, racing across the car park and scurrying for cover under an overflowing wheelie bin. Instinctively I whistle for him. I used to like cats.

The fire door opens, catching me off-guard. I spin around and find myself face to face with a nasty-looking big bastard covered in tattoos. Thank God we're on the same side.

'I'm looking for Chapman,' I tell him, remembering the name Sahota told me to ask for.

'Who is?'

'I am,' I answer without thinking.

'And who are you, you fucking idiot?' he sighs, taking a step forward and forcing me away from the building, into the middle of the car park. He rests his hand on the hilt of a monstrous knife with a vicious, serrated blade.

'My name's Danny McCoyne,' I answer quickly, trying to disguise my nerves and sound confident. 'Sahota sent me here.'

At the mention of Sahota's name the thug visibly relaxes. He looks me up and down again, then stands to one side and ushers me into the building. I do as he says and wait for him to follow as he pulls the door shut again and secures it with a heavy wooden crossbeam. He leads me through the ground floor of the building. My eyes are slow to adjust to the darkness indoors and I trip down off a slightly elevated wooden stage area. He looks back at me and shakes his head.

Inside, the club is as dilapidated as everywhere else, but nothing like the stupid, outdated images I'd got in my head. The floor is littered with the broken remains of dirty polystyrene ceiling tiles; makes me wonder: if the ceiling's this bad, how strong is the rest of the building? Disappointingly (but not unexpectedly) the bar has been completely stripped. There's a row of spaces on the mirrored wall where the optics would have been. Christ, I could do with a drink, just to calm my nerves. I feel more anxious in here than I did walking through the centre of town when I was up to my neck in Unchanged bastards and well-armed enemy military.

My chaperone obviously doesn't want to talk. He leads me along a wide corridor, through another, much smaller second bar, and up a long staircase. There are four doors leading off a square landing. Three of them are open, and I can see at least one or two people in every room.

He opens the remaining door and I follow him into a large room which is almost as big as the main bar area we walked through on the floor below. It's sparsely furnished, but largely undamaged. The light is dim, but I can make out several wooden crates of supplies stacked up against one wall. A guy is sitting on his own at a table in the far corner using a laptop, and there's another asleep on a mattress under a curtained window.

As soon as I enter the room a woman gets up from where she's been lying on a threadbare sofa. She's hidden in the shadows, but something about her is familiar. I'm sure I've seen her before. Is she Chapman?

'Who's this?' she asks. Her voice has a trace of a gentle Irish accent which is beaten into submission by the abrasiveness of her tone.

'Says he's looking for you. Says Sahota sent him.'

My unwilling guide disappears, his job done. The woman walks towards me, stepping into the light. I immediately recognise her, but I can't remember where from. Was it this life? My old life?

'The slaughterhouse,' she says.

'What?'

'The slaughterhouse, few days back. You're trying to remember where you saw me before. You were there with the guy with the smashed-up hand and foot and I—'

'You were the one telling me not to bother with him 'cause he'd be dead soon,' I interrupt, suddenly remembering where we met.

'That's right. And he was. I'm Julia Chapman.'

'You're a happy soul, aren't you?' I say sarcastically as I shake her hand, recalling how blunt and matter-of-fact she had been when we spoke before. She nearly crushes my hand with her vice-like grip. She's just trying to let me know who's in charge.

'I'm a realist,' she answers, 'and I'm focused. And so should you be. I tell you, when this war's finished, I'll be the first one up and dancing at the fucking party and the last one to sit down. Until then, though, all I'm interested in is fighting.'

'Bit of a coincidence, though, finding you here.'

'You reckon?'

'I thought you were busy recruiting for Ankin's army.'

'I still am.'

'So why are you here?'

'To make sure Sahota gets the right people too.'

'So are you trying to tell me you followed me into the city?'

'I'm not trying to tell you anything, but yep, something like that. There were a few more people involved, and it wasn't just you we were watching.'

'Don't believe you.'

'Believe what you like, pal, it really doesn't bother me. Thing is, we are where we are, and where we are is here. It's what we do next that matters most.'

'If you say so.'

I wonder if she always talks this much bullshit or if she's trying to impress me by exerting her authority? She looks me straight in the eye and for a second I think she might be about to throw a punch.

She bites her lip and turns away. 'Come here. I want to show you something.'

I follow her out of the room and across the landing. We walk through another part of the building, where two more fighters are resting in the shadows. They glance up at me as I pass them, but they don't move.

She leads me out onto a narrow verandah, then we use an unsteady stepladder to climb up onto a debris-strewn flat roof-top. There are large puddles of water covering much of the ground. A pair of deckchairs have been left under an improvised shelter made of a stretched-out tarpaulin. The views across what remains of the city and the exclusion zone are vast and panoramic. Looks like they've been using this place as an observation point. Smart.

Julia leads me to the edge of the roof overlooking the refugee camp in the centre of city. The view is incredible, not just because of its scope, but also because of the sense of scale and perspective it gives everything. In every other direction all I can see are abandoned buildings and immense swathes of empty land. Our land. No trace of the Unchanged.

'Takes your breath away, doesn't it?' Julia's soaking up the sight, staring with palpable hate deep into the city where hundreds of thousands of Unchanged refugees are cowering in squalor. Their closeness still makes me feel uneasy.

'Is this what you wanted to show me?'

'It is, but don't just look at it, *think* about it. *Feel* it, even. Right across the whole of the country, our enemies are hiding together in places like this: thousands of them, crammed together in the space of just a few square miles, stacked on top of each other, hardly able to breathe. Now turn around and look at what we've got. Out beyond the city boundary you can walk for miles and hardly see anyone.'

'I went back to where I used to live,' I tell her. 'Couldn't believe what little space we had to ourselves . . .'

'And you know what makes it worse?' she continues, not listening to me. 'Those idiots still have faith in the people who are supposed to be leading them, not that they ever see them or hear anything from them. Christ, they don't even know who they are. They're just clinging desperately onto the rules and organisations that used to keep their pathetic little lives ticking along, trusting in a system that was dying long before we ever appeared.'

'Can you believe we used to—?' I start to say before she interrupts. Her over-the-top enthusiasm for all of this is frightening.

'You know, some of those fuckers still think they're going to be protected, that everything's going to work out all right for them in the end. Thing is, you and me and everyone else – we know different, don't we?'

'They'll never win,' I answer quickly, standing my ground as an unexpected gust of wind threatens to blow me forward. 'They can't.'

'And that's why what we're going to do is going to have such an effect. We're gonna pull the carpet out from under their feet.'

'How many of us are here?'

'Including you, ten.'

'Is that enough?'

'We're not the only group. There are others. I know Sahota wants to get more than a hundred of us in place, ready for when the time's right.'

'And you think this is going to work?'

'No question. The Unchanged can't trust each other. Christ, they can barely bring themselves to look at the person next to them any more. I mean, there's never been any real trust between strangers, but now they've got it into their heads that anyone could turn on them at any second. So there's real fear in the air, all the time, a tension and uncertainty that's never going to disappear. The more of them who can cram themselves inside the city walls and the longer they're in there, the more that fear increases.'

'So we just walk in there—'

'—and light the fuse. That's right. They're right on the edge. I give 'em a week at most, ten days if they're lucky, and that's even without us getting involved. They've got no food, no sanitation, no medicine, and what with the floods—'

'Makes you wonder how they've lasted this long.'

'Have you been in there yet?'

'Coming here just now.'

'So you know what it's like?'

'I saw enough—'

'Thing is, they're all out for themselves, whether they'd admit it or not. Every one of them will do all that they can to survive, and screw everyone else. Self-preservation means everything to them. It's all they've got left.'

'So when do we do it? When do we go in?'

'It's up to Sahota. He'll know when the time's right.'

'And how will we know?'

'We'll know, trust me!'

'So do we just sit here and wait?'

'We do tonight, maybe tomorrow too. Then we'll be told to get into position. Could be hours after that, might even be days. We get in, bury ourselves deep, then explode. It's a small sacrifice to make.'

Sacrifice? The word makes me go cold. I'll fight alongside these people, but I don't intend sacrificing myself, not while there's a chance Ellis might still be out there.

'So we do enough to push them over the edge, then get out?'

'We do enough to push them over the edge, then keep pushing,' she answers quickly, sounding annoyed by my obvious lack of enthusiasm. 'What we do in the city is all that matters. You don't think about the future, getting out, leaving the fight, nothing like that. If you're left standing at the end of all of this, well done you, but if you're not, well then, that's too bad. This is way bigger than any of us.'

With that Julia walks away and leaves me alone on the roof. I watch her go, feeling like I've just shut myself away with a group of kamikaze cult members.

PART VII

Mark had to find more food. He didn't want to think about what would happen if he didn't. Impossible choices would have to be made. He didn't understand how it could have come to this. Kate had to eat, she was his obvious priority, but who next? Gurmit Singh could go to hell as far as he was concerned, but what about Kate's parents? Her dad was in his late seventies, her mum not much younger . . . could they really justify wasting precious supplies on them at their age?

Christ, what was he thinking? Leaving them to starve? And he needed to eat because he couldn't bear the thought of Katie and their child trying to survive in this nightmare world without him. And what about Lizzie, what was her position in the pecking order? And as for that thing she kept tied up in the bathroom . . . Mark cursed the day he'd agreed to let her stay with them.

The hotel room diagonally opposite room 33 was empty now. He'd heard noises there a while earlier and had watched through the peephole in his door as the occupants had fled. He wasn't sure exactly what had happened – someone cracking under the pressure of this impossible situation and being hunted down as a Hater, he guessed. The soldiers hadn't come to investigate (they never did any more) and there were at least two bodies still in the room, but he didn't care. As soon as he'd seen the rest of them thunder down the stairs in what looked like blind panic he'd known he'd have just a couple of minutes to get in there, strip out anything of value, then get out before other refugees claimed the precious space.

Mark felt like a CSI investigator trying to piece together a murder scene as he stood in the small room, which was a mirror image of the room where he and the others were living. He stepped over the first corpse, a woman, who was lying on the floor, her face grey, and savage welts and bruises covering her neck. In the opposite corner sat a man who he assumed was either her partner or her brother. He was slumped in a chair, blood pouring out of what looked like razor slashes across his throat and wrists. The cuts were still dripping. He was the one who'd snapped, Mark assumed. Looked like he'd taken his sudden aggression out on the woman, then killed himself in guilt and shame – what a pointless waste of lives.

But there was no time for sentimentality. He began searching for food, looking in the same hiding places he used in the room across the landing, and found a few scraps, nothing much, but it was better than going back empty-handed. At least he'd be able to—

A piercing scream cut through the uneasy silence and he knew immediately that it was coming from room 33. He grabbed the food, tripped over the outstretched legs of the dead woman and ran. He was horribly afraid he already knew what was happening; he could hear her. She was loose.

Mark reached for the door and pushed it open at the exact same moment Gurmit Singh pulled it open from the other side. He sprinted into the room, dragging Singh back inside, and kicked the door shut behind him. He couldn't risk Singh getting out and telling anyone what they were keeping in here – not that they'd be able to understand him, but it was still too great a risk. Kate's mother was screaming: a constant, ear-piercing wail of absolute terror.

The kid was on the bed, naked but for a dirty grey vest. Though her wrists were still bound together with a plastic tie, her legs were free, and her tiny hands were wrapped around Kate's father's throat and she was repeatedly yanking his head up then slamming him back against the wooden headboard. Kate and Lizzie both tried to pull her off the old man but she refused to let go, her claw-like fingers digging into his skin and holding on with a vice-like grip. Mark pushed them both aside and wrapped his arms around the little Hater's waist. He backed away from the bed, dragging both the girl and the old man with him until Lizzie was able to prise her daughter's fingers off his scrawny neck. He fell back onto the mattress. His wife was still screeching, her eyes screwed up tight, and Mark badly wanted to hold a pillow over her face until she shut up . . .

'For God's sake shut her up! And what the hell happened?' he asked, grunting in effort as he struggled to hold onto Ellis. He wrapped his arms tighter around her chest, trying to restrict her movement, but she leant her head forward and bit down into his forearm, getting a mouthful of the sleeve of his thick jacket. 'Where's her bloody gag gone?'

Before anyone could answer, Ellis jerked her head back again, cracking against Mark's chin, and he bit down hard on his tongue. He yelped with pain, but didn't let go of the little monster. Though less than half his size, she continued to wriggle relentlessly and with incredible ferocity, refusing to give up. Mark was absolutely certain that if her hands had not been tied, several – if not all – of the people in the hotel room would almost certainly be dead by now. He shuddered.

Ellis made another desperate bid for freedom, arching her back then relaxing, doing it again, this time kicking her feet back, catching Mark full in the balls. She managed to wedge her foot against the nearest wall and pushed, and the sudden movement caught him by surprise and sent him reeling backwards. There was a sickening thud as he slammed against the opposite wall and he lost his grip. Ellis squirmed away from him and raced back towards the pensioners in the bed, but this time Kate was waiting for her and smashed her across the face with a heavy telephone directory. Stunned, Ellis dropped to her knees.

'Don't!' Lizzie shouted, running towards her daughter as Kate stood over her, ready to strike her again. She barged Kate out of the way, crouched down and thumped a hypodermic needle into Ellis' bare thigh. Ellis yelped with sudden pain and ignoring the needle still stuck in her skin, she spun around and lashed out at her mother with her bound hands. Her jagged nails tore into her mother's skin and ripped down it, leaving three parallel lines of welling blood.

And then her hands fell away. Eyes glazed, she tried to stand up again. She took two steps forward then fell and hit the grimy carpet face first. She tried to pick herself up again but she was out cold before she'd lifted her head.

The room fell silent, even Kate's parents becoming quiet, her mother in shock and her father concussed. Gurmit Singh, who'd been cowering against the door with his hands over his head, stood up and reached for the handle.

Mark also stood, the throbbing pain in his bollocks beginning to subside, and shouted at him, 'You open that door and go out there and you won't get back in again. Your choice.'

Singh looked at him. Mark didn't know for sure whether or not he understood, but he was deeply relieved when he hesitated with his hand on the latch, then stopped and trudged slowly back to the armchair he'd claimed as his own.

He stepped over Ellis' inert body and pointed down at her. 'Evil,' he hissed. He jabbed his finger at the door. 'Nasty bitch! Get gone! Not here!'

While Kate was busy dealing with her catatonic parents, Mark held Ellis still as Lizzie lashed her legs together with a length of nylon washing-line, then gagged her again. She rubbed antiseptic cream from an almost empty tube on the countless sores and abrasions which covered her skin, caused by weeks of struggling against her binds.

'What the hell happened?'

Lizzie put down the tube and wiped away her tears. She was obviously trying to stay in control. 'I'm running out of pills,' she admitted. 'I've been giving her half-doses. I was just trying to clean her up. I thought she was out cold, but she must have just been asleep, or maybe she was trying to trick me, or—'

She stopped speaking and began to sob as she started stroking her daughter's greasy, tangled hair. She shuffled back as Mark dragged Ellis into the bathroom and chained her to the base of the sink pedestal.

'How many of those shots have you got left?' he asked.

'That was the last one.'

'And the pills?' He backed out of the bathroom and shut the door.

Lizzie didn't answer until it was fully closed and her daughter had disappeared from view. 'A week at the most.'

'Jesus . . .'

'What am I going to do, Mark?'

'That thing has to go,' Kate interrupted, shouting from across the room and pointing accusingly at the bathroom door. 'Get it out of here, because if you two don't, I will.'

Mark walked over to her and reached out to put his arms around her, but she pulled away. She leant against the wall and slid down it, cradling her distended belly.

'That *thing*,' Lizzie sobbed, 'is my daughter!'

'She *was* your daughter,' Kate quickly replied. 'Christ knows what she is now. She's more animal than human.'

'I know that, but what am I supposed to do?' Lizzie asked, sitting on the floor opposite and holding her head in her hands. 'You tell me what I'm supposed to do?'

'Just get rid of her. She's one of *them*, Lizzie: she's a *Hater*. She won't stop fighting until she's killed us all—'

'I know, but—'

'But you don't, do you? You *don't* know! She killed your boys – how can you even stand to be anywhere near her when she took your sons from you?'

'I can't,' she whispered, pulling her knees up to her chest and bowing her head, ashamed by her own admission. 'I don't want her here either, but I don't know what else I can do. I'm her mother, and that has to count for something, doesn't it?'

'You could turn her over to the military.'

'You know I can't. We've been through this. As soon as they've got her they'll put a bullet in her head.'

'So?'

'I can't let that happen,' she snapped, anger suddenly evident in her increasingly desperate voice. 'You're right, Katie, I should never have brought her here, but what else could I have done? If I just let her go now, she'll start killing, and they'll hunt her down. Even if I could get her out of the city she wouldn't survive. She won't be able to find food or keep warm or look after herself or—'

'Tough. We should just do it.'

'How would we get her through the crowds?' Mark asked, trying hard to remain practical and focused, not letting the fraught emotions cloud the situation.

'Pump her full of drugs, then. Give her everything you've got left. Kill her, for Christ's sake.'

'Katie—' Mark began to protest.

'I can't hurt her,' Lizzie sobbed, 'she's my daughter, my own flesh and blood – regardless of what she's done or what she might do, I still have to protect her.'

30

'Are you McCoyne?'

I sit up quick. Eyes are blurred – where am I? No chains, dull grey light . . . I look around until I can make sense of my surroundings. It's one of the upstairs rooms in the social club. I found these cushions on a sofa downstairs and—

'Are you McCoyne?' the voice asks again from somewhere behind me.

Neck's stiff. I look back over my shoulder and see a figure standing in the open doorway. 'Yeah, what's the problem?'

'No problem. Come with me.'

He turns and disappears and I've got no choice but to follow. The building is cold and I jog across the landing to catch up with him. I recognise him now. His name's Craven. Julia introduced me to him yesterday. I think he's her right-hand man.

We enter the largest upstairs room. Julia and another man are sleeping here. Craven gestures for me to sit down next to him at a table in the corner and he fires up a laptop. I realise I saw him using it when I first arrived.

'Have we got power here?' I ask, noticing that there's a power cable connected to the back of the computer. Dumb question.

'Sort of,' he answers. He sounds as tired as I feel. 'There's electricity a few streets away. We've just run a lead here to keep the laptop going.'

'What, an extension lead?'

He looks at me, dumfounded. 'Yes, a fucking extension lead.' He shakes his head and turns his attention to the laptop. I watch as he logs onto some kind of central database. Is this

235

the same system that Mallon was talking about? My know-ledge of this kind of thing is limited and I don't want to piss him off any more than I already have by asking him how the hell he can connect to anything from here, or even what is there left to connect to? There are all kinds of things hanging out of the back of the machine – wires running into small black boxes and the like – and I guess the secret's there, somewhere.

My mind wanders as I watch him working. I stop thinking about what it is he's doing and instead I just look at the bright display and listen to the sound of the keyboard clicking as he types. I used to hear that noise all day, every day at work. It takes me back . . .

'Sorry about the early wake-up call,' he mumbles, still con-centrating on the screen. 'Access to the system's intermittent so we have to make the most of it when we can. They're usually running automatic maintenance at this time of day so the security's easier to bypass . . .' His words fade away as the screen changes and he concentrates on entering more details.

'There . . . got it.'

'Got what?'

He slides the laptop over to me.

'We're in. Enter your details.'

'What details?'

'Your name, date of birth, last known postcode.'

I start jabbing at the keyboard with two fingers. It's months since I typed anything.

'Wait,' he says. 'Danny short for Daniel?'

'Yes.'

'Put your full name in.'

I do as he says.

'What's all this about? What are we doing?' I ask.

'Killing you,' he replies without a hint of sarcasm.

'Killing me?'

'Thing about this war,' he says as he takes the laptop back again, 'is that it's made everybody's priorities change. Every-one's worried about their physical safety, and some of the things which used to matter now get forgotten about or overlooked. This is a prime example. This is just about the only national system that's still running outside of defence, and anyone with half a brain can hack into it and make alterations.'

'But what exactly is it you're doing?'

'Is that you?' he asks, angling the screen back towards me.

I scan the details. 'Yes, that's me.'

'Right,' he continues, working his way through various menus and submenus. 'Ah good, you're dead already!'

'What?'

'They've got you down as being dead. Tell me, did you ever have one of those neck tests or a mouth swab?'

'Yes, why?'

'Because that's where most of this information comes from. They used it as kind of a census. They tried to test pretty much everyone when everything first kicked off. It's a "who's what", rather than a "who's who", if you get my meaning.'

'Sort of. Anyway, I'm not dead!'

'According to this you are.' He clicks a button and scans another screen. 'Hunter's Cross. Ring any bells?'

'Doesn't mean anything to me.'

'It's a gas chamber. They've got you down as being killed there.'

'I ended up inside one of those places, but I got out when it was attacked.'

'There you go, that explains it. They probably marked you off as being dead when they sent you down. Close shave, eh?'

'Too fucking close!'

'That's it then,' he says, starting to close up the laptop. 'You can go back to sleep now.'

'Wait a second,' I say quickly, putting my hand out and stopping him from closing it. 'Can I—?'

He seems to immediately know what I want. He's probably done this for plenty of other people before me. 'Be quick,' he whispers. 'If Julia catches me letting you do this she'll have my bollocks.'

My hands are suddenly shaking with nerves. I look down my details on the screen, but there's nothing on there that I didn't already know (apart from the fact that, apparently, I'm dead.)

'How do I—?'

'Looking for family?'

'Yes, my daughter.'

'Start there,' he says, pointing at the bottom of the screen. I click on a button marked 'other people listed at this address'. There's a pause of several seconds, then a blank screen is returned. My heart sinks.

'How old was she?'

'Five.'

'Either she hasn't been listed or she's listed elsewhere. Try searching on her name.'

I enter Ellis' details and press search. Still nothing.

'Was she with anyone?'

'Her mother and brothers.'

'Search for them then.'

I try Elizabeth McCoyne – no match. In desperation I try my son Edward. He's listed at an address I don't recognise, as is his brother. They're both listed as dead and, just for a second, I feel a sharp pang of pain. It quickly fades when Craven starts making noises.

'Come on,' he whispers, 'that's enough. Julia will have a fucking fit.'

'Wait a second,' I say quickly, desperate not to let go of the computer yet.

'Now!'

'Just one more—' I turn back to the computer and cover the keyboard as I type. I search for Elizabeth Parker, suddenly remembering that Lizzie only took on my name informally, for the sake of the kids. She always used her given name on official forms. I stare at a blank screen and frantically flashing cursor. Craven looks over his shoulder. The faster I need a result, the slower this system seems to get.

'Come on . . .' he says, sounding agitated.

It finally returns a screen full of results – eight Elizabeth Parkers are listed. I scroll down to the right date of birth and click on Lizzie's entry. She's listed at a hotel and I quickly memorise the address. The Prince Hotel on Arley Street – I think I know it. Chancing my luck, I click the 'other people listed at this address' button once more and just manage to scan down the first part of a huge list of names when Craven wrestles the laptop away from me and slams the lid down. I think I saw Mark Tillotsen – he's one of my cousins – but there was no sign of Ellis.

I get up and turn around. Julia is standing behind me.

'Whoever it was,' she warns, 'forget them.'

'm scavenging downstairs for food, hunting through deserted kitchens and bars that have already been ransacked countless times before, hoping to find an overlooked stash of supplies to supplement the crappy rations I've had since I got here. At the back of a counter, tucked away behind a broken cash register, I find three small packets of peanuts. I swallow the contents of the first in a single mouthful, then do the same with the second. I shove the third into my trouser pocket for later. There's precious little time to think about food these days, but when I do get to eat I realise just how much I've missed it. Maybe one day I'll get to sit down to a proper meal again – if I survive the next couple of days that is.

There's a half-open door behind the bar I hadn't noticed before. I lean inside.

'Who the hell's that?'

I back out of the low-lit storeroom quickly, startled by the voice from the darkness. The door lets in a little light and I can see someone in the corner, sitting wedged between two piles of empty boxes. 'Sorry, I . . .'

The man looks up and I recognise him from last night. His name's Parsons. 'Doesn't matter, mate.'

I've only been awake for a couple of hours, but already the drawn-out tedium of waiting to fight is getting to me. The idea of a conversation, any sort of distraction, is appealing. 'What you doing in here?'

'Keeping out of the way.'

'Why? You pissed Julia off or something?'

'Show me someone who hasn't.'

I know what he means. Being around Julia reminds me of

working for Tina Murray, my sour old bitch of a supervisor back at the PFP. Wonder what happened to her?

Parsons gestures for me to come closer. I do as he says, then slide down the wall and sit next to him. It's stiflingly hot in the social club this morning now the sun's up, but the dark store-room is refreshingly cool.

'So are you ready for this?' I ask. 'Ready to go out there and start fighting?'

''Course I am,' he answers, almost too quickly. 'Can't wait to start killing again. Can't wait to see them panic when we get given the word.'

There's an awkward silence.

'You don't sound convinced.'

The silence continues as he thinks about what I just said. Then, 'I'm not. I mean, don't get me wrong, I know what's got to be done and I know this is probably the only way to make it happen. It's just that . . .'

'You don't want to die?'

'Exactly.'

'Me neither,' I admit. 'Who does?'

'No one in their right mind. They're all talking about this battle like it's a holy war or something and it's doing my head in. I don't want to be stuck in the middle of the city when they level the place like they did London.'

'But it's got to be done. You can't deny that.'

'I know . . . I'm just nervous, you know?' he admits, keeping his voice low. 'I can't stand all this hanging around. You know what it's like when you know you've got to fight, you just want to get on and do it.'

He's right. It's a relief to find someone else who's willing to speak candidly about how they're feeling. Almost everyone else is too busy spouting propaganda and bullshit bravado to dare admit that they're apprehensive about what's coming. They talk like I imagine Brutes think – focused on the kill at all costs.

'You been here long?' I ask.

'Got here about half a day before you.'

'And were you at that convent place with Sahota?'

He nods his head. 'We've all been through that. Quite the eye-opener, eh?' Parsons stares into space, thinking hard. I sense there's more he wants to say, but he's not sure whether he should speak. Perhaps he thinks I'm testing his dedication to the cause?

I study his tired face. He looks about ten years older than me, and I wonder what it is we have in common that made us both suitable fodder for Sahota's organisation.

'So did you believe any of it?'

'What?'

'All that stuff the Unchanged were spouting at Sahota's place? Breaking the cycle and all that crap?'

I don't answer immediately. Can I trust this man? Now I'm wondering if he's the one testing my allegiance.

'Some of it,' I answer, being deliberately vague. 'What about you?'

'I agree with most of it, up to a point. What Sahota said scared me more, though. I get the feeling they're just using us as—'

He stops suddenly.

'Problem?'

'Listen!'

I quickly get up and go back out into the bar. Someone's banging on the outside of the fire exit I entered through yesterday. Apart from me and Parsons there's no one else down here, and I realise it's down to me to confront whoever's out there. I move quickly across the room, grabbing a broken pool cue to use as a weapon, then stand by the door and wait. The hammering continues. The door's solid – no way of knowing who's out there without opening it up.

'Do it,' Parsons hisses from across the room. Cowardly fucker, why don't you come over here and open it? Rather than argue, I take a deep breath, tighten my grip on my pool cue bludgeon, then open the door. There's a teenage girl standing in front of me, looking as tense and unsure as I did when I first arrived here. She only looks about fifteen. She's one of us.

'I'm looking for Julia Chapman,' she says, her voice surprisingly confident and strong.

'Who is?' I ask, remembering back to my own arrival here.

'My name's Sophie Wilson,' she answers, handling the situation far better than I did, 'and I've got a message for her from Sahota.'

I let her in, quickly checking around the back of the building to make sure she hasn't been followed before shutting and barring the fire exit.

I lead her through the eerily quiet building, Parsons following us at a cautious distance. I take her upstairs to where I last left Julia talking to Craven, but she's not there. He points up at the ceiling. I head up to the roof, covering my eyes at the sudden brightness. The sun is huge in the clear sky high above us. Julia's sitting in one of the deckchairs under the tarpaulin, looking into the city through a pair of binoculars. She lowers them when she hears us approach.

'This is—' I start to say.

'You're Julia?' Sophie interrupts me, and when she nods, goes on, 'I'm Sophie Wilson, and I've got a message for you from Sahota. He said to tell you that I'm the last one.'

'And did he say anything else?'

'Yeah, he said to say: Town Hall, south side. Six a.m. Five others.'

Julia looks at her for a second, absorbing what she's been told. 'Thanks, Sophie. I suggest you get some rest while you can. There might still be some food left downstairs. Ask one of the others and they'll show you.'

Sophie heads back down without question, leaving me with Julia. Parsons hovers behind us nervously.

'What did her message mean?' I ask, feeling like I'm the only one who's not in the know.

'It means there's as many of us here as there's ever gonna be. It means it's time.'

I look straight ahead, determined not to let her see how nervous I'm suddenly feeling.

'South side?'

'South side of the Town Hall is where he wants us to base ourselves,' she answers, looking through the binoculars again. 'It's where I thought he'd want us to be, close enough to the military to cause them problems, far enough out not to be suspicious.'

'And five others? What was that all about?'

'That means five other groups like ours. That's not so good. We were hoping for double that – but it should still be enough, though.'

'And where will they be?'

'I don't know and I don't care. All I know and all you need to know is that we'll go where we're told to and cause fucking chaos when the time's right. Between six groups of us, their military won't know which way to turn. The panic will spread fast and, before you know it, the whole city will be fighting. And if we do it right, before long there won't be a city left.'

'There won't be anything left,' Parsons mumbles under his breath.

I sit down on the edge of the roof and stare into the distance. The Unchanged camp looks like a massive, dirty black machine from here. Clouds of grey smoke billow up from between buildings like belching exhaust fumes. Helicopters buzz through the air like flies around a corpse. There's no point denying it: being this close to the enemy makes me want to march in there and start killing – or it would if I didn't feel the odds were stacked against us. It's probably just me; maybe I should have more faith? But like I keep telling myself, I don't want to die.

'Just imagine it,' Julia says wistfully, looking deep into the distance, 'imagine when we start to fight and they start to run, when they panic and try to get away from us and run straight into the next battle . . . Christ, it'll be beautiful! It won't take much, you know, just the minimum of coordination from us will be enough to start it off and they'll do the rest themselves. There'll be a chain reaction, and we'll be able to sit back and watch them killing each other.'

I know I should keep my mouth shut, but I can't. 'Except we won't, will we?'

'Won't what?'

'Once we're in there, there's no way back out.'

'That doesn't matter. All that's important is wiping out the enemy.'

'But at what cost?'

'We can't co-exist, end of story. The cost is irrelevant.'

I know I'm making things worse for myself but I can't help it. 'What good is winning if you're dead? What did they used to call that, a Pyrrhic victory?'

'A what?' Parsons asks.

'A Pyrrhic victory.' Julia sighs. 'It's when you win the battle, but the end result leaves you fucked too.'

'Great,' he grunts.

'You're wrong,' she says to me, putting down the binoculars and standing up, 'and you need to stop talking like that.'

'How am I wrong? Once we're in the city, there's very little chance of any of us getting out alive, is there?'

'It's a sacrifice we have to make.'

'And where exactly will your great mate Sahota be while all of this is going on? Watching from his office? When we're gone, who's going to be left – just kids and Brutes?'

She shakes her head. 'You come up with an alternative and I'll listen. Do you want the Unchanged to survive?'

'Of course not, but—'

'But what?'

'But there's got to be a better way.'

'If there was, don't you think someone like Sahota would have come up with it by now? If there was any alternative, don't you think we'd have tried it? None of us wants to die—'

'My point exactly.'

'—but if your death results in the death of hundreds of the enemy, thousands even, then it has to be worth it, doesn't it?'

I don't bother to respond. She's bought into this completely, like a brainwashed old-school terrorist about to embark on a jihad. Even if my death were to result in tens of thousands of Unchanged being killed, I still don't want it to happen. And what about Ellis? I'd rather fight steadily and have this war drag on for years than sacrifice myself today. I can't stand the thought of not seeing her again.

Julia's not going to let this go.

'You need to focus on what's coming,' she says, a sneering, threatening tone in her voice. 'Craven said you were looking up information about your family earlier. Forget them, who-ever and whatever they were. Your only allegiance now is to us, and nothing else matters apart from what we do when we get back into the city.'

She stares into my face then walks towards the stepladder. She stops and turns before she disappears down. 'If you screw up when we're in there,' she warns, 'then so help me, I'll kill you myself. This is too important for an idiot like you to fuck up.'

I watch her go, gritting my teeth. Parsons quietly takes her place in the now-empty deckchair. I forgot he was here.

'Thanks for the support.'

'I'm with you, mate,' he says, shielding his eyes from the sun, 'but I've got enough sense to know when to keep my mouth shut.'

32

Heavy cloud filled the sky during the late afternoon and early evening. As the light fell we were called into the main upstairs function room and weapons were handed out. I was given a gun, a few rounds of ammo and several grenades, but I don't think I'll use them. More to the point, I don't know *how* to use them, even though Julia and one of the others tried to show us. I'll stick to my blades.

Since this war began I've fought alongside hundreds of men and woman, maybe even thousands. Who they were and what they were capable of didn't seem to matter until now. But standing in the bizarre surroundings of the rundown social club, I looked at the ten other fighters heading into town with me and tried to imagine how each of them would fight, how they'd kill. The two women – Julia and Sophie – appeared totally unfazed, ready to face anything, and most of the men were similarly focused. Only Parsons and a guy called Harvey looked as nervous and agitated as I felt. Harvey is a huge, lumbering hulk of a man. He wears glasses with ridiculously thick lenses and because he suffers from acute asthma he sounds like Darth Vader. He also has appalling halitosis – you can smell him and hear him long before you see him coming. Poor bastard. He comes across as being a bit backward and I wonder how much of what's happening he truly understands. Still, he must have something between his ears if they reckon he'll be able to keep control of himself once he's out in the city surrounded by hundreds of Unchanged. I'm not convinced myself.

We leave the social club well before three a.m., splitting into four pairs and one group of three, staggering our departures and each taking a different, pre-arranged route to the rendez-vous point at the Town Hall. I'm with Craven, the computer guy, and we follow the towpath alongside a canal which cuts through what used to be a busy residential area. This place used to be a vibrant, noisy suburb of the city. The nearby university caused the local population to swell during term times and the narrow streets were full of cheap shops, restaurants, cafés, bars and pubs. Everywhere is silent now and the only resident I can see is floating face down in the murky canal.

We've been walking for almost an hour, but the towpath has taken us almost all the way into the very centre of the city. We reach a steep flight of steps leading up to the street and as we climb them, our closeness to the heart of town becomes apparent. We emerge in the middle of a lifeless crowd of terrified Unchanged. No one even looks at us as we pass through. Most of them just stare into space, waiting. I expected this to be infinitely harder, but somehow I'm now able to swallow down my emotions, to hold the Hate, not start killing them because I know they'll be dead before long anyway. Seeing Sahota's plan realised will result in many more deaths than I could ever cause by myself. If everything happens as predicted, the city will have fallen by this time tomorrow. Maybe I can bear to be beside them because, for the first time in as long as I can remember, the Unchanged are not my only focus. I have another agenda. Since we left the social club all I've been able to think about is getting deeper into town, giving Craven the slip and heading for the Prince Hotel. I'll search for Lizzie and then, when I've made her tell me where she last saw Ellis, I'll use the chaos as cover and try to get away.

'Down here,' Craven says, changing direction and leading me along a tight passageway filled with people. I look into their vacant faces, and I feel nothing but contempt for them. They remind me of what I used to be before the Hate: beaten, wretched, resigned. They cower in the shadows, waiting for a salvation which is never going to come. The Hate has stripped away their identities and their purpose. They are empty, just waiting for death to come along and end their misery. Standing here, ankle-deep in this scum, there's a part of me that wants to stay and see Sahota's plan fully realised. I do want to watch these people burn.

The road we're now following runs along the edge of a military enclosure. Everything looks very different tonight, but I'm sure this used to be a council depot. Tall railings surround the place and there's a massive concentration of soldiers at the gates. The enclosure is comparatively well lit, thumping petrol-driven generators powering floodlights. The number of refugees under our feet here is greater too, attracted like moths to the light and noise. Craven and I weave through the milling masses with our heads held high, without a fucking care, and no one even gives us a second glance.

'I can see why Sahota picked this spot,' I say quietly as we begin a slow descent down the sloping main street which leads to the Town Hall. Even now it's still an impressive building: a huge, mock-Grecian hall complete with ornate carvings and rows of huge white stone columns. The civic square around it is seething with people, most of them camped out on the cold, hard ground, wrapped up in coats and blankets, their misery illuminated by more well-spaced lights. There are signs that there used to be something like a soup kitchen operating from here – abandoned tables, empty gas cylinders and empty tins of food rolling around in the suddenly vicious wind.

'It's perfect,' Craven agrees. 'There are thousands of them here, and they're all at breaking point. They probably came here looking for food and shelter and got neither, so they just dropped where they were standing and gave up. They'll riot in a heartbeat once we start on them.'

I look around as we pick our way through the sprawled masses. He's right. There's an unspoken tension in the air here, much more fractious and intense than any I've felt before. There's an uncomfortable stand-off between civilians and the military too. I don't know which side is more wary of the other. Maybe that's the real reason why the soldiers are here in such numbers.

As we pass a large stone statue its distinctive dark outline strikes a sudden chord. For a second I remember this place as it used to be. On the rare occasions I'd get a proper lunch break from work, I'd sometimes walk here to get away from the office and everyone in it. Once or twice I met Lizzie here, back before the kids were born—

'There's Sophie,' Craven says, nudging me in the ribs with his elbow. She's standing on the opposite side of the square. 'Go find yourself a spot.'

We separate as planned. Each of us will disappear into the crowd until the time to attack comes. It'll look less suspicious if we're all spread out – not that it matters; when the fighting starts no one will care who threw the first punch or fired the first shot. I find a narrow gap midway along a low wall, between two sleeping refugees, where I stop and wait.

There's a still-functioning clock on the side of the Town Hall, just visible from where I'm standing. It's a little after four, so less than two hours to go. The Prince Hotel is no more than a mile from here. I'll wait for a little while before I make my move. If I go off too fast there's a chance I'll be seen and followed.

Trying not to make it too obvious, I look around for the others. Craven and Sophie I've already seen. I see Parsons on my right, and another man whose name I don't know sitting perched on the plinth of the statue in the centre of the square. Harvey is leaning up against the same wall as me, a little further along. His size makes him easy to pick out in the crowd.

And there's Julia, sitting right in front of me. There's just a handful of people between us. I catch her eye and, stupidly, I almost acknowledge her. She has a dirty blanket draped over her head, hiding all but her eyes. Bitch is staring straight at me, watching my every move.

250

33

It's been pissing down with rain for the last twenty minutes. There's no shelter here and I, like everyone else, am soaked to the skin and freezing cold. I've been crouching down beside the wall trying to keep myself covered, but the rainwater's running down the gentle slope of the packed square and forming deep puddles around my feet. The conditions don't bother me – I'm surrounded by Unchanged and getting ready for what amounts to a suicide attack; a little water is the least of my problems – but when other people start to move around me I know I need to go with them, to keep up the illusion. I follow two of them, stepping over the person immediately to my left who hasn't moved in as long as I've been here. Someone grabs my arm and I know who it is before I turn around. I can hear him breathing.

'Is this it?' Harvey asks, his voice low but still too loud. 'Is it time?'

I keep my voice down. 'Not yet, too soon. I'm just getting out of the rainwater.'

I try to move but he keeps hold of me.

'Where you going?'

'Somewhere drier.'

'I'll come.'

'No, it's better if we split up. If people see us together they'll—'

'Doesn't matter. Not long now.'

'I know, but—' I shut up when the deafening rumble of a sudden, booming explosion fills the air. There's a moment of silent shock in the square as everyone is taken by surprise. It lasts no longer than a second, then all hell breaks loose around me.

The mass of people who've been huddled on the ground begin to get up and start scrambling for cover. Is this it? Has the signal to fight been given early? I look around but apart from Harvey there's no one I recognise anywhere close in the mass of refugees suddenly crisscrossing all around me.

My arm is grabbed again. 'It's not time,' Julia yells in my ear, shouting to make herself heard over the sudden noise filling the square, 'don't fight! This isn't it – get up towards the statue.'

As I do as she says, I can sense her following my every step. I look up and see that a surprising number of the people in the crowd ahead have now stopped and are standing still, looking back in the direction from which I've just come. Other panicking refugees continue to weave around them.

One of our men is already standing on the statue. He sees us coming and beckons us closer. He points out into the distance. 'Some dumb fucker's got their timings wrong.'

I'm still being shunted from every angle, but I manage to pull myself up next to him and look back. Behind the Town Hall I can see a high-rise office block is on fire. There's a necklace of fierce flame burning about two-thirds of the way up the side of the building, and it's taking hold with incredible speed. I can see people in the windows above the flames, illuminated by what's happening below them. Some have started to jump, choosing instant death when they hit the ground over waiting for the fire and smoke to get them.

'This isn't right,' I say, thinking out loud, trying to shield my face from the driving rain.

'What isn't?' the man next to me asks as he reaches into the pockets of his jacket for his weapons.

'Why there? If you want to cause panic at ground level, why start fighting halfway up a tower block?'

'It wasn't us,' Craven shouts, wading through the masses to get to us.

'How do you know?'

'It's a helicopter – you can see it sticking out of the side of the building. It looks like it was just an accident. You know, I guess it was only a matter of time – you can't look up anywhere in this place without seeing something in the air, but everything's so dark now that buildings like that must be pretty hard to make out. In this weather it's even worse. It looks like the idiot pilot must have flown straight into it.'

Julia plucks Harvey from the crowd and pulls the five of us closer together, no longer concerned with trying to remain invisible. The other people around us couldn't give a damn who we are or what we're doing. I doubt most of them even notice us.

'We have to keep waiting,' she says. 'This is only going to help us.'

'We should do it now,' Craven argues, 'capitalise on it. Sahota wanted more groups—'

'We wait,' Julia repeats. She's had her orders and she's sticking to them.

I stare at the crash for a few seconds longer, watching the flames crawling and licking up the sides of the high-rise, swallowing the tail of the helicopter. The fire moves with incredible speed, eating up the higher floors of the block in massive gulps. The destruction is beautiful, almost hypnotic . . .

But then something happening down here at ground level tears my attention away from the building: people are starting to flood into the already packed square. Like a dam that's burst its banks, a deluge of desperate refugees is suddenly washing towards us. They've been forced out of their flimsy shelters and squalid refuges around the base of the burning building. Some are coughing violently, their lungs filled with acrid smoke and dust; others are injured, burnt, or bruised and cut by falling debris. And a lot are just panicking, following the flow, and their fear and confusion is invigorating. Experiencing their terror this close makes me feel superior, *strong*: they're running blind from the immediately perceived danger without giving a second's thought to what they might be running towards.

Suddenly the air is filled with more thunderous noise: another explosion – and this time it's coming from the opposite direction and I'm sure this has to be one of ours. A swollen balloon of flame billows up in the darkness about half a mile from here. It disappears quickly, but its after-effects remain. Surely another surge of refugees will start moving this way and they'll hit the others head-on . . .

'That's enough,' Craven says. 'Come on, Julia, let's just do it. We won't gain anything from waiting.'

They can do what the fuck they like. I'm going. This is my last chance to find Lizzie before all hell breaks loose and I'm going to take it. I climb down off the statue and, leaving Craven and Julia arguing, I start to move back through the crowd. The sudden bewilderment and panic of the Unchanged makes it possible for me to ignore them and resist fighting. I know these people will be dead soon – I don't have to kill them myself. I glance up at the clock on the side of the Town Hall as I'm swallowed up by the masses. Quarter to five. If Julia has her way I've still got an hour. Or have I? Has the fuse already been lit?

The constant movement and heavy rain is disorientating and I'm struggling to get my bearings. I push my way deeper into the hordes of Unchanged and I'm almost at the furthest edge of the civic square when the burnt-out ruin of a nightclub looms up in front of me and I realise I'm moving in the wrong direction. People are trying to force their way in both directions through an alleyway at the side of the ruined building, and none of them making any progress. I turn around and walk straight into Parsons. He stands in front of me and blocks my way, looking as desperate and lost as one of the Unchanged. He has a grenade in his hand.

'Is this it, McCoyne?'

'No,' I tell him, 'not yet. Julia says we should—'

'I think it's time.'

'Not yet,' I say again, shouting to make myself heard. 'She's up there by the statue. Go and speak to her. See what she says before you—'

'It must be time,' he shouts over the rain. 'I can't stand all this waiting—'

'Parsons, don't! It was just a helicopter crash. And the other explosion—'

He doesn't say anything else, but just pulls the pin from his grenade. A sudden surge from the crowd shunts him sideways and I try to move back as he manages to get his balance and stand straight again.

'Throw the fucking thing!' I shout, gesturing wildly.

Disorientated, wracked with nerves, Parsons just looks at me. I shove him hard in the gut, sending him tripping down the slope, and he starts colliding with refugees, knocking them over like bowling pins. He topples back and is gone, immediately snatched from view by the hordes.

I put my shoulder down and run as fast as I can in the opposite direction, forcing my way through the masses. I trip over a body on the ground and stumble forward, barely managing to stay upright. Instinctively, I reach out and grab hold of someone, another startled refugee, using him to haul myself back up and keep moving forward. He tries to grapple me down, but I push him out of the way, knowing that in seconds I'll be the least of his worries. This one has more fight in him than most of them and he manages to cling on to the corner of my coat. I yank it from his grip and duck to one side when he takes a swing at me. I'm trying to focus on getting away. I shove him down, praying that I won't be able to—

For a fraction of a second the world is filled with brilliant white light and a noise so loud I think my head's going to burst. I'm thrown down by the force of the explosion behind me and for a moment all I can do lie there, sandwiched between fallen Unchanged. I pull myself to my feet and when I look back I can see a space in the crowd and a dark, shallow pit where, just seconds ago, countless people were crammed together. Now there's nothing, just smouldering debris. I turn and run while the shock quickly fades and panic begins to fill the air.

People are running in every direction, trying to get away from the square, and I allow myself to be carried along with them, using their bulk as camouflage. For a moment I smile: none of them know who or what I am, and none of them care. Away from Julia and the others I'm suddenly as irrelevant and unimportant as everyone else, and the anonymity is welcome and reassuring. Running shoulder to shoulder with the enemy, I realise that desperate need to kill these people that I've felt since the Change has all but disappeared. Maybe it's because these people are all dead anyway?

There's less than an hour to go now until Sahota's moment of glory, but I don't think the city will last that long. A phalanx of helicopters is thundering overhead, and one of them peels off and begins firing on some unseen target close to the burning high-rise, causing the crowd around me to start moving with even more panic and speed.

Above the heads of the stampeding masses I see something I think I recognise: the distinctive angular outline of a tall, recently built apartment block. As I run towards it there's another sudden detonation and the front of the building explodes outwards in a sudden swollen bulge of fire and heat. I turn away from the immediate blast and duck down as thousands of tiny, razor-sharp shards of glass begin raining down around me. Most of the crowd instinctively try to turn back and run the other way. Dumb fuckers.

I keep moving forward, knowing that the ground around the centre of the blast will be relatively clear now, with just the dead and dying to get through. I run past the burning remains of the building, zigzagging through the carnage, dodging chunks of concrete and twisted lumps of metal and flesh.

I look up: there are people trapped on the upper floors. A woman is shoved from a third-floor window and lands on the pavement just ahead of me, hitting the ground with a wet thud like rotten fruit. It's wonderful to see and part of me wishes I could find somewhere safe around here to sit and watch the whole city burn.

I'm back to shoving my way through the enemy masses again. I thump heads with another man and he pushes me away angrily, his eyes full of hate. Instinctively I reach for my knife, but I force myself to let it go, fighting against everything I believe in. The need to kill might have subsided, but the desire's still strong. I'm like a junkie who's been clean for years but who's now surrounded by an endless supply of their drug of choice. Once I start killing, will I be able to stop? If I lose control now all hope of finding Lizzie will be gone for ever, and although I don't want to have to face her again, without Lizzie there's no chance I'll ever know what happened to Ellis. This is my last chance.

I spot another momentary gap in the crowd, at the middle of a crossroads. This place used to be one of the busiest intersections in town, with backed-up queues of traffic all day, every day. I climb up onto the roof of an abandoned MPV – the kind of car I always wanted, me the family man – and look around me. I've been running in the right direction, but I think the Prince Hotel is still about half a mile further on. Apparently endless swarms of people are still trying to escape the carnage behind me, fighting with each other to make it through the madness. As more explosions suddenly light up the area around the Town Hall and the civic square behind me, the beauty and simplicity of Sahota's plan comes sharply into focus. Did Julia cause those last blasts, or Craven, or one of the others? Has she finally given the order to attack? If it's like this now, I think to myself, how bad will it be by six o'clock?

A helicopter crawls across the sky overhead, filling the air with thumping noise and momentarily illuminating me with its sweeping searchlight. I jump back down to the road and keep running.

34

Recognition and familiarity brings nerves, even fear. Not far now. The hotel's almost in view, and every step I take is bringing me closer to Lizzie, and to knowing what happened to my daughter. What if I'm too late? What if Ellis is lost, or dead? Suddenly turning tail and heading back to the Town Hall to fight to the death alongside the others feels like the easier option.

I take a shortcut through an eerily empty supermarket, in through the loading bay and out towards the smashed display windows, but before going outside again I stop and stand in the darkness, giving myself a moment to take stock of the chaos unfolding all around me. The behaviour of the Unchanged population is changing. Although there are some who are still clinging to the meagre protection of the shadows, desperate not to be seen, it looks like most have joined the growing exodus away from the centre of the city. They're moving as a single, snaking mass now, each following the person in front, no one consciously choosing the direction in which they run. Their sudden reliance on the safety of numbers yet again exposes the pathetic weakness and vulnerability of the Unchanged.

I move on alone: neither weak nor vulnerable.

I run along a narrow street, pausing to look around when I reach the Arley Road. I'm struggling to see anything through the hordes of people flooding down this major route – and then I spot it: the Prince Hotel is fifty metres or so further up the road, looking pretty much exactly as I remember, its imposing frontage just becoming visible in the dull first light of dawn.

The rain has finally stopped, leaving the damp air smelling

fresh and clean, all the dirt and decay temporarily washed away.

What the hell am I doing? I suddenly feel guilty and weak. I should be back by the Town Hall fighting with the others, so why am I all the way out here on my own? Logic says that after three months of this violence and unpredictability, Lizzie could be anywhere – Christ, she's probably *dead*. Craven told me the Unchanged computer system was inaccurate and easily manipulated. I saw it myself, because I'm sure as hell not dead – not yet, at any rate – so why have I put so much faith in what I saw on the computer screen?

I guess it's simple: it's because I've got nothing else. There's no alternative. This is my last chance and I can either take it or give up on Ellis for ever. I take my axe from my belt and a knife from inside my coat and I hold them ready. I feel detached from everything now. There's the Unchanged on one side, my people on the other and then, standing alone and wedged right between the lot of them, me.

I sprint away from the side of the road and charge deep into the river of people still flooding out of town. The first few stragglers I collide with are pushed away with hardly any effort, and it's not until I'm close to the centre of the road that I have to start killing to keep moving. It's the only option left now if I want to get through, but I know I'm doing it because it's the only way to keep moving, not because I actively want them dead.

I'm carried along with the flow of barely human flesh, so deep and so strong and fast-moving that I struggle to lift my arms. I manage to raise the axe and bring it thumping down between the shoulders of a man directly in front of me. I spin him around, the blade still buried in his back, then pull out the axe and kick him down. A woman behind is forced forward by the mass of people and when she trips over the body on the ground I hack at her too, slicing the axe deep into her neck. Two down, now, and even better: the piled-up corpses act like a rock in the middle of a stream, channelling the flow of refugees around me on either side.

I'm braced for their outraged reaction, but it doesn't come. These people have seen and experienced so much; all they're interested in is getting away, and screw everyone else. Another man trips over the bodies on the road and collides with me and I swing the axe around and hit him in the pelvis. As he falls away I'm suddenly standing in an unexpected bubble of space – but not for long as a tall, powerfully built man breaks ranks and hurls himself at me. He's much stronger than me and all I do is hold out my knife . . . and watch as the stupid bastard impales himself on the blade. Another one sees what's happened and rushes me, and now I think they're finally beginning to realise what I am.

I duck out of the way of his amateurish attack and instead he collides with a teenage girl. A bald man with wild eyes helps her up and out of the way, then turns on the other man and punches him in the gut.

I continue to move backwards, working my way across the road as, in my wake, more desperate, panicked fights break out. Whether they're trying to get away, trying to help each other or trying to find me, it doesn't matter, their reactions are all the same. They fight, and once they've started, they keep fighting. I'm forcing my way through the mob with relative ease, now, hacking and slicing only when I have to. All around me the Unchanged are turning on each other, and I'm quickly forgotten.

Breathless and bloody, I reach the front of the hotel. I cross the forecourt and climb the steps up to the door, forcing my way inside just as several people are forcing their way out. Christ, I feel weird – strangely invisible, and high on a euphoric mix of adrenalin and nerves. If I am feeling any fear, it's masked by the immense satisfaction, excitement and relief of finally having killed again. I hadn't realised how much I'd missed that buzz.

But as I disappear into the vast, dark building, a sudden

wave of terror hits me. *Lizzie might be here.* She might be standing next to me right now, for all I know, because I can hardly see anything. What was I thinking? How am I supposed to find her in here? Did I think I was just going to be able to walk up to the reception desk and ask for her room number?

As I scout around the ground floor, the full implications of my short-sighted lack of planning really hits home. This is a mistake. Time is running out. The city won't last much longer and my only remaining option is to check every bloody room. For half a second I consider turning around and just wading back out into the crowds to enjoy the killing for as long as I'm able – but then I think of Ellis again, and I force myself to stay calm, stay in control. I know I don't have any choice but to keep moving.

35

The ground floor of the hotel is deserted, and it's easy to see why. The carpet is soaked with water and there's a tide-mark on the wall about half a metre off the ground. The wallpaper is hanging off in strips and the whole place smells of rotting waste and untreated sewage. I thought there would be more people in here. I guess most of them were washed out with the floodwater that has obviously flowed through the building in the last couple of days. Others will have left when the fighting started. Am I too late – has Lizzie already gone? Was she ever here at all?

My feet squelching on the waterlogged carpet, I head upstairs. As I climb the long, straight flight of steps to the first floor I have to knife a fucker in the gut for trying to barge past me. He nearly sent me flying; now I watch as he goes rolling over and over until he lands in a bloody, groaning heap at the very bottom.

I start checking the rooms on the first floor. The first few are empty and I'm halfway down the landing when a door flies open and three terrified Unchanged men come sprinting out, carrying as many bags and boxes as they can manage between them. They can't see me over everything they're carrying and one of them knocks me to the ground. Instinctively I get up and start running after them, but it's too late and they're already gone. Doesn't matter. Have to concentrate. Have to focus. *Let them go.*

The next three doors are open and the rooms are empty. They're all foul, indescribably squalid, full of the residue of the refugees who've been forced to live here together for weeks on end. The carpets are covered with a layer of waste and abandoned belongings, so deep that I don't see the curled-up body of an elderly man until I feel the fingers of his outstretched hand crack under my boot.

Back out on the landing, I force myself to slow down. Need to try and apply some logic here. The hotel's emptying, so there's no point checking any of the vacant rooms. If the doors aren't locked, I decide, there's no one there.

I start hacking at the next locked door I find. I can already hear the bastards inside the room screaming with panic. I keep working, then shoulder-charge the door open when I've done enough damage to loosen the latch.

One of the occupants runs at me, brandishing a chair leg. I sidestep him, then shove him across the landing, sending him crashing into the wall opposite. There are three other Unchanged in the room, with a fourth trying to get out through an open window. The light's low, but I can see enough to know that I don't recognise any of them.

They're of no interest to me so I turn and head back out to the landing, pausing only to knife the fucker who comes back at me for a second go with the chair leg.

The lock on the door of the next room is broken, but it's held on a chain. It opens just far enough for me to see inside. No sign of Lizzie, but a grey-haired woman grabs hold of the door handle and pulls it shut, snatching it from my hands. Another room empties as I approach and this time I just press myself back against the wall and let two more sobbing Unchanged stumble past.

Almost all of the second floor is empty, and Lizzie's not in any of the rooms that are still occupied. In a room near the staircase on the third floor I find a small girl sitting alone in an armchair that dwarfs her tiny shape. In my haste and desperation I think for a second that it might be Ellis. It's dark, the dull dawn light just beginning to seep in through the cracks between the wooden boards which have been nailed across the window. It's only when I touch the girl and she slumps forward that I see it isn't Ellis, and it's only when she doesn't move again that I realise she's already dead, abandoned by whomever she was with.

The door to the last room on this floor is open slightly but it slams shut as I run towards it. I barge it open before they can get it locked. Three Unchanged women and a man begin shouting and screaming at me in a language I don't understand. Sounds like Polish or Russian or something . . . I turn and leave and one of them follows me back out into the corridor, still shouting. She grabs hold of my legs, pleading with me for help. I kick her off and keep moving.

Top floor. Running out of options.

There are more locked doors up here than I've got time for. I stop outside the first. I can hear voices inside so I start chopping at the lock with my axe. My arms are beginning to feel heavy, but the rotten wood splinters easily and the door flies open. Lizzie's not here and I move on. I can feel their relief when I turn my back and I hear them shoving furniture up against the door to seal themselves in as soon as they've slammed it shut.

The next two doors facing each other are both closed. I jump the sprawled-out body of a Chinese man and press myself up against the first of them. I can hear a man's voice ranting in Urdu or Punjabi or something, so I immediately turn my attention to the other and start chopping at the wood around the latch.

I stop for a second when I hear another deafening explosion outside and a flash of white light pierces the boards on the windows, illuminating everything like a strobe. It's impossible to gauge the distance, but that sounded close – too close. I can still feel the vibrations through my feet as I start chopping again. This door is more stubborn than the rest – it's newer than the others, probably recently replaced. I guess I'm not the first person to have to try and break into a room here. I grunt with effort as I hammer the door again and again, desperate to get through.

PART VIII

With his face pressed hard against the spy-hole in the door, Mark stared in disbelief at the man trying to bludgeon his way into the room directly opposite.

'What is it?' Kate asked, trying to pull him away. He didn't answer. He couldn't answer. How could this be? How had he found them – was it just coincidence, or the cruellest stroke of bad luck imaginable? Had he been looking for them – but how could he have possibly known they were here? He looked over his shoulder at Lizzie, standing in the far corner, the stunned expression on his face obviously speaking volumes.

'Mark, what is it? What the hell's the matter?' Kate demanded again, her voice now frantic. He ignored her, staring at Lizzie, who started to move towards him. As if she already knew what was outside, she tried to push Mark out of the way, but he stood his ground, turned back and pressed his eye up against the tiny glass button in the door again.

Danny McCoyne. He hadn't seen his cousin in almost a year, but it was definitely him, he was sure of it: his cousin Danny – his mum's sister Jean's son, the kid he'd messed around with at countless boring family gatherings and parties when they were growing up. The miserable no-hoper with the dead-end job who'd ended up saddled with too many kids in a too-small flat. The notorious waster, cited by other members of the family as a prime example of how not to do things. Danny McCoyne: Lizzie's partner, now a murderer. A Hater.

Outside on the landing, McCoyne continued to hammer against the door, and Mark found himself feeling overwhelmed by the anger and hatred so visible on his cousin's twisted face. He was shocked, appalled by what Danny had become. He'd always been a gangly, awkward kid and he'd not changed as he'd grown up, but that uncertainty had been replaced now with focus, ferocity and a vicious intent. To Mark, Danny McCoyne now personified the previously faceless Hater menace, and he felt his legs weaken with nerves at the thought he was about to be forced to confront him.

Lizzie grabbed Mark's arm and yanked him out of the way. She pressed her eye against the spy-hole briefly then staggered away from the door, recoiling in shock at the sight of the Hater in the hallway. The room around her was filled with noise – Kate's panicked screaming, Gurmit Singh's constant, unfathomable tirade – but she didn't hear any of it. *How the hell could he be here?*

'Will someone tell me what's wrong?' Kate pleaded, desperate for information.

'It's Danny,' Lizzie mumbled, her voice barely audible.

'What? But how could he—?'

'Keep your voice down, Katie,' Mark warned.

'Let him have the kid,' Kate shouted, moving forward. Mark pushed her back away from the door, but she cried, 'Come on, Mark, let him take her. Give her to him. Get the little bitch out of here. We'll be safer if—'

The noise from the landing got louder and louder. Mark shoved her back towards her catatonic parents, then ran back to the spy-hole and peered outside again. As he watched, McCoyne finally forced his way into the room opposite. He disappeared inside, but was back out again just a few seconds later, and this time there was no question as to where he was heading next.

'Get back!' Mark hissed as he stumbled back towards the others, sweeping them away from the door. He grabbed the baseball bat, the only thing they had in the room to defend themselves with, then herded Kate, Lizzie and Singh around the foot of the double bed, gesturing for them to get down and stay out of sight.

'Is he—?' Lizzie started, but the sound of the first flurry of blows from the axe against the door rendered her question obsolete before it had even been fully asked. The door rattled and shook in its frame.

Mark looked at Kate, who cowered alongside her parents, then turned and faced the door again, desperately trying to give the impression he was ready to fight when all he really wanted to do was run.

The Hater in the hallway booted the badly damaged door open and sent it clattering back against the wall, splinters of wood flying in all directions. He charged into room 33, straight into Mark, who ran towards him to try and head him off, baseball bat held high. Mark clumsily swung the bat at his cousin's head, but he missed by a mile, wrong-footed by the sudden speed of events, the close confines of the cluttered room and the utter terror which he felt in every nerve of his body.

McCoyne grabbed the end of the bat on its fast upward arc, yanked it from his grip and threw it out of reach across the room.

The Hater stopped.

He thought he recognised the man in front of him. Mark? Mark Tillotsen? *Cousin Mark?* Was it really him?

The unexpected appearance of a face from his old life caught him completely off-guard. For a split second he stood there in numb silence, staring at the other man, his head suddenly filled with memories and emotions which had been suppressed or long-forgotten, ever since he'd first tasted the Hate. He rocked back on his feet, hardly even blinking, as another explosion outside shook the entire building.

Then Mark lunged at him again and someone else screamed something unintelligible from the far corner of the room and he snapped himself out of his sudden trance and remembered Ellis and Lizzie and why he was there.

He caught Mark as he leapt forward, grabbing his collar, spinning him around and smashing him up against the wall, then dropping him onto the floor in a crumpled heap. Mark rolled over onto his back and lay groaning at the Hater's feet.

McCoyne sensed more movement. Another one of them was attacking—

He looked up as Lizzie ran towards him. Her face was tired, old and drawn, her cheeks and eyes were sunken and hollow, but he knew immediately that it was her. 'Lizzie, I—'

She swung the baseball bat around and smashed him in the side of the head.

36

I hear them talking, but I keep my eyes shut. My hands are bound to radiator pipes behind me and my ankles are tied together. There's blood in my mouth, trickling down my throat. Someone trips over my feet but I force myself not to react. I half-open one blood-caked eye and see Cousin Mark trying to drag a pregnant woman away from me.

She sees that I'm awake and squirms free of him and she turns back and boots me in the gut. I can't defend myself. I take the full force of her foot right in my stomach, and I'm doubled up with pain, gasping for air and choking on the semi-coagulated blood in my nose and mouth.

Christ, that bitch is wild. It takes two of them to pull her away from me and hold her down. If I didn't know better she could almost pass for one of us. Maybe she is? Maybe she's been conditioned to hold the Hate like I've learned to?

Mark and an Asian man keep the pregnant woman away at a distance. Why the fuck have they got an Asian man with them? I wonder briefly. Lizzie strides across the room and grabs my shoulder and pulls me over until I'm sitting upright, my back against the radiator.

She looks straight into my face, then slaps me so hard I almost fall back down. 'You killed my dad, you fucker,' she spits. 'I loved you and you killed my dad!'

What am I supposed to say? She's right, and I don't regret it. I could kill everyone in this room and not give any of them a second thought. Except Lizzie, perhaps. I can't take my eyes off her. It's suddenly like we've never been apart and for a single brief and foolish moment the irrevocable difference between us seems trivial and unimportant.

She slaps me again and though I try to turn away she still hits me with full force. The pain's good; it wakes me up. I start trying to get my hands free of the plastic ties they're using to hold me.

'We should kill him,' the pregnant woman snarls, holding her swollen belly.

'That'd make us as bad as him,' Lizzie answers quickly before turning her attention back to me. She's nervous, scared. She forces herself to talk to me. 'Why are you here?'

'I've been looking for you,' I answer quickly.

'Haven't you hurt me enough?'

'It's not about you. It's Ellis – I need to know what happened to her.'

'Why?'

'Why do you think? She's like me, Lizzie. She should be with me.'

'What, so you can let her loose outside to kill? So you can let her run wild and—'

I stare her in her face. I'm still trying to get my hands free behind me. 'I want to take her with me. I want to look after her and take care of her. I don't want her out there fighting on her own.' I'm being honest. I wonder if she'll understand . . .

'I don't want her fighting at all. She's just a kid—'

'I just want her with me, Lizzie. I want to keep her safe.'

Lizzie slumps back and drops to the floor opposite me, her head in her hands. The Asian guy is still mumbling and cursing at me from the corner of the room. The pregnant woman watches my every move, as if she doesn't dare to look away. Mark tries to appear collected and in control, but I can sense his terror. I feed off their collective fear. It's empowering. Even together they're no match for me.

'He's here to kill us,' Mark says. 'Katie's right, we should have just got rid of him. This was a bad idea.'

I spit a lump of bloody phlegm onto the carpet. 'I'm not interested in any of you. Just Ellis. Let me know what happened to her and I'll go.'

'Don't listen to him. Let him go and the fucker will kill us—'

'I won't. I can control it – I'd never have got this deep into the city if I couldn't. I can hold the Hate. They taught me.'

'Who did?' Lizzie asks.

'People like you.

'This is bullshit,' the pregnant woman yells. 'Why you?'

'Not just me. Others too.'

'But why?'

'Haven't you heard what's happening outside? It's a co-ordinated attack,' I explain, suddenly desperate for Lizzie to understand. 'I came here with other fighters, but I broke away to try and find you.'

'I don't understand—'

'I'm not interested in killing any of you. I just want to know what happened to Ellis. Tell me what happened to her and I'll go and you'll never see me again—'

'Let him take her,' the pregnant woman yells, 'the evil little bitch—'

'Shut up, Katie!' Mark yells.

What did she just say? I can't believe what I'm hearing. This must be bullshit – she can't really be here, can she? How could they have kept her hidden, and stopped her from attacking them for so long? I look from face to face in search of an explanation.

'Ellis is here?' I say at last.

'In the bathroom,' the pregnant one shouts, trying to get up again, pointing at a door in the wall opposite me as my cousin pushes her back down and tries to cover her mouth.

'Here? But how—?'

Still slumped on the floor in front of me, just out of reach, Lizzie starts to sob.

'I couldn't let her go. I knew she was like you, but it didn't matter. Even when she killed the boys, I couldn't bear to let her go—' Her words dry up as tears take over.

I keep trying to move my wrists and I'm bending and

stretching my legs, trying to break my bonds. Got to get up and get to Ellis—

'He can take her,' says the pregnant woman. 'Let him take her.'

'We can't trust him,' Mark snaps at her.

'Does it matter? Throw the pair of them out the door and let them take their chances—'

Another thunderous explosion interrupts her. They're getting closer and more frequent now. At this rate the city will have fallen long before six a.m.

'She's right,' I tell Lizzie, begging for her to listen properly to me. 'I promise I won't hurt you. I'll take Ellis and you'll never see either of us again.'

My cousin picks up the bloodied baseball bat. 'As soon as we let him go he'll turn on us,' he says, sneering at me.

'For fuck's sake,' I scream at him in frustration, 'will you just listen to what I'm saying? I don't want to kill any of you—'

'Come on, Lizzie,' the pregnant woman says, calmer now, lowering herself down and kneeling down on the floor next to her. 'You said yourself you can't help her. This is the best option for all of us.'

'She's right,' I agree, as if they're going to listen to anything I say.

Lizzie glares at me. She's in an impossible situation – whatever choice she makes, she loses. No matter what she is and how I feel about her now, I'm surprised that it still hurts me so much to see her like this.

She's starting to cry. 'I can't. I just can't let her go—'

'You don't have long,' I tell them. 'The city doesn't have long. I can get her out of here before it's too late, get her to safety.'

'You've hardly got any medication left for her, Liz. You can't hold her if she's not sedated. Have you thought about that?'

'Of course I have,' she sobs, looking back and staring at the pregnant girl. 'I just can't stand the thought of her being out there on her own. She's only five—'

'But she won't be on her own,' I interrupt. 'She'll be with me.'

'Come on, Danny,' she sighs, wiping her eyes. 'You were hardly the world's greatest dad at the best of times. What chance has she got with you now?'

'More chance than she's got without me. Look, you're not thinking straight. Stay here and you're all dead. This is the best option for her. The only option . . .'

The hotel room is momentarily silent, the only noise coming from outside. Vibrations shake the floor and walls. Even the Asian man has finally shut up.

Lizzie holds her head in her hands. 'I just can't. You don't understand. She's not like you remember, she's—'

But before she's finished speaking, the pregnant woman lunges towards me, catching me and everyone else completely off-guard. She grabs my head and pulls me forward, then leans down behind me. I try to shake her off, but she's too heavy and I'm squashed under the bulk of her unborn child. As quickly as she attacked she's up again. She stands opposite, holding one of my knives in her hand. What has she done? Has she cut me or—?

Wait . . .

My hands are free.

My legs are still tied together, but I push myself off the wall and reach out for Lizzie. She manages to scramble back out of the way, but the other woman's not as quick. I grab her right foot and pull her over and she hits the ground right in front of me. Mark tries to react, but the Unchanged are reassuringly slow and by the time he's made a grab for her I've already got her held tight. I wrap one arm around her throat and hold the knife to her face. Stupid bitch. At least I've temporarily silenced the constant fucking noise coming out of her mouth.

I lean forward and cut the ties around my ankles, then slowly stand up. Mark starts to move towards me again but I prick the woman's cheek with the tip of the blade and the sight of her blood and the sound of her half-choked screams is enough to stop him.

I kick the bathroom door open and it takes a second for my eyes to adjust to the gloom. Lying bastards! It's empty. She isn't here. There's a thin mattress on the floor, some sheets, empty bottles of water and the remains of medication, food wrappers . . . but no Ellis. I can smell her scent, but she's gone.

'Where is she?' I yell, turning back around and holding the blade up to the woman's eye.

'She's safe,' Lizzie answers. 'Let Kate go, Danny.'

In desperation Mark tries to run at me again but, like all of his kind, he thinks too long instead of acting on instinct. I'm far faster than he is and I see him coming a mile off. Even with the weight of this bitch in my arms he's no match for me. I kick him in the bollocks and send him reeling.

'Where?' I yell again.

'Let her go and I'll take you to her,' Lizzie says. She sounds calm now, in control.

I stare into her eyes again, and tighten the pressure around the other woman's neck. Is she telling the truth? Do I have any choice? I could be in touching distance of Ellis, but without Lizzie I might as well be miles away. Mark rolls around at my feet, groaning.

'Please,' he whimpers pathetically.

I could kill her but I don't. Suddenly all I can think about is Joseph Mallon. I can see his face, and I can hear his damn voice echoing around my cell, telling me not to fight fire with fire, to break the cycle. Was he right? As the city crumbles around us, can I risk not following my instinct and letting these fuckers live? Could it really be that the more I fight today, the more I stand to lose?

I let the woman go and she falls to her knees and crawls away on all fours, gasping for air. Lizzie walks over to me, stopping only when we're almost touching.

'I just need to know that you'll look after her and get her to safety.'

'Where is she?' I shout, struggling to keep control, not to attack her. 'Just tell me where.'

'I need to hear you say it, Danny.'

'I promise you, Lizzie, I'll get Ellis as far away from the city as I can. I'll look after her, I promise. She's all I've got left.'

'Then you've got more than I have,' she sobs. She looks into my eyes and I can't look away. 'We moved her last night,' she finally admits. 'We couldn't risk keeping her here any longer.'

'What have you done with her?'

'She's safe. Mark and I were going to try to get her out of the city. It was the lesser of two evils.'

Mark reaches into his pocket and pulls out a set of keys. He pulls himself up and throws them to Lizzie. 'Take him.'

'I can't,' she says, beginning to cry again.

'It's the only option. Listen to what's happening outside, Liz. It's all fucked. He's right, at least she's got a chance this way.'

'But what if—?'

'I won't hurt you,' I tell her, meaning every word, although I don't know if she believes me. 'All I want is Ellis. Take me to her and you'll never see me again.'

'Just give him the keys,' the pregnant woman says. 'Let him find her for himself and you stay here with us.'

Lizzie wipes her eyes. 'No, I'll take him. I just want to see her again, one last time.'

37

There's a fire escape at the rear of the hotel, iron stairs running down the back of the building. Lizzie, watching me like a hawk and carrying a knife I know she won't dare use, pushes me down the landing and around a corner towards an innocuous-looking grey door. It's already been forced open. She gestures for me to go through.

'Where is she?' I ask as I step outside, shouting to make myself heard over the sounds of battle which fill the air. We stand at the top of the zigzagging metal staircase bracketed to the back of the run-down old building. She points in the general direction of the streets behind the hotel, but I can't see anything specific. The sun is rising and below us the city is beginning to burn. A fleet of planes and helicopters are taking off from somewhere far over to our left.

'There's a garage,' she answers breathlessly. 'The front of it has collapsed, so it's difficult to get in or out. We locked her in the back of a van.'

'If this is a trick, Lizzie—'

'No trick,' she says quickly, and I know she's telling the truth. We're wasting precious time: Ellis is close. I start climbing down.

There's another car park at the back of the hotel, and a small patch of wildly overgrown garden beyond it. Lizzie leads me away from the building, down a path that's barely visible through the long, damp grass. The sky is still filled with heavy grey cloud, but it's slowly beginning to brighten.

'This way,' she whispers, catching her breath after a series of exploding flashes light up the early morning gloom for a fraction of a second. A low-flying helicopter gunship rumbles overhead, heading back towards town.

I follow her to the end of the path where there's a tall wrought-iron gate.

Lizzie bends down and shifts a broken lump of paving slab that's keeping it shut and the gate swings open. She pauses before going through and ducks back into the shadows as a group of people run past. I watch them as we step out into the open: three figures chasing a fourth down a cobbled alley. They corner the lone runner, drag him to the ground and kick the shit out of him. It's impossible to tell who's who – am I watching the Unchanged being hunted down, or is that one of my people cornered? It doesn't matter any more.

'Move!' Lizzie hisses, shoving me forward again. There's another gate in a wooden fence opposite and we cross the alley and go through. I can tell immediately by the number of rusting car parts and piles of tyres and mangled exhausts that this must be the place.

I follow her through a side door into a dusty office. It's dark and I walk into the back of her when she stops suddenly. She grabs my arm and leads me further forward, until she finds a torch she obviously left here previously. We go through another door and down a single steep step into what must be the main workshop. The air's cold and the noise we make echoes off the walls. She shines the torch further ahead and I see that the front of the building has collapsed in on itself, sealing it off from the street.

'Over here.'

We walk around the back of a jacked-up car to the furthest corner of the workspace. There's a white and blue van parked with its back to the wall. Its front wing is a light matt grey colour, primed and waiting to be painted by a garage employee who's never coming back. As we approach the rear of the van I see there's a light on inside it. Lizzie pushes me out of the way and unlocks the door. She opens it as far as she can and slips through the gap and I follow her.

Lying flat on her back in the middle of the van, chained to the front seats, her wrists, legs and ankles bound together with plastic-covered washing-line and her mouth gagged, is Ellis. My little girl is awake and alert, her beautiful brown eyes darting from Lizzie to me and back again. She looks straight at me, but I'm not sure if she remembers. She's wearing only a dirty grey vest and knickers, and her tiny body is covered in cuts, scratches and bruises. Lizzie leans over her and she immediately reacts, arching away from her, then trying to lunge forward and attack. The longer I look at her, the less familiar she becomes. She snarls and hisses through the gag like a frightened animal.

Lizzie, Ellis and me all together again. I never dared dream this would really happen. Suddenly the noise of the battles outside and the helicopters and explosions all around us don't matter. Everything that I have left is in the back of this van. I swing my rucksack off my shoulders and open it up. I pull out Ellis' doll and Lizzie takes it from me and holds it close, tears running down her face.

'You went back?' she whispers.

'Looking for you,' I tell her.

Lizzie moves Ellis' wild, unkempt hair away from her eyes and tries to show her the doll. She recoils from her mother's touch, desperately trying to pull away. Lizzie's unfazed – I guess she must be used to this now. Ellis' eyes show no recognition, no understanding.

'It would have been easier on everyone if she'd just stayed with you,' she admits, 'but how was I to know after what you did?'

'I know.'

'I didn't even realise she was like you until a couple of days after you'd gone. I really didn't expect it – I didn't even think it could happen. One minute she was sitting there with her brothers, the next . . . I was out of the room for less than five minutes, honestly, and I came back in and saw her with Edward—'

She starts sobbing again, and as her tears drip down onto Ellis, she wriggles and squirms as if they're corrosive acid drops.

'Why did this have to happen, Danny?' Lizzie asks. She knows I can't give her the answers she wants.

'It wasn't because of anything you did or didn't do,' I say. 'It wasn't a matter of choice, not for any of us. None of us could control it, or predict it . . .'

She smiles and wipes her eyes. 'Remember how hard we used to think we'd got it? How wound up we used to get with the kids?'

'How could I forget?'

'You hated your job; I couldn't stand being with the children, Dad was sick of bailing us out all the time . . .'

'I know. I remember.'

'I'd do anything to have it all back how it was.'

She's right. In spite of everything, sitting here with her and with Ellis lying between us, part of me knows she's right.

'I wish I could be back there,' she continues, reaching down and resting her hand on Ellis' shoulder. Ellis flinches and tries to roll away, but Lizzie ignores her violent reaction. 'You, me, Ellis and the boys in the kitchen of our shitty little flat, fighting over the TV, or who'd eaten whose sweets or something stupid like that.'

'Me too,' I say quietly, surprising myself with my admission. Another explosion reverberates around the garage, followed by the sound of dust and debris raining down on the roof of the van. This van is like a cocoon, temporarily isolating us from the chaos of the rest of the world, but I can hear the intensity of the fighting outside continuing to increase.

'We can't stay here,' I tell her. 'It's not safe.'

'I know.'

'I have to go. I have to take her with me and get her away.'

Lizzie nods and wipes her eyes again. She looks down at Ellis and smiles, then crouches down next to her and picks up the knife she was carrying. Ellis tries to lunge at her, the chains still holding her back. For a split second I think Lizzie's going to attack her, but I watch her face and I know that she won't. She can't. She removes the washing-line which has been wrapped around Ellis' legs, then slides the long blade between her bare ankles and draws it up, cutting through the plastic ties which bind them tight. Ellis immediately reacts, kicking out at Lizzie with incredible unrestrained fury and anger.

'What are you doing? Get out of here, Liz. Just go . . .'

'Hold her, Danny,' she says.

I admire her calm. I lift Ellis up, her legs still thrashing, and wrap my arms around her chest as Lizzie removes the padlock and chains which have kept her anchored to the floor of the van. Her ferocity and strength is remarkable and I struggle to keep hold of her. Lizzie removes Ellis' gag and her head immediately lurches forward as she tries to take a bite out of her mother's face. Lizzie ducks out of the way, then lowers the blade towards the ties binding her wrists together.

'You should go,' I tell her. 'Get back to Mark and the others. Try and get away from here while you still can.'

She shakes her head and starts to cut.

'Let her go, Danny. I just want to hold her before you take her.'

'Don't, Liz, she'll—'

The plastic ties pop open and Ellis immediately lunges forward, her incredible strength taking me by surprise. She flies at Lizzie, landing in her arms and smashing her back against the side of the van with a sickening thump. For the briefest of moments they're locked in an embrace, Lizzie burying Ellis' face in her chest, not wanting to let her go. I watch the pair of them in the low light, huddled close together. They could be anywhere: saying goodbye in the school playground, sitting on the end of Ellis' bed last thing at night, keeping her warm when she's just come in from outside—

The expression on Lizzie's face changes. Her eyes screw shut with pain and she opens her mouth to scream, but no sound comes out. Ellis pushes her away and looks at me, blood covering the bottom part of her face. She spits out a chunk of Lizzie's flesh, turns back and attacks again.

I shuffle back into the corner and cover my head as she rips her mother's body apart.

38

Blood-soaked and panting hard, Ellis sits in the opposite corner of the van and watches me. What has she become? Does she even remember who I am? She hasn't tried to kill me. I know she'd have attacked if she thought I was a threat.

'We have to go, Ellis. We have to get away from here. It's not safe. People are going to try and kill everyone here. Do you understand?'

There's no reaction, and no time to wait for an answer. I take her rainbow-coloured jumper out of my rucksack and edge closer to her.

'Put this on. Keep you warm.'

I reach up to put it over her head. She swipes it out of my hands. I pick it up and try again, but she's not having any of it and I drop it. She hisses at me and pushes herself further into the corner. Poor kid. It's hard seeing her like this. I'd naïvely expected her not to have changed much. Maybe I'd just been trying to convince myself she wouldn't be like the kids we found at her school. She'll be better now we're together.

'Come on, we're going,' I tell her, forcing myself to move. I grab the knife and torch in one hand and Ellis' wrist with the other and drag her out of the back of the van. We hit the ground and she immediately tries to pull away from me, but I won't let go. I drop the torch, shove the knife into my belt and lean back into the van again. With outstretched fingers I reach the long length of cord they'd used to tie her legs together. It's wet with Lizzie's blood.

Ellis keeps pulling against me, and her strength and persistence are hard to control, but I manage to keep hold and pull her close enough to tie one end of the cord around her waist like a leash. Christ, there's hardly any meat on her at all. The chubby puppy fat I remember around her belly has gone. She's lean and sinewy now – just skin, muscle and bone.

I tie the other end of the cord around my own waist. 'In case we get separated, okay?'

Still no reaction.

'Ellis, can you hear me?'

She looks into my face, but she doesn't respond. Now that she's attached to me I let her go and she immediately darts away, almost dragging me over when the cord pulls tight. I try to haul her back but now she's fighting against me constantly.

'Stop! Ellis, sweetheart, it's Daddy!'

Now I'm struggling to keep my footing. And in the brief lightning flash of an explosion outside, I see that she's trying to undo the cord. I run towards her and scoop her up into my arms again, and she starts kicking and squirming to get free.

'Calm down,' I whisper, my mouth next to her ear. 'Please, Ellis, just stop . . .'

But my words have no effect. I've got to get us out of this garage. Maybe she'll respond better if she can see me clearly and if she can see what's happening around us. Disorientated, I head the wrong way and find myself trying to get through the rubble at the collapsed front of the building. I double back on myself, past the open van and Lizzie's body, trying to retrace my steps back out. Someone shines a light in my face and I can't cover my eyes so I instinctively screw them shut. I almost drop Ellis, but manage to hang on.

'Let her go,' a familiar voice orders.

'Julia? How did you—?'

'I followed you. We knew you were looking for your kid and Craven showed me what you found on the system.'

'But what about the plan? The fighting?'

'What about it? Have you seen what's happening out there? The chain reaction's started without us, McCoyne. They're turning on each other.'

'So you've got what you wanted. The city's falling apart and—'

'I can't let you take her. Kids like this are the future. We need them more than you can imagine—'

'She's staying with me.'

'You don't understand, Sahota and Preston both—'

'No, *you* don't understand. Ellis is my daughter and I'm responsible for—'

'Your only responsibility is to this war.'

'I'll take her back to the others. I promised Preston I'd—'

'Do you think I'm stupid? If I let you go you'll disappear and we'll never see either of you again. I can't take that risk. She's coming with me, and you should be proud to let her go. We'll take her and she'll help us hunt more of them down until the last one's dead. Your kid's already more of a fighter than you'll ever be and you should—'

'She's my little girl. I don't want her to fight.'

'You dumb bastard, do you think you have a choice? Just let her go.'

I don't answer but run forward, trying to find a way past. Julia comes at me and I drop Ellis to defend myself. Another flash of the torch blinds me for an instant and the sudden tightening of the cord as Ellis darts away pulls me off-balance.

Julia swings a punch and catches me on the side of the head. I'm knocked back and sent reeling by the unexpected angle of her attack. I trip over something hard and heavy in the dark behind me and find myself on my knees in some kind of oily inspection pit. I feel the cord tighten again and I immediately grab it and try to pull Ellis back. It gets even tighter, then goes taut, then drops down loose as Julia cuts through it.

'Ellis!' I shout as I scramble out of the pit. Julia drops her torch and for a split second I catch a fleeting glimpse of her shape as she sprints through the office and back outside, barely managing to drag Ellis behind her. I chase after them, through the wooden gate then out along the cobbled passageway. It's packed with people, far more than before, all of them running to escape the carnage which is steadily consuming the centre of town. Can't see Julia – she's just one among hundreds now.

I follow the stumbling crowd until we reach the end of the passageway. I look in all directions, shouting for Ellis, but my calls go unanswered, most probably unheard. Too many people. I start to wade through them, unable to see anything through the waves of foul, barely human flesh that constantly crash into me. I grab the knife from my belt and start slashing into those nearest to me – I'm not interested in killing, I just want them out of my way. The sun's almost up now but the light's still poor and dirty smoke is drifting everywhere like horror film fog.

Someone grabs me from behind and I spin around to defend myself, but they're not attacking, just trying to get through. I'm on my back in the gutter in a puddle of rancid rainwater before I know what's happening. My wrist cracks against a kerbstone and I drop the knife. I reach out for it but it's kicked away by one of the stampeding crowd and before I can get up someone's planted a boot right in the centre of my chest. Suddenly struggling to breathe, I roll over and manage to crawl away through the forest of legs. Other Unchanged trip and stumble over and around me but I force myself to keep moving until I get to the side of the street, where there are fewer of them.

I'm next to a badly decayed body in a deserted shop doorway when my hand rests on a length of metal tubing about a metre long. It looks like it was a fencepost, or maybe part of a road sign, but it'll make a decent weapon. I use it to help me get up, then head back into the crowd again, swinging it around like a samurai sword. On a vicious upwards arc the jagged end of the tube catches an Unchanged woman on the side of the head, tearing her flesh from below her ear up to the corner of her eye. I swing the tube again and another goes down. It's like I'm cutting down crops, scything a path through the chaos.

There's an overturned wreck of a car in the middle of the

street. The crowd splits to go around either side of it but I climb onto it. The burnt-out skeleton is precariously balanced on its roof and it quivers and vibrates with my every move. Another helicopter flies overhead and I instinctively duck. I turn around to watch it disappear back over the city centre—

And then I see her.

I'm surrounded by a sea of heads but back in the direction from which I've just come, there's a break in the crowd, a small, unexpected gap. Though it's a struggle to see through the smoky haze and the constant, uncoordinated activity, I glimpse a flash of remarkably fast movement – it's Ellis, finally free and unrestricted, and she's killing at an incredible rate. I can see her leaping from victim to victim with ferocious speed and intent, using nothing but her hands and teeth to kill. She wraps herself around each one of them, doing enough damage to fatally wound them, and then moving on to attack her next victim before the previous one's dead. Even after everything I've seen, my daughter's ruthless, savage brutality is incredible, both awe-inspiring and terrifying in equal measure.

There's Julia. I steady myself as the upturned car rocks again, and watch as she chases after Ellis. She's holding onto the cord with one hand and chopping at the Unchanged around her with what looks like a meat cleaver in the other, but she's struggling to keep up. Ellis is too strong and too fast for her.

I swing the metal pipe out over the side of the car like a golf club, taking out several more refugees and almost decapitating one of them. I jump down into the space where they were standing then hold the tube out like a lance and run forward, shoulder dropped, towards where Julia and Ellis are fighting. I follow the trail of bodies, tripping over outstretched limbs and slipping in the pools of blood and gore that Ellis has left in her wake. An unusually aggressive Unchanged comes at me with a machete. The downward sweep of the blade grazes my shoulder, but it does little real damage and I'm gone before he can take a second swipe.

Julia's dead ahead of me now, being virtually dragged along by Ellis even as she continues fighting. Yet another helicopter powers overhead, this one releasing a volley of screaming missiles into the crowd nearer to the centre of town. I can feel the heat of the missiles as they scorch through the air above me, and the shockwave from the explosions in the distance almost knocks me off my feet. Julia lifts her cleaver and chops it down into the shoulder of a slow-moving Unchanged man before the vibrations knock her off-balance too. She steadies herself and pulls back on Ellis' leash, but the momentary delay is enough for me to catch her.

I grab hold of her shoulder and spin her around. 'Let her go, Julia. She's my daughter.'

Distracted, the cord almost slips through her fingers. She drops her weapon, snatches back the plastic-covered line with both hands and tries to wrap it around her wrist. Her face is bruised, her right eye swollen purple and almost completely shut. Did Ellis do that to her?

'Help me with her,' she demands.

'Help you?' I yell back, using the metal pole to shove an unsteady Unchanged out of the way. 'Are you serious? Let her go—'

'We have to get her out of here. Help me!'

More missiles explode, vast swollen bulges of intense orange flames rising up from the area around the Prince Hotel. That's far too close for comfort. What choice do I have? I drop the pole and grab the cord, taking the strain from Julia, and together we begin to reel Ellis in. I catch a glimpse of her through the swarming crowds. We're dragging her back, but she's still fighting, grabbing as many Unchanged as she can, sinking her teeth and claws into their skin, slashing and tearing at their flesh. She's just a metre away now, still pulling against us, but unable to overcome our combined strength. Julia runs and grabs Ellis by the waist, lifting her clean off the ground, making her drop the body of a young Unchanged kid mid-kill. She manages to squirm around in Julia's grip and I'm forcing myself between them to take my daughter from her, but Ellis unintentionally elbows me in the face, catching me full force between the eyes, and blood begins pouring from my nose.

Julia staggers away, trying to keep hold of Ellis while deflecting the constant barrage of kicks and punches coming from her. My girl is like a child possessed, fighting with a savage strength and intensity way beyond her years. They disappear into the crowd again for a few heart-stopping seconds as I spit out blood from my broken nose, until I catch sight of the washing-line on the ground and I drop down and grab hold of it, reeling Ellis in again.

I'm too late: she's sitting on top of Julia, her thumbs sunk deep into her bloody eye-sockets, repeatedly lifting her head up and smashing it back down onto the tarmac. Her skull's cracked, blood pouring from it, but she's still thrashing her arms wildly, though there's no strength left in her, only movement.

Ellis squeezes again and this time Julia stops suddenly, her limbs falling heavy to the ground. Ellis lifts Julia's head and slams it back down once more, then she looks up at me and springs away. The washing-line whips out of my hands, burning my skin.

'Ellis!' I scream.

My daughter leaps up at another Unchanged woman who's running towards her. The woman catches her with surprise, and is slammed back down onto the road, overcome by the unexpected force of the attack. Ellis kills her, then stands up and drags another one down, then another, and another, and I'm transfixed – until an Unchanged man barges into me from the side and I grab his collar, flip him over and smash the sole of my boot into his face.

The exhilaration is incredible. Suddenly, now that I have Ellis with me, this is all that matters. Another one of them comes at me with a knife and I grab his hand and twist it around with such force that I hear his elbow pop and crack, then plunge the blade into his own chest. I pull the bloody weapon back out and then, without thinking, grab a handful of hair from the head of another, yank it back and draw the knife quickly across its exposed neck, feeling it slice easily through flesh.

Beside me Ellis launches herself at a kid just a little older than she is. The kid fights back, almost getting away, before Ellis forces it over to the side of the road and smashes its head through a low window.

And this, I realise as I kill again and again, without meeting any resistance, is what I'd always said I'd wanted. I'm fighting freely, without restriction or fear, with Ellis by my side, doing the same—

Except she's not here. I've lost sight of her again. I shout her name, but the chaos around me now is all-consuming. The helicopter is circling overhead again, and the panicking crowd is pushing me further and further back. I try to carve my way through the horde, but it's like trying to swim against the strongest current imaginable. Through a momentary gap I see Ellis racing away, moving diagonally across the street, jumping from body to body, from kill to kill, slithering through the crowd. She jumps up onto the back of one unsuspecting man, snaps his neck – I marvel at her strength – then leaps over to her next victim before the first corpse has fallen. Then she's gone again, lost in the midst of the madness.

What has she become? She's a savage, feral monster, a million miles removed from the Ellis I knew and remembered, but she's still my daughter. Seeing her like this is heartbreakingly sad, but at the same time there's a part of me that's incredibly proud of what she is now and how bravely and strongly she's fighting.

I've got to get to her.

I'm struggling to keep going. I'm panting with effort, my legs heavy and lungs empty, barely able to keep moving, and yet the tide of Unchanged refugees coming towards me is endless. I try and force my way between them, but every time I take a step forward I'm pushed several steps back. Got to keep moving. Can't stop now—

The roar of another missile fills the air. It hits the side of a building less than a hundred metres ahead, puncturing a hole in the wall and exploding outwards, showering the entire street with debris. When the explosion fades, everything becomes silent and still. I stand motionless as the last few refugees to have escaped the blast continue to push past me. I slowly move closer to the blast zone as the sound gradually begins to return; the screams and moans of the injured and dying, a single car alarm that's somehow still working, the crackle and pop of flames, the hiss of fractured pipes . . .

I can't see Ellis.

I stand alone at the edge of a massive expanse of rubble and fallen bodies. Around me, a few people begin to move again, crawling through the debris, slowly picking themselves up and staggering about aimlessly. I walk deeper into the madness, slowly at first, then starting to run. I trip and slide over the remains of people under my feet.

Where is she?

I run faster, barely managing to stay upright in the midst of the carnage. The closer I get to the epicentre, the fewer complete bodies there are. I look down and all I can see now are dismembered limbs and other, less recognisable chunks of bloody meat.

I can't move, can't think straight, the stench of smoke and burning flesh filling my bleeding nostrils. I can't focus. I can hardly breathe. Have I lost her? Against all the odds, Lizzie kept Ellis safe for weeks on end. Just minutes with me and she's gone. So much for my promise. *I can't give up.*

There are more people moving all around me now, some of them disentangling themselves from the bloody wreckage, others continuing to flood forward from the centre of town, picking their way through the gruesome ruins, the explosion just delaying their escape temporarily. I slowly cross what's left of the street, trying to see through the smoke and haze to line myself up with the buildings close to where I last saw her.

As I get nearer I drop to my knees and start to crawl through the bloody mire, pushing away the grabbing hands that reach up at me, desperate for help. My knee sinks down into the open chest cavity of a young Unchanged man, physically forcing his last breath from his lungs. Another one of them catches hold of my coat and I prise its surprisingly strong fingers away when I see a small, child-size hand sticking out from under two heavy cadavers.

I drag the corpses out of the way, desperate to dig Ellis out from beneath them. She's face down on the tarmac, a pool of deep red, almost black blood spilling out around her head. I put my hands under her shoulders, pull her out and turn her over, but it's not her. Thank God. I drop the body and keep moving.

There are Unchanged moving all around me again now. Most are injured, all are terrified. I increase my speed, determined to find Ellis, throwing wet chunks of human remains over my shoulder as I look for any sign of her. Then I see it – the severed end of the plastic washing-line.

As more bombs explode around me, showering me with dust and dirt, I pick up the end of the cord and follow it back, terrified at the thought of what I might find at the other end. I catch sight of a bare ankle that's smaller and thinner than the rest and haul another bloody body out of the way, jumping with surprise when it opens its eyes and screams in pain and grabs hold of me.

There – underneath another corpse – I think I see Ellis' shock of untidy brown hair . . .

I pull more bodies away, excavating my way down to the ground, until I uncover her tiny, emaciated body. She's not moving. I shake her shoulder, but there's still no response. I lean down until my ear's just millimetres from her mouth, but it's impossible to hear or feel anything. I grip her wrist in my hand and check for a pulse, but there's nothing. I pull her up until I can lift her and hold her in my arms.

She looks like she's sleeping, and for the first time since I found her she looks like *my* Ellis again, the precious little kid

I used to tuck up in bed at night and fetch breakfast for in the morning, the noisy little bugger who made my life hell but who I loved more than anything else in the world. She's bruised and blood-soaked, and beautiful.

I check her neck for a pulse again, not even sure if I'm doing it right. Did I just feel something? I prise her eyelids open and her pupils are wide, fully dilated – but she doesn't react to the light. I hold her close, her head next to mine, and for a second I'm sure I hear something. I concentrate, shutting out everything else, and then I hear it again. The faintest whisper of a shallow, rasping breath. She's alive. I've got to get her out of here.

39

The skies overhead are filled with movement and noise. Missiles, mortars and rockets whip across the clouds and detonate around the city centre. Helicopters buzz overhead, a few observing, most of them attacking, firing into the crowds below.

The bulk of the refugees are following each other like sheep, sticking to the main roads out of town and not even bothering to consider whether those in front know any more or less about the situation than they do. They are running blind, finding the illusion of safety in numbers. There are hundreds of them moving down the wide ring-road which, as many of them must know, will eventually swing around and take them straight back into the dying heart of the city.

There's another way.

On my left is an enormous pile of smouldering rubble where there used to be a multiplex cinema. Still carrying Ellis in my arms, I leave the road and run around the edge of the ruins, following the perimeter of a wide, tent- and caravan-filled car park which has been almost completely abandoned. On the far side of the site is a steep embankment, along which runs one of the train lines out of the city. While thousands of those dumb bastards have stuck to the clogged-up roads, I can already see that there are just a handful of people up there following the train tracks out of town.

Ellis starts to move. Thank God for that. It was only a small flinch, but it was enough, and I sense she's going to be okay. I hold her tight as I climb up the embankment, quickly reaching the top. As I start running along the side of the track, I'm still instinctively watching out for trains I know will never come.

My feet dig into the gravel which feels like wet sand, making every step take twice as much effort as it should.

From this relatively high vantage point, I can see clearly in most directions. I look back over my shoulder at what's left of the city behind us. Massive sections of it are on fire now. The skyline has changed hugely, in an incredibly short period of time. Huge landmark buildings that were standing tall and proud when I arrived here just a few hours ago have been destroyed, changing the skyline for ever. Even from this distance and over the endless noise I can still hear the sounds of thousands of people fighting, and the relief at having escaped from the heart of the battle with my daughter is immense.

I keep running, exhausted, but forcing myself to keep going. We're probably safe at this distance, but I want to get even further away. As the train track snakes away towards the suburbs, the desolate ruins of housing estates spring up on either side of us. Even out here there are people in the streets; I see scores of terrified Unchanged refugees who've fled the city and are looking for shelter, only to be intercepted by people like me and Ellis. Where the hell did so many of our fighters come from? Were they already in the centre of town with us? The answer becomes clear as I see more and more of them approaching, coming in from outside the city and crossing the exclusion zone. Word must have reached them that the refugee camp is imploding – or is this a planned attack? Are these the advance troops from Ankin's army?

Another helicopter flies overhead, this one so low that I instinctively drop down to my knees and bend forward to protect Ellis. She shuffles in my arms again and groans with pain. I hold her closer to my chest and look up as the helicopter flies past and away. Then another thunders over us, then another . . . they're all flying away from the city. I stand up and watch as even more gunships follow the first three.

Finally, I start moving again and, as the combined noise of the powerful engines begins to fade, I become aware of another sound, this time much closer, and on the ground. Beyond the ruined houses on my right there's a large expanse of parkland, and even from this distance I can see there's a huge amount of activity there. There are battles raging in the streets around the park and a massive convoy of vehicles is leaving the grassland and driving off onto the surrounding roads. Another helicopter takes off, from somewhere close this time. It climbs quickly into the early morning air, banks hard to the left and follows the path of others before it.

Ellis starts to wake up and move. She grunts and squirms in my arms but I just tighten my grip, determined not to let go.

'Stay still,' I tell her, not knowing if she can hear me or if she understands, 'please, sweetheart . . .'

The train track cuts through the housing estate and runs parallel with the edge of the parkland. I've never seen it from this angle, but this place used to be Sparrow Hill Park, I'm sure of it, though it's unrecognisable today. The sprawling expanse of well-tended grass I remember is now a vast mass of abandoned tents and Portakabins: though obviously once filled to over-capacity with refugees, much of it now is conspicuously empty. Huge swathes of the camp have been washed away; several stagnant lakes are all that remain after the floodwaters swept relentlessly through the site.

There are people fighting on the track up ahead, so I run down the embankment and begin to weave through a dense copse of brittle-branched trees to try and get closer to the park. Already I can see movement on the other side of the trees.

I hold Ellis even tighter as she tries to get away again. Her rage is increasing the closer we get to the Unchanged and I can feel how badly she wants to fight – but I won't let her. It's too dangerous here.

Through the trees and I hit a wire-mesh fence. Something's different here. I can't put my finger on it, but I sense something's wrong.

As I work my way around the wire-mesh fence looking for a way through, the penny drops: the Unchanged military are evacuating. It's their stock response when they realise they've lost control of a building, an area or even a city – withdraw as many of their people as they can to a safe distance, then bomb the hell out of what's left. I saw it at the hospital, at that office block with Adam, and a hundred times before that. And Christ, now I know exactly what happened to London. They lost control, the same way they have here. And their response then? They levelled the bloody place. More than ever, I know I have to get us away.

Ellis manages to free one of her hands and slashes at my face. Blood dribbles down my cheek and when I lift up my hand to wipe it away she shoves both her fists up under my chin and pushes my head back, then she knees me in the gut and breaks loose. I sprint after her. I see she's heading towards where a truck has crashed through the fence and come to a sudden stop wrapped around the base of a tree trunk. It can only just have happened. The half-dead driver is hanging out of the door and when he sees us he starts groaning and begging for help. He's Unchanged, and when Ellis jumps up at him, the force of her sudden attack throws him back across his cab. By the time I get up to her he's already dead, but she continues to kick and slash at his lifeless body, her instinctive aggression taking over. I grab her hair and pull her back towards me, managing to get a grip under one of her shoulders. I drag her back out into the open.

'Off!' she yells, her voice guttural and hoarse, sounding more like a warning howl than a properly formed word.

'We have to go, Ellis,' I tell her. 'We can't stay here – it's too dangerous.'

I drag her behind me into the park. She's still kicking and thrashing furiously but her short arms can't reach my hands to break my grip. I run across the boggy grass towards the chaotic activity up ahead. There's a bottleneck at the single exit where Jeeps, huge trucks and other armoured vehicles are all vying for position to get onto a track that's barely wide enough for any of them. All around the vehicles, refugees and soldiers on foot are trying to escape from the park. People are fighting with each other in their desperation to get away, but there are no other people like us here. This is Unchanged versus Unchanged.

A khaki-coloured Land Rover pulls away and skids through the mud before coming to a sudden halt at the back of the ever-growing line of vehicles. No one pays us any attention as I run towards it. The driver tries to weave through the stationary queue and push his way in. He is focused on getting away from here before the inevitable carpet bombing begins. But there's no way through for anyone. A helicopter hovers overhead, broadcasting a pointless announcement which is all but inaudible over the racket of so many impatient, over-revving engines.

The driver of the Land Rover is distracted, arguing with one of the other soldiers in the back. This is our chance.

I haul Ellis up close and whisper in her ear, 'Kill them, honey.'

I yank open the back door of the mud-splattered vehicle and literally throw her inside. I slam it shut again and wait for several anxious moments until the bloody face of one of the soldiers is smashed up against the window, cracking the glass. I pull open the front door, drag the driver out onto the grass and stamp hard on his face until he stops moving. I jump into his still-warm seat and lock the doors. Behind me Ellis stands on the chest of one of the dead soldiers, ripping out his throat with her bare hands.

'Good girl,' I tell her. 'Now sit down and hold on.'

The way ahead is still impassable, and there are more soldiers running towards us now, more interested in the vehicle than either their fallen comrades or us. As the nearest one reaches for the door I shove the Land Rover into reverse, skidding back across the grass and knocking one of them down. Into first gear and I accelerate forward over his broken legs. We're struggling to get traction on the soggy ground for a second, but the soldier's body helps the wheels to finally get a grip and we career away.

'Hold on,' I tell Ellis again as we slip and slide through the mud. I follow the curve of the boundary fence, looking for the way we came in, hoping I'll be able to squeeze around the other side of the truck and get out again. There it is.

I accelerate up over the collapsed wire-mesh fence. The side of the Land Rover scrapes along the side of the fallen truck and we're out. I'm steering madly – hard right, then hard the other way, then changing direction again – as we weave through the trees. Behind me Ellis is being thrown from side to side, but the soldiers' bloody corpses are at least providing her with some cushioning.

'Put your belt on,' I tell her again.

She doesn't react.

I wrench the steering wheel hard over again, then grip it tight as we burst out through the trees, crash through a low picket fence and swerve onto a narrow residential road that's swarming with people who are scattering as we power towards them. Ellis slams herself up against the window, beating her hands against the glass, desperate to get outside and start killing again.

There's a traffic island up ahead, and the rest of the vehicles that've managed to escape from the park are driving around it. I accelerate the wrong way around the island and force my way into the fast-moving queue. We hurtle along a wide road that's virtually clear on one side. More refugees dive out of the way as we approach. The road climbs up over a high fly-over supported on huge concrete struts, and now I know where we're heading. This was obviously the Unchanged military's main route in and out of their refugee camp. In less than a mile we'll reach the motorway.

I'm distracted as the truck in front smashes into a person trying to sprint out of his way. The body goes spinning over the crash barrier at the side of the fly-over and tumbles down a twenty-metre drop. Our speed is such that I dare look down for only a fraction of a second, but that's enough for me to see that the area of town below us now resembles a vast battlefield. The fleeing refugees have collided head-on with an army of our fighters marching into the city and they're no match for our people. My brief look shows me a bloodbath of unprecedented scale and brutality.

The front of the Land Rover clips a lump of concrete and I almost lose control. I try and focus again as we start our descent towards the motorway, Unchanged military vehicles ahead of us and behind. Ellis has started throwing herself at the door, trying to get out, oblivious to the danger.

'Sit down,' I shout at her, reaching into the back and trying to grab her arm. I manage to catch her wrist, but she won't budge. Christ, she's strong. She straightens her legs against the back of the front seats and the harder I try and pull her forward, the more she resists.

As this road widens and merges with the motorway, two vehicles try to overtake me at once, an articulated lorry on one side and a Jeep on the other. Still struggling with Ellis, I accidentally ram the lorry and it veers off to the right and hits the metal crash barrier running along the central reservation. The back end jack-knifes and blocks two of the three lanes behind us. In the rear-view mirror I watch as more vehicles smash into the lorry, filling almost the entire road with a tangled mass of crushed metal. A few manage to swerve around the wreck and keep moving.

Ellis lunges at me from the back and as I lift my hand to protect myself I manage to get a hold under her armpit. I drag her forward, flipping her over through a full turn and bringing her slamming down hard on her back on the passenger seat.

'Sit down!' I yell at her, and finally the volume and desperation in my voice has some effect. She backs away from me and moves towards the door, pulling up her knees and curling herself into as small a shape as possible. 'Put your belt on, Ellis,' I tell her. 'Do it!'

She doesn't react, but I ignore her, focusing my attention on getting as far away from the city as possible. I overtake a large armoured transporter on the inside. There's a flash of light and a thunderous noise directly above me and I brace myself for another missile explosion, but it's just more helicopters, fleeing from the fallen city along with everyone else. I look at the speedometer and I see that we're doing more than ninety miles an hour – more than a mile and a half a minute. We might be six or seven miles away already, maybe more. Is that far enough?

'We've got to get away from there, you understand?' I yell over the noise of the engine. I snatch a look over at Ellis. She's cowering on the seat next to me, half-naked and covered in blood and grime. She is staring at me, her huge brown eyes unblinking. The poor kid's in shock, traumatised by everything that she's seen and done since we were last together. If only Lizzie hadn't taken her away from me. She'd have been better off with me there to explain everything.

I turn to smile at her reassuringly. 'Listen, we'll find somewhere safe to stop, then we'll—'

Her eyes have moved away from my face and towards the windscreen and I turn back to focus on the road myself. I quickly steer us onto the hard shoulder, out of the way of a lumbering army truck – we almost ran into the back of the slower vehicle. We rumble over the hard shoulder, the tyres brushing the edge of the grass verge and churning up clouds of grit and dust. I yank the Land Rover back on course, the sudden movement making Ellis slide over to the right. I look at her again: her gaze remains fixed, staring into the sky.

'What is it?'

She doesn't answer, but it doesn't matter, I can hear it now. Even over the Land Rover's straining engine and the cacophony around us I can make out a high-pitched whine. And then I see it: a single dark speck, racing across the sky towards the city at an unimaginable speed. Must be a jet or—

Fuck! It can't be . . .

The accelerator pedal's already flat on the floor but I try and push it down harder still when I realise what it is I'm looking at. With one hand I reach across and shove Ellis down. She yelps in pain and protest and tries to fight me off, but I ignore her cries and keep pushing until she slides off the seat into the footwell.

'Get down!' I scream, my voice hoarse with panic, 'get your bloody head down, *now*—!'

She looks up again, and all I can see are those beautiful brown eyes staring back at me. She tries to move again, but I push her back. 'Don't look up, Ellis: whatever you do, don't look up . . .'

And then it happens.

There's a sudden flash of intense white light so bright that it burns. I screw my eyes shut, but I can still see everything as the incandescent light and sudden, scorching heat wraps all the way around us, filling the Land Rover, burning my skin and snatching the air from my lungs. It fades almost as quickly as it came, but the darkness which takes its place is equally blinding. I'm thrown forward as we smash into another vehicle ahead of us, and in the fraction of a second I'm looking out I see that the motorway has become a single solid mass of smashed cars and trucks.

A howling wind swallows up the Land Rover and hurls us and everything else forward again. I try to reach out for Ellis, but I can't find her. I lean over, but I can't feel her. The Land Rover's spinning now – feels like it's rolling over and over, being hit by debris from all angles. I'm thrown back in my seat again, and the back of my head smashes against the window.

Try to move but I can't.

Try to focus but I can't.

Try to speak but . . .

40

How long? Hours, minutes, or just seconds? Everything is still, much quieter than it should be. I slowly prise my eyes open, not knowing what I'm going to see. The windscreen of the Land Rover has shattered, though it's still holding. The glass is crisscrossed by hundreds of tiny, snaking cracks. We're straddling another wreck, and the nose of our vehicle has been shunted up into the air. Lying back in my seat, all I can see in front of me is an angry yellow-grey sky. It's the colour of bile.

Ellis moves. I try to lean across, but my neck's stiff. I reach up to massage it, but my skin feels wrong – moist, raw. Must have been burnt. Ellis shuffles again, and I try to twist around.

Then I freeze. I feel my bladder loosen involuntarily.

The force of the crash must have spun the Land Rover around, and what I can see now through the passenger window is the single most terrifying thing I have ever seen. Between here and what used to be the city, almost everything's on fire. There are flickering flames everywhere, and the ground is scorched and black. The city itself – my home, the place where I lived with my family, where I worked and played and struggled and fought – it's gone. A thick climbing column of dark grey smoke rises straight up into the sky from its dead heart. At a height I can't even begin to imagine the smoke balloons out into the unmistakable shape of a mushroom cloud.

Ellis climbs up onto the passenger seat next to me. Thank God I found her. If I'd been any slower or any later, or if I'd have waited any longer she'd be gone now, vapourised in the blinking of an eye, along with so many others. Lizzie, Josh,

Edward . . . they're all gone. I start sobbing. The flat, Joseph Mallon, Julia . . . Don't know why I'm crying – is it shock, or relief, or sorrow?

Ellis looks at the explosion in the distance, then turns and looks at me, her brown eyes locked onto mine. I try to talk to her, but I can't make the words come out. My throat is burning dry. My lungs feel like they're filled with smoke. Is she in shock too? For the first time since I found her she's quiet and subdued.

'We'll wait here 'til it's safe,' I tell her in a voice that doesn't sound like mine, 'then we'll find somewhere better, okay?'

She looks at me, but she still doesn't react. Then she looks at the broken windscreen.

'Snow,' she says. The first proper word I've heard my daughter say in months.

'Not snow,' I tell her, watching large grey clumps drift down and settle on the cracked glass. 'It's ash. Dirty. Poison. Make you sick.'

She slumps back in her seat, and beyond her I can see the mushroom cloud. Even now, after all that's happened, it's a terrifying and humbling sight. The ultimate symbol of the Hate. Who did this?

'We're going to find a house,' I tell Ellis, still watching the cloud, not knowing what I'm saying now, or why, 'and we're going to stay there together, you and me. I know it's hard to understand what happened with Mummy and Edward and Josh, but one day we'll work it out, and when we do, you'll—'

She springs up from her seat and throws herself across the inside of the Land Rover, leaning on my chest, shoving me back into my chair and pressing her face hard against the glass.

I can't move, I'm pinned down by her weight. She's following something, watching it circling us. With lightning speed she scrambles over the seats into the back of the car, trampling over the soldiers' corpses. She yanks at one of the door handles, trying to get out.

'Don't, sweetheart,' I shout, trying to turn my aching body around so I can pull her back into the front. I manage to catch hold of her, but she wrestles herself free. 'You can't go out there—'

She squeezes through the gap between the seats, pushing me aside, and lunges for the door. I lean across and cover the lock. She shakes the handle violently and screams with frustration.

'Ellis, don't,' I plead. 'You have to stay here with me. You can't—'

A sudden round of gunfire from somewhere close interrupts me and I turn and look out of the window on my side. There are people out on the motorway now, hundreds of them. Mostly they look like our people, but there are Unchanged soldiers among them too. Our fighters outnumber them. They're hunting them down.

Ellis lunges at me, trying to get past. I wrap my heavy arms around her waist and try to pull her closer, but she kicks herself free. I'm too tired to keep fighting. She shoves me away and the back of my head cracks against the window. Her constant, violent movements make the precariously balanced Land Rover shift and it starts to slip to one side.

'Ellis,' I say, but she recoils from my touch and scrambles away.

She pushes against the windscreen in frustration and when the broken glass starts to bulge outwards she does it again. And again. I want to stop her but I don't have the energy. There's blood on her hands now, but she carries on thumping the glass regardless, desperate to get out.

Finally, with a grunt of effort and anger, she breaks through the windscreen and scrambles out onto the bonnet of the Land Rover. My door's blocked by another crashed car and all I can do is follow her out. I crawl over the front of the vehicle. The metal is still hot. Most of the paint has been scorched away. Shards of glass grind into my belly.

I drop down onto the tarmac, losing my footing when it's

further to fall than I think. I get up quickly, breathing hard. The air out here is bone-dry and foul-smelling.

Ellis has already darted away and I follow her, moving out from the shadow of the crashed Land Rover and into the open. I look along the motorway in either direction. It's a single mass of stationary vehicles now. Many of the Unchanged drivers and their passengers are dead. I can see them wedged behind the wheels of their wrecks or with their bloody faces smashed up against windows. Some have survived: one of them emerges now from the back of an overturned truck a short distance away, but before he's taken more than a couple of steps, Ellis has attacked. She's jumped onto a car, then leapt at the disorientated Unchanged man, landing on his back. She's smashed him down to the ground with incredible brutality.

A pack of fighters race past me. They've been waiting out here in the wasteland, and now they pick their way through the convoy like vultures, stripping the meat from Unchanged bones, hunting out the survivors and tearing them apart. Up ahead a Brute thunders along the road unchallenged, making kill after kill after kill. Any Unchanged resistance is quickly crushed. Even those who try and run are chased down and killed.

Ellis lunges at another one and disappears from view. I swallow hard and force myself to move. My leg hurts. I look down and see that there's blood dribbling down from my right knee. My trouser leg and boot are stained wet-red.

'Ellis, wait—' I try and shout, but my voice is nowhere near loud enough. I find her on the ground alongside a Jeep, leaning down over another body. She looks up at me and a chunk of bloody flesh drops from her mouth. Was she *chewing* it? I reach out and grab her wrist before she's able to get away. 'Too dangerous here. Need to get under cover. Come with me . . .'

She prises my weak fingers off and crawls away, searching for the next kill. She brings down a dazed, blood-soaked woman who's already half-dead, pulling her down to her knees. Ellis grabs a fistful of her hair and smashes her face into a charred car door, again and again, denting the paint-stripped metal more and more with each impact. I haul myself towards her, using other wrecks for support. Up ahead the towering mushroom cloud is beginning to lose its shape. That makes me even more afraid: it means soon the air will be filled with poison, if it's not already. I throw myself down at Ellis again and wrap my arms tightly around her. The pain in my bloody knee is almost unbearable, but I have to ignore it. Ellis is all that matters.

'You have to come with me. We'll both die if we stay out here . . .'

She puts the soles of her bare feet against the misshapen car door and straightens her legs, pushing me back until I over-balance. With one leg already weakened, I fall back. She bites down onto my hand, drawing blood, and I let go. She stands over me, one foot on either side of my body. I look up at her, covering my eyes from the fine dust and ash which is falling faster now.

I reach up and snatch her hand again as she sees another Unchanged and tries to run. I won't let go. I can't let go. She screams and pulls and kicks at me, but I won't let her go.

'Stay with me, please . . .'

Ellis drops down onto my chest and stares into my face. What's she thinking? Does she understand any of this? Another Unchanged trying to drag itself to safety distracts her and she starts to move.

I grip her wrist even harder. 'Don't go.'

She clenches her free hand into a fist and hits me. I try to stop her, but she hits me again, and again and again and again until my face is numb and my eyes are almost swollen shut. Too tired. Can't fight back.

I feel her get up.

There's so much I need to say, but I can't get even the first word out. I'm aware of her looking down at me, breathing hard, my blood on her hands.

'Ellis,' I start to say, but she isn't listening. She looks up, and sprints away. I turn my head and watch as she disappears into the maze of crashed vehicles, searching for her next kill.

All I can do is watch her go.

41

Cold, body shaking . . . Breathing in dust.
The fighters are long gone. Ellis is long gone.
Empty.
Everything's lost.

Still lying in the road, curled up in a ball. Stomach churning, legs and arms aching. Head pounding. Throat dry, lungs scorched. Warm wind gusting. Swirling sky black above me. Light's fading. Stench of burning meat is everywhere. Been here for hours, face down on the tarmac.

Heavy footsteps.

Someone standing next to me. A soldier? Stay still. Don't move.

'Found one,' he shouts, face hidden, voice muffled by a gas mask.

'Worth taking?' someone shouts back.

'Not sure.'

He kicks me in the gut to see if he gets a reaction. I look up, but I don't move. I feel the Hate rising.

'Well, has it still got two arms and two legs?'

'Yes.'

'And is it breathing?'

'Think so.'

'Then chuck it on the truck.'

He bends down, grabs hold of my shoulder and picks me up. He hauls me across the road, my feet dragging in the dust.

Have to try and fight. It's all I've got left. Everything else is lost.

With what feels like my last breath, I straighten my legs, stand tall and wrestle myself free. Unarmed and uncaring, I shove the soldier away with all the force I can manage. Caught off-guard, he slams face first into a wreck. I spin him around and rip off his face mask. I need this fucker to know how much I hate him when I kill him.

He throws me back. He's much stronger than me. I fall, my injured knee giving way. I wait for him to attack, but he picks me up again.

Is this how it ends? Is he going to kill me now?

Wait – he's like me. He's one of us.

'Easy, Tiger,' he grunts, pushing me forward again. 'Save it for the Unchanged.'

Too tired to protest. I feel anger, pain. Relief.

He leads me through the motorway chaos, and when my legs buckle again he picks me up and puts me over his shoulder like a sack of potatoes. I can't fight. Can't react.

I open my eyes and try to lift my head. Hard to see anything. More soldiers wearing gas masks are dragging or carrying people over this way. We reach a flat-bed truck and he pushes me up. Grabbing hands reach down and help me and once in I fall back against the side of the truck, struggling to breathe. Dirt and ash has ground into my cuts and burns, but I'm too tired to care. Too tired to feel the pain.

I'm empty.

Everything's lost.

For half a second I try to look for Ellis, but I know she's long gone. I look around at the faces of the people crammed into the back of this truck. They're all like me. They're all fighters. We're no longer people, just fighters. I guess we're all of us conscripted into what remains of Ankin's army, or another force like it.

I was stupid to believe I could sidestep this war, that I could escape from it with Ellis. What's left of the world is now entirely governed by the Hate and I have to be ready to fight and to kill until the last trace of the Unchanged is wiped from the face of the planet. Only then will the situation change.

My daughter is gone, lost long before I found her. Now all I have left is the Hate.

Exhausted, I close my eyes and let the darkness swallow me up.

I need to rest and recover and be ready for what's still to come. I have no choice, no option.

The hardest battles are looming large on the horizon.

Acknowledgements

I'd like to thank a number of people for their help and support.

First, and perhaps most obviously, to John Schoenfelder at Thomas Dunne Books in New York and Jo Fletcher at Gollancz in London; thank you both for your tireless enthusiasm, observations, recommendations, guidance, and suggestions.

To my family and friends, thank you for your patience, tolerance and unwavering belief and support over the last few years as I've negotiated this particularly crazy section of my haphazard and largely improvised 'career path'. Particular thanks to my long-suffering wife, Lisa, who never questions why she regularly catches me researching subjects as diverse and unsavoury as genocide, germ warfare, secret underground bunkers, torture techniques and countless other topics!

Finally, and most importantly, to those of you who've read and enjoyed my previous books, thank you for coming back for more! Particular thanks to those readers who've been with me since the very early days of giving away thousands of free downloads of *Autumn* and all my subsequent adventures with 'Infected Books'. Some of you read *Hater* when it was self-published in summer 2006, and you've been waiting since then for this sequel to arrive. It's finally here and I hope you enjoy it. I promise you won't have to wait anywhere near as long for the conclusion to the trilogy!

To everyone I've listed above and to anyone else I should have mentioned but didn't, thank you.